DAVE!

(A Novel from the Future)

Parts 1-3

DAVE!

This page intentionally left blank. Do not draw on it.

PART I:

THE INVADERS

CHAPTER ONE

To: voluptuosus.mendosus@texo.org;   scammon.brenda@emoveo.net;
danglybits@servitus.org;   dazzyduks@nhfd.edu;   mateo@servitus.org;
dirtyphil@paratus.net;   marcrichardauthor@outlook.com;
lilybushhammer@texo.org; drills4rgent@gallileo.com; gofigger@thesalad.net

CC:

Subject: Chain

December 23, 2030

Hey everyone,

To those reading this email, I want to say thank you. I'm trying this little social experiment before it's no longer possible for anyone to do social experiments. Plus, my wife left me and I'm bored. I don't understand it. I came home, and there she was, sitting on the couch, sobbing. The mascara making really unattractive streaks down her face, giving her a bawling Tammy Faye look. Reluctantly, I asked her what's wrong. Her answer to my very legitimate question was a very uncalled-for slap across the face. It wasn't the first time I had been slapped by her, but this one had some real meat to it. In fact, I can still feel it, if I think hard enough about it. Apparently she had some sort of idea in her head that I was cheating on her. I could care less about chasing strange. I don't even like the familiar, never mind the strange. Sucks to say, but I've never had much of a sex drive, even as a teenager. Could be low testosterone. Maybe it's the fact I've always felt like an old man trapped in a young man's body. In either case, I had always been that way, and she knew it when she married me. Anyway, there was no convincing her that I wasn't sleeping around The lipstick on the collar was just the design of my shirt. She bought it for me for Christmas, for fuck sake. I tried explaining all this to her, but she didn't buy it. She didn't buy any of it. So much for trust Anyway, here I am in an empty house. She's gone, and all she left me with of hers was her Terence Trent D'Arby CD collection. She said she could only listen to "Wishing Well" so many times. Whatever. I don't have a CD player, anyway (I don't think anybody does), so they're of no use to me. I suppose I could find an old ripping program and upload them, but what would be the point? I can only listen to "Wishing Well" so many times, too. I would trade every one of those CDs to have her back, but it's pointless in even thinking about it; her mind's made up.

So here I am, writing this chain letter. All of you on my email list know who I am, but I'm hoping you will forward it to all of your friends, and add some stories of your own. Tell about your lives, tell about how you feel about the state of the world. Send the email to all friends on your list, and hopefully they'll do the same. Keep this thing going. At least until email ceases to exist. Before the earth breathes its last breath, which may be sooner than we all think.

My name is Glenn Richter. I live at 125 Westboro Baptist Church Lane, Missouri. Once upon a time, not so long ago, I was a fairly successful real estate salesman. My claim to fame, and also my biggest sale, was selling an Oprah Winfrey impersonator an impersonation of Oprah Winfrey's mansion. I made a pretty good living. I wasn't rich, by any means, but I did all right, if I do say so myself. I was sitting on top of the world. Or at least, I was sitting somewhere around Finland. Recently, though, I had to quit my job as my wife was spreading rumors around town that I was a philanderer. I couldn't really disagree, the main reason being I had no understanding of that word. But when I learned what it meant, which happened to be right before I caught her crying in the living room, and was able to call bullshit, it was too late. My reputation was ruined, and sales plummeted. No one trusts a philanderer.

I was a millennium baby, born on May 5, 2000, and grew up in a really small town in Kentucky. My father was a pipe fitter, or at least that's what he called it. Some call it "porn fluffer". Not a very prestigious job, and he'd often come home smelling of stale chlorine and coconut oil, but it paid fairly decent, and he was able to purchase a house in the suburbs, right outside of Loserville. We lived there with my two brothers. My brother Dennis, after he turned sixteen, decided he wanted to be my sister instead. My brother Cody was, and still is, a good-for-nothing drug addict. I say good for nothing, but he's actually pretty good at scoring me drugs, when the mood hits me.

My mom was absent. She went insane shortly after my birth, and the last anyone had heard of her, she was living under a bridge by the Cumberland River, acting like a troll and demanding bridge crossers answer three questions before they pass. Since traffic went by at a rather quick pace, no one really understood what she was asking, so most just threw change out their windows.

So, this country. Dammit. It all started, I think, when Mel Gibson won the election of 2026. We thought we knew what we were getting. He seemed like an honest, down-to-earth type of guy. All of his racism and fascism and drunken ramblings were out in the open, so we thought he had nothing to hide. We thought. But everyone has something to hide. Everyone has an agenda. You, me, the mailman, the guy selling chicken wings from the front stoop of his apartment building, everyone. Every right winger's dream, to build a wall across the Mexican border, came to fruition. But he didn't stop there. He put a border wall around the entire United States, which included the borders of Mexico and Canada, as well as both coasts. Even republicans found that a little excessive. A lot of tax dollars were spent on that. That, and military. We decided to give up Alaska and Hawaii. For one reason, it didn't make sense to build walls around them if none of us citizens could get in. We would have to build two very expensive highly-reinforced tunnels or bridges. The second reason, and what I feel to be the most important, is all of those offers that companies gave away, like McDonald's two for one deal as well as their Monopoly game, were not valid in Alaska and Hawaii. Maybe there were other reasons, too, but I don't work for the government, so I don't know.

I, for one, miss being able to go to Hawaii for vacation. We used to do it all the time when we were children. Dad set aside a lot of his fluffer money for us to be able to take vacations as a family. While I spent most of my time hang-gliding, beach-lounging, and para-sailing with Dad, my brother Cody spent most of his time stoned as hell on Maui Wowie, and trying to score heroin; whereas my brother Denise, who was once Dennis, spent most of his time taking in the very large vagabond transgender scene that Hawaii had to offer. Selfish.

Now back in the day we never would have thought that Mel Gibson would have been elected president in 2026. Not because he's a prick, not because of his time being spent making Apocalypto II (I thought the first one was awesome. The sequel, were it to ever be finished, would probably do as well as most sequels do), but because it was 2026. A number that is not divisible by four, and therefore, not an election year. But toward the end of Donald Trump's reign, he decided he wanted "a couple more years". This became somewhat of a slogan for his campaign, which was kind of lame and too vague to be much of a slogan, I thought. But he was so revered at that time, that people walked around carrying signs and wearing shirts that had that slogan on it: A COUPLE MORE YEARS! (My guess is he wasn't that revered, and he paid to have his support teams seem larger than they actually were. And why not? He could afford it. The same way he paid to have protesters protest his own rallies.)

And so it happened. Trump was in for another couple years, which threw off the schedule of any future elections. Furthermore, to keep things consistent, they also changed the schedule of the Summer Olympics and Leap Year so that they could still fall on the same year as election years, as they always had been. This would apparently make things less confusing. Now, those are two international events, so you would think the rest of the world would put up a stink. But we're America, so fuck you. (Of course, you know, that became America's slogan.)

So yeah, Mel and that crazy wall. I realize that after 9/11, things changed for the worse. We suffered more frequent terrorist attacks. America's distrust of Muslims grew. But we could have done something other than get every card-carrying Muslim out of the country, and send them to the Middle East. Most of them didn't even hail from the Middle East. There were Muslims from Africa, China, the UK, and even ones born right here on American soil. Not only was shipping out all the Muslims wrong, the plan itself was expensive and poorly thought out. They were sent away with a small amount of "gate money", much like prisoners get upon release, which helped ease their burdens a little. Maybe. But this gate money was funded on the taxpayer's dime. Also, even though we got rid of the majority of them, some were left, and those, more often than not, happened to be the actual terrorists. Only the law-abiding ones left on their own recognizance. Also, we had no great plan to keep them from sneaking back in.

Donald figured he could get the wall built in those couple more years he had. That was a long shot. Masons were no longer allowed to exist, as they were thought of to be part of some cult, which was no longer allowed here. So there were really no skilled brick layers. But he gave it a try, and actually got a fair amount done, at least across the Mexican border, before his term was up and Uncle Mel finally got his turn in office to complete it.

He made us call him "Uncle Mel". He thought that "Mr. President" sounded "too stuffy". Now, I had my share of crazy uncles. One even insisted that he hailed from a meteorite that crash landed on earth back in 1806. Now, that would make him not only very old, but also very dead, as he would have burned up when the meteorite hit the atmosphere. Yeah, I had my share of crazy uncles, and I didn't need one more. And I never had an uncle as crazy as old Uncle Mel. He had his share of stupid agendas, but priority number one was getting those walls up. We soon ran out of brick and concrete, and what was erected was a combination of brick, steel beams, chicken wire, wood, and "old-fashioned American ingenuity". Whatever that was. Not very effective, but it was something, I guess. There were parts of the wall that were nice, that even had some decorations and some potted plants hung up, and those were the parts they tended to show on television. But we all knew how the rest of it looked. A lot of us lived by the ugly parts.

If the wall was the end of it, I could probably live with it. I mean, I don't really know any Muslims or Jews, so it doesn't really affect me personally. It sucks, however, I could deal. But there's far more to this regime than some stupid barricade. Right at this moment, there are more poor people living in America than there have ever been in history. There are more legislations preventing any sort of anarchistic movements. Nowadays, you can't say anything bad about the government. Trump passed laws preventing what he called "libel and slander" against his administration, making it a civil violation to even comment on something so innocuous as Trump's hair. You could get the shit sued out of you. Nowadays, it's a criminal violation, not a civil one, and you could end up in federal prison for badmouthing the government. Of course, you'll note here that I really don't give a rat's sweet fuck about the law. I'm not going to continue living under this dictatorship and smile the whole time. Stalin's dead. Hitler's dead. Hussein's dead. Bin Laden's dead. This type of autocracy should have died along with them. Alas, here we are. The end of the world is coming, friends.

Maybe my mom's craziness is genetic, and I'm being paranoid. But what tells me otherwise is I'm not the only one who thinks this way. We can't all be crazy.

Something is going on. Society as we know it is in for some major changes. I don't know what, or how long it will take, but we are on a downward slope to hell.

Anyway, Merry Christmas. Hope all is well with you guys. Ciao.

Glenn Richter.

To: Billy.G.Abbott@mailinator.com;
Elizabeth.C.Abbott@mytrashmail.com; atqui@mugio.com

CC:

Subject: Re: Chain

December 27, 2030.

My name is Adrock Abbott. I was named after some rock star from the 1980's I think. Or a hip hop guy. I don't know. Nobody listens to that crap anymore. I'm 12 years old and I don't want to be writing this, but my mawm is making me. My mawm makes me do all kinds of things I don't like. Sometimes she makes me make my bed and clean my room. Sometimes she makes me rake the lawn. Sometimes she makes me go to the wall and yell at protesters with her. I don't want to do any of those things. My da makes me do all this crap too, but I like him better because he's my da. Anyways, my mawm says if I write this letter than we can go out for ice cream. Which is, like, a big deal, because they can never afford to go out for ice cream. They usually just buy some crappy Hood ice cream at the grocery store, and it's not even a flavor I like. It's usually chocolate or something, and it tastes like feet. They want me to write about my life experiences. But they also tell me I don't have any life experiences yet because I'm only 12. I'll be 13 next month, so I don't know what they're complaining about. They say this letter is important, because I am the future generation. I don't really know why this letter is so important tho. They said hobbies so I will tell you that I really like going on hikes by myself. It's the only way I can get away from the Rents. They let me go in the woods, and they probably hope I get eaten by a bear. That would be a cool way to die tho. Bears are pretty awesome. I like to go out there and look for cool shit I can't see in my house like pincones and birds and stuff. It's fun to get the little acorn hats and blow them like whistles. I can blow them really loud and make the whole neighborhood ANGRY! I do it sometimes till mawm tells me to stop. I have a skateboard I like to ride, but I don't have a helmet anymore since someone stole it. The Rents don't want me riding it without protective gear so I do it only when they're not home. Which is a lot of the time actually. My most fun thing to do with the skateboard is I like to get those bang snaps that explode when you throw them on the ground, and I put them at the bottom of my hill, and I start to ride down the hill and try to hit them with my skateboard wheels. I do ok most times. Mawm and da say the protesters are hurting our country, and they're dirty people, so sometimes I throw the bang snaps at them. Hahaha. But then one time someone threw a rock at me so I don't do that anymore. Who throws rocks at kids? Jeez. I also have a playstation that is like 1000 years old but I play it anyway because we have like 1000 games for it. It's stupid and the grafix are lame but it's fun to. I was in third grade when the Rents pulled me out and now they home school me. Which is so easy because and also I am learning a lot. As you can see I am a pretty good speller but I suck at math. I think da has given up trying to teach me that. Who cares about math? One time I found a stray dog and asked the Rents if I could keep it. They said ya but then when I got it home it had the mange, and they made me get rid of it. I thought it wasn't very nice to just let it go out into the wild so I bashed in it's head with a rock. There aren't a lot of kids my age to play with so mostly I just hang out by myself. I do have one friend who's name is Pickles. We get together sometimes and throw rocks and crabapples at passing cars. Pickles has his own apartment. He has a playstation XX but he doesn't let me play the really good games because he says it's too violent for kids. He's 24 years old. He's ok. When I grow up I want to be like Pickles. He never got married and he runs a website, which he says I can't look at because I'm too young. Anyway I think maybe this is enough for a letter. Now let's go get some fucking ice cream! Mawm will make me take out the swear word. Whatevz

Sincerely,

Adrock

To: ddawg@compleo.net;   trace.hudgins@nequities.net; gavin73volo@veritas.org;

nimium@certo.net;   calypsokid@oportet.net;   63313@compleo.net; d3vin@certo.net

CC:

Subject: Re: Chain

December 27, 2030

Glenn, you're a good friend of mine, so I won't rag on ya too bad. I'm not religious, and I think that saying the end of the world is coming is a little much. While I will agree that the wall is a piece of shit, it's not the idea of the wall that's bad. It's the fuckin wall itself. I mean, wood? Seriously? Have we learned nothing from the three little pigs? Wood is good, but if you want to build a wall that old Habib wolf can't blow down, you need to find something better than wood. Did you know that over ¾ of the goddamned wall is wood? That leaves 75% of the wall that can be broken through with a chainsaw, or even a chisel. Next thing you know, some do-good left wing nut jobs are gonna get it in their heads to send chainsaws to Iraq, just like how we sent guns to Iran a bunch of years ago. Then they'll be coming over here to rip the wall down. Has history taught us nothing? Fuckin chainsaws, man.

My name is Dale "Irongut" Malloy. I come from Blackburn, Oklahoma, I'm a self-made businessman, my business being none of your business. I earned the nickname Irongut when I ate the 93-pound steak at Jimmy's Taco House. Being famous for their tacos only, which I think are pretty mediocer, they couldn't cook a steak for shit. And the steak was tough and burnt to shit and took me eight hours to chew my way through, but I was promised a T-shirt, and my friends also promised that they would all call me Irongut from that point on. I didn't have a nickname yet, and Irongut sounded pretty badass. So I ate the damn thing. I am not to be confused with Linda "Irongunt" Fallon, who only ate their 84-pounder. Please don't call me Irongunt.

I joined the Outlaws and was with them for a few years, but then one day when I was out riding my bike, my pantleg got caught in the spokes. This was the bicycle Outlaws, not to be confused with the other Outlaws. We may not have been as fast, but we were just as tough. Anyway, my leg got caught and I took a tumble and it knocked out my front tooth and now I whistle any time I say my S's. That was enough for me. I only had 30 or so more teeth, and I wasn't going to give them up for nothing. Bicycles are dangerous. Kids, if you're reading this, think twice before you pedal.

We were a poor family growing up, and I blame it mostly on the fact that no one in my family voted Republican. Also, my daddy liked to play them slot machines. And the slot machines liked to eat his take home pay. Our house was falling apart. Literally. Some nights, when the winds got bad, ma would make my brother and I sit up in the attic and hold onto the rafters as tight as we could so we didn't lose our roof. Sounds cruel and abusive, but my brother and I didn't want to lose our roof either, so it was something we felt we had to do.

For extra cash, we would put on shows in our backyard and charge people 30 bucks to see em. My mother would get out her washboard and my dad would get out his Jew harp, and my brother and I sang. Mostly folk songs about the Lord or some shit, and we were way out of tune. Soon people got bored of the singing and wanted to see something else. So we started finding a way to steal animals from the zoo and put on a show with those animals. Everybody loved the monkeys and shit. And everybody would be covered in shit cause, you know, monkeys. We even had some raccoons that would eat right out of peoples hands. We had a dolphin in a tank, and a couple pythons in some glass cages. When a tiger ate someone in the audience, we then figured it was time to start stripping instead. We set the animals free, and they probably ate a few more people, but then we started taking off our clothes, and people cheered and cheered.

So we did that for a while. Anyways, we weren't really ever able to get our way out of the poorhouse, despite the additional revenue the shows were bringing in, cause Daddy would just go run out to Reno and be gone for days, coming back totally broke. I made a vow right then and there that when I grew up I was gonna be rich.

I made it halfway to rich. I'm comfortable. Some say there's no middle class, but I am proof otherwise. I pay my share of taxes, and I feel like I own a piece of that damn wall. So you can see why it makes me sick when I see people outside protesting about it. All over the place, in every town, they got people out there with signs, blasting Pink Floyd, screaming about tearing it down. Christ, we just built the fucking thing! How would you like it if you just built this giant house of cards, or Legos thousands and thousands of miles across, and someone came and just tore it down? No, I say the wall's there, just leave it there. But it's happening. They've already started chiseling away at the weaker parts. If only we invested some more of our tax dollars into getting more guards for the wall itself, then nobody could tear it down in some sneaky way. Things are turning to shit real fast.

Anyway I hope y'all got everything you wanted from Santa Claus this year. I got me a sailboat. Which was dumb in hindsight because I got nowhere to sail it. But I figured I had money to burn, and you know what they say, you can't take it with you. Come to think of it, I can't take the sailboat with me either. Oh well. It makes a nice lawn piece.

See ya,

Irongut

DAVE!

To: voluptuosus.mendosus@texo.org; scammon.brenda@emoveo.net; gracie4@paratus.net; efil4zaggin@texo.org; mateo@servitus.org; dirtyphil@paratus.net; marcrichardauthor@outlook.com; lilybushhammer@texo.org; drills4rgent@gallileo.com; therealdeal@peristalisis.edu

CC:

Subject: Re: Chain

December 27, 2030

Glenn, I love you, but I have to say I'm more than a little offended that you would trivialize my gender issues the way you did. When will you grow the hell up? Calling me "Denise". Saying that I didn't ever hang out with Dad because I was too busy partying with the homeless transgender folks in Hawaii. Remember all the times Dad wanted you to go have a catch with him, but you were too busy to toss the ball around? I had to go do it, despite my tendencies to "throw like a girl". Remind me why I love you again? You were never really there for me. To this day, you're, ah fuck it. I'm not here to air our dirty laundry. If you don't get it by now you never will.

Anyway, my name is Starlet, contrary to what my brother says, and yes, I was technically born a dude, but I don't really like to talk about it. I know it interests people, but I'm not interested in discussing it. I don't feel any different than anyone else. Some people are born with a cleft palate, some are born with a third nipple, some are born with six fingers, I was born with a dick. Whatever. It's a birth defect. It bothers me that we all cry about the cleft palates of the world, and are all, "Oh, this poor child needs surgery," but when a girl wants to get her dick removed, a feature that shouldn't be there in the first place, people get all up in arms. Bah, I could go on and on. I suppose I'm fortunate living in a time where people are at least a little more understanding. I'm also fortunate to have had my surgery when insurance still covered it. Some folks nowadays are forced to live with the defect. Forced to live in the wrong body. I can't even imagine.

Look at me, here I am talking about it when I said I wouldn't. Moving right along…

I was, and still am, part of the protests that are going on around the country. I live in Frenchville, Maine, so I have easy access to the border wall. Frenchville sucks. All of Northern Maine sucks, actually. For those of you who live in this state, you know this already. For the others, I guess the best way to describe it is, it's like a remote Alaskan village, with all the alcoholism and none of the charm. There are very few work opportunities here. You can get a job as a forester easy enough, if you enjoy breaking your back all day. Or you can go work at one of hundreds of meth labs, if you want to get all exploded and shit. I got a job at a convenience store. I feel quite fortunate that I am a gorgeous woman with no manly features, except for maybe my big hands, which a lot of the women up here have anyway. There are more than a few rednecks up here who wouldn't understand if they found out that I "used to be a dude". I live here because of its proximity to the border. I don't know why I chose here to live, as there are thousands and thousands of border towns to choose from. I guess part of it is because Maine is a beautiful state. Part of it is because there is a lot less violence against citizens here than in most border towns. The government is much too busy worrying about our coastline and our border with Mexico than to worry much about Canada. I'm not one for violence. All I want to do is carry my little sign on my days off, listen to Pink Floyd (yes, we do listen to The Wall way too much. I do wish there were more albums about walls.), and hope for change. Sure, we all line up along the borders to protest, but it's about more than the wall. Don't get me wrong though, that is a big part of it. But it's what the wall symbolizes more than anything Intolerance. Hatred. Mistrust. Bigotry. Not only for others, but for our own people. These were mostly Americans that were forced to flee, to cash in the freedoms we had once granted them for a life in the desert. I for one understand what it's like to be the target of discrimination.

Being that the Canadian border was the least of our concerns, and that lumber is plentiful and cheap up here, this is the stretch that was mostly made out of wood. Regarding what Irongut said, I have not seen any foul play as far

17

as chipping away at the border. I can't speak for everywhere, but I really don't see it as being much of an issue. There really is no point in destroying little pieces of the wall. Even if people could sneak in, it's highly unlikely they'd last long, without getting caught. They'd be the only ones without the requisite American Citizen tags implanted in their forearms.

Heh, back when I was a child, if I would have stumbled across this letter, I would think this was written by an insane person. Or some science fiction author with a wild imagination. But it's all true, as you all know.

It didn't take long for these changes to happen. The Republicans are fucked. For a group whose sole mission in life is to get the government out of their affairs, they sure as hell like imposing their beliefs on every citizen, and weaseling their way into our private lives. They have this country so fucked up. They love to preach about the Constitution, but when it comes right down to it, they are absolutely ripping it to shreds. Let me break it down.

First Amendment: Freedom of speech, religion, press, all gone. Those in power may point to the fact that we are able to protest without consequences. That will absolutely be the next thing to vanish. I'm scared to death every time I go out to the wall that there will be riots, and I will be assaulted. Or killed. Yet I do it anyway, because it's the right thing to do.

Second Amendment: This is the only one they left alone. My God, if they fucked with the peoples' rights to own guns, they'd have a mutiny on their hands.

The Third Amendment nobody cares about, as usual.

The Fourth Amendment: Gone. The police don't need a search warrant for anything anymore. They can search your home, your car, your body cavities if it came to that. The seats in my car are all ripped up from the last time I was pulled over by a cop. Yes, I was speeding. Give me a ticket. I was totally cooperative with the officer, had my license, registration, insurance card. Everything was in order. But I think that cops nowadays must get some sort of incentive for finding anything even remotely incriminating on a person's person. It's the only reason I can think of. Up here, the chances of getting pulled over are slim to none, since most of the towns lack a police force. Hell, most of the towns up here lack a name. So everyone speeds. And drives drunk.

But if you happen to get pulled over, you will be pulled over by the sheriff or deputy or someone with much larger authority than any everyday police officer. And I assume they have more to gain by finding shit on people. So the sheriff asked me to get out of my car, and proceeded to rip the thing apart. He did find a bit of a joint, which no one really cares about, since weed was made legal here fifteen years ago or so. There were no empty beer cans or anything like that. No secret conspiratorial files tucked away under my seat. No empty lipstick cases filled with cocaine. Nothing. He seemed pretty defeated, and let me go with a nice chunky ticket. I was told to have a nice day.

Amendments 5 through 8: There is no such thing as a fair trial anymore, as everyone in power is corrupt as fuck. There are more people in prison today than there ever have been, about half of them there for crimes they didn't commit, and the other half there for crimes that deserve no more than a slap on the wrist or a fine or some small amount of jail time. You can "plead the fifth" all you want, but if the police want you to confess to something, prepare to sit in that dimly lit room with your little cup of water or ginger ale for a long long time. They will get a confession out of you. If not, you'll end up in prison anyway for obstructing an investigation.

The Ninth Amendment: Most of our other rights not included in the Constitution have been infringed upon. As you all know, we have very little rights left.

The Tenth Amendment states that the federal government possesses only those powers delegated to it by the states or the people through the Constitution. Hahahahaha. This has been a farce for a long long time.

The Fourteenth Amendment is obviously gone. We all know that. The only ones who are true American citizens are the white ones who were born here. There is no more "becoming" an American Citizen. We outlawed that while Trump was still in the White House.

The government interprets the Constitution as they see fit. Words get twisted, contexts get changed, depending on who you are. It's like Christians with the Bible. Since there is no Ultimate Truth, what truth there is is skewed depending on your situation. This has been an issue from day one, when it was written, but the majority of our rights have disappeared within the last few years or so.

The corruption runs deep. From Uncle Mel, to congress, to the judges, to the cops, to a lot of American Citizens. There is no escape, really. Everyone is a rat, everyone gets an incentive to be a rat, and no one can be trusted. This email will get reported, I'm sure. But nobody really cares about anyone bitching and moaning about the government. We've always had the right to do that, and there's really no harm. You can't write an editorial defaming the president or anything, but I can say whatever I want in an email to my friends. It's harmless, really.

The middle class has been all but eliminated. A non-biased survey run by CNN estimated that only one percent of the population is middle class. Five percent are rich, and ninety-four percent are in the poverty zone. One would think all we would have to do is redefine what "poverty" is to skew the numbers back to normal, but most people can barely afford to eat, and to me that means they're poor. Millions upon millions are in debt so far there is no possible way for them to ever dig themselves out in their own lifetimes. The banks know this, yet they grant loans anyway. Government bailouts are an awesome thing.

Glenn, you may be a lot of things (A liar, a thief, a man with a stupid haircut, and an asshole) but you are not a cheat. You loved Jessica with all your heart. She was your everything. I don't think you would ever do anything to jeopardize that. My guess is that a rumor got started from high up. It spread first to your wife, then all around town, that you were a womanizer. This caused you to lose your job in real estate. A successful real estate agent is about as middle-class as it gets. I think it was the government that caused your unemployment, throwing one more below the poverty line. Of course, it can never be proven. Nobody ever knows where rumors begin, but they usually end in devastation.

The government runs everything now. And I mean EVERYTHING. Television networks used to be privatized. Now they are government-run. The gov't funds movies, tv, internet sites like Youtube, and some of the more popular journals. They even got to some of the novelists. American literature is absolutely chock full of propaganda. It started out as just another way to fish for dollars. Put some money into projects that you know are going to bring back revenue a thousandfold. They saw other countries doing it, and figured it was high time to get into that game. I almost applaud their efforts. Capitol Hill is now Capital Hill. They are bringing in trillions of dollars from the entertainment industry. Job well done.

But they didn't stop there. Oh no. I don't think I'm too far off base when I say they have begun to censor everything. I'm not talking about sex and violence; in fact, there is more sex and violence on tv and the Internet and in movies than there ever has been. They know enough to give the people what they want, and that's more garbage for their eyes. There are a few things that I am talking about, however.

First, the commercials. Interspersed among the normal ads for mops and laundry detergent, are the pro-government ads. "Do your part. Sign up for IRON" Iron being the Immigrant Removal Operations Network. Bullshit tattling scheme that encourages people to call into a hotline to turn their neighbors in if they suspect them of any involvement with any "Occupy" movements, or anything anti-government related, outside of carrying signs. Also on the tattle list would be those who are practicing Muslims, illegal aliens, it goes on and on. Jews have recently been added to the list, thanks to Uncle Mel. There are other ads as well, special messages from Uncle Mel, horse shit that they think people want to hear. They have rigged Tivo and Instaplay so that you can still skip the commercials about dog food and hairspray, but not the ones the government produces. Those you have to watch. Or at the very least keep on in the background while you put together your favorite jigsaw puzzle.

It won't be long before they start censoring actual content. I notice there are a lot more pro-government, rah rah for the United States movies out now. They have to be very careful and do this a little at a time, creep into America's subconscious, or else people will tune out. And there aren't enough like-minded people who actually enjoy those films and shows yet. They have to be careful not to alienate their audience. Brainwashing is a slow process.

And it's not just entertainment. The government has their hands in almost everything now. The food industry, the fashion industry, soon the housing market, etc. etc. It used to be Republicans were scared of communism. That was the number one fear in the 1980's, and during the 2010's it was all about spreading fear of any sort of Socialist movement. The Republicans wanted Washington to stay the hell out of people's business. I don't know what happened. I think the fear of terrorism and the fear of uprisings got bigger than their fear of communism. They learned that free thinkers can be dangerous. The thinking spreads quickly, sometimes too quickly for the powers-that-be to contain effectively. So little by little, they are trying to weasel into everything, brainwashing the masses and making money at the same time. It's a no-brainer, really. Why can't they see that they're becoming everything that hate?

I could go on, but my chicken's boiling. No, that is not a euphemism. TTFN.

Starlet Richter

To: dddevilmaycare@texo.org; travis@emoveo.net; nickmarydrew@paratus.net; readmybooks@texo.org; godiswatching@servitus.org; mrbfpfan@paratus.net; glampyre6@texo.org; drills4rgent@gallileo.com; fatty@jarvis.org

CC:

Subject: Re: Re: Chain

December 28, 2030

HI there.

My name is Marc Richard. Starlet has been a good friend of mine for a few years now. She used to live in Portland, which is the biggest city Maine has, and is far more accepting of the LGGBTQDMTF lifestyle than the towns up north. I understand, though, that she had a mission. And I can't blame her. I would be there too, but I'm not much of a protester. I'm a very big creature of habit; I like my routine. I get up, have some coffee, write a bit, take the dog for a walk, write a bit more, and watch the tube. I don't see where protesting could fit into my daily routine. I prefer to be lazy, leaving the protests to others, and hopefully reap the benefits later on when some change is actually made. Plus, I like Portland way too much. We have our fair share of protesters here, too, but the ones along the wall seem to be making the most noise and drawing the most attention.

I agree with Starlet when she says the middle class is being eliminated. I try to make a meager living writing books, and I'm marginally successful at it. By "marginally successful", I mean that I keep below the poverty line; being a successful author is not what it used to be, with so many self-published and wonderfully talented writers clogging up the market. I wouldn't want to make much more money, because I'm certain that someone would see to it that my books were not only banned from Amazon, but eliminated from bookstores as well. This is another way they are censoring entertainment. They haven't taken control of all the industry yet, as Starlet has said. But they sure make it difficult for the little guy. The independent authors, movie directors and producers, are slowly being squeezed out of the market. We can't have people being too successful on their own, and making too much money. There is no way to really "get rich" anymore. You pretty much have to be born into it.

Anyway, I'm not going to get into my own personal history, because you can read it in my book It'll End in Tears. While we're on the subject, I have other books as well. Degrees of Separation, Harm's Way, Those Eyes, and Sorry. Shameless plugging? You bet! I'll take it anywhere I can get it. The only way for me to keep putting food on my plate and affording this shithole of an apartment is to keep promoting. Also, if you could please leave a review, those are just as important as sales.

Glenn suggested I turn this email chain into a book, but I'm kind of hesitant for a couple reasons. One being I've done the email chain thing before, in my book It'll End in Tears (which, by the way, you can also most likely find in your local bookstore, if you can find a local bookstore). I really prefer coming up with new material, rather than copying and pasting emails and journals and calling it a novel. It's lazy and unimaginative. The biggest reason, though, is this email chain will hopefully far outlive me. I think change is coming, it's inevitable, but not for a long while. I'll probably be long in the ground before we see any real progress. No, I'll leave the publishing duties to someone else, if they're so inclined.

With that thought, I'm outty. I have nothing constructive to say; just figured I'd say hi.

Marc Richard

Visit www.marcrichardauthor.com for more information.

To: voluptuosus.mendosus@texo.org; scammon.brenda@emoveo.net; gracie4@paratus.net; efil4zaggin@texo.org; mateo@servitus.org; dirtyphil@paratus.net; marcrichardauthor@outlook.com; lilybushhammer@texo.org; drills4rgent@gallileo.com; therealdeal@peristalisis.edu

CC:

Subject: Re: Chain

February 2, 2031

Hey, it's me again. Miss Starlet. So here we are, a month later and so much has happened. After all this picketing, all this shouting, all the standing around with our thumbs up our collective asses, we are finally doing something more productive. We're bringing down the wall!!! Finally!!! And I am so happy to say that I am in the front line. We are the Topplers! We will not be deterred!

Let me preface this a little. Those along the wall have a tendency to spread word very quickly about things. Most of these words are, more often than not, rumors. I think people got bored doing nothing but holding signs, listening to Pink Floyd, and shouting chants, so fanciful stories started to surface, I guess to keep things interesting. Some of the more fantastic ones were that old Uncle Mel was, in fact, an alien from another planet outside of our solar system. And I can see why this rumor would be easily believed. Humans aren't supposed to act this way. The power in the White House was becoming more and more…I don't know. Is weird the word? Corrupt? Both. Weirdly corrupt. It seemed that nothing productive was being done. All that false camaraderie, all that us vs. them mentality that appeared to some to be bringing the American people closer together, was actually dividing our planet. The theory was that his species had been watching our planet for a long time from his eye in the sky, and it didn't take long for him to come to the conclusion that ours was the most fucked-up country on the planet. Once Trump took office, it was easy as butter falling off an egg for an alien race to infiltrate our government and continue to segment the human race, building a snowball of hate and mistrust among the people. I can see how this claim could appear to have some validity, but I don't buy it. I think it was nothing more than projecting. Is it that impossible to believe that we, as a country, really are that awful, that we have to blame our twisted government on some extraterrestrial shit?

Another rumor is that our commander-in-chief is Jewish, and he's filled with such self-loathing that he felt it necessary to rid the country of all the aspects of himself that he couldn't stand. Also, that he had a micropenis. I think I remember people saying the same thing about Hitler. I don't buy it.

Another rumor was that the center of the earth was made out of cream cheese, and we were all living on a really delicious bagel.

So you can see what I mean about boredom spawning rumors. And I thought the thing about the Topplers was just a rumor. But it's not. It's all over the Internet. The video is up on Youtube. In just a few short months this fucking wall is coming down.

Shit, gotta go. Chicken's burning. And that is a euphemism.

Starlet

CHAPTER TWO

My name is Eric Tisdale, and I am what some may call a hustler, but I prefer to think of myself as a pool shark. I shoot a mean game of pool. I used to have my own pool table, till I sold it. What a bitch it is to move a pool table. Now I spend most of my time at the bars hustling strangers for pocket change. I had a real job once, then shit happened. I am not putting this in an email for reasons which I think will be abundantly clear. There's nothing else to say, anyway, without getting too deep into things certain people shouldn't catch wind of. The rest of this is, at least for now, for my eyes only. Sorry to break your little chain, Glenn, but you never really liked me anyway, nor I you, and the email chain is a stupid idea to begin with. Nobody will ever publish it, even as a history text. It's dumb. I've known Starlet from way back when we were teenagers. We met in Hawaii, on the beach. She was drinking her virgin daiquiri and I was drinking my glass of hot milk. I was down in the dumps, feeling like such a loser. My girlfriend of three years had just run off and joined a cult, and left no forwarding address. The second I met Starlet I thought, now, here's a kindred spirit if ever there was one. We started talking; I told her all about my tale of woe, she told me of her troubles, with her mom being a troll and everything. We hit it off, and we have been friends ever since. If only Starlet would have moved out to California when I asked her to, things would be a whole lot different. Not only could she have been one of the Invaders, she could also have been a lot better understood. It seems like every third person I run into around here is gender-fluid. Although, you have to be careful using that term. Some folks, if they don't identify as such, find that term highly

27

offensive. Some prefer to use the term "gender-liquid", and some like the term "gender-viscous". Some even like to be called "sir" or "ma'am", whatever that's about. To each their own, I guess. It gets very confusing for me, as I'm sure it does for a lot of people. Anyway, she would have been much happier in Cali, is what I'm getting at.

I was there the day the Invaders came to be.

I was sitting there in my living room, watching Mr. Bean (I love that guy), when an Uncle Mel ad/ PSA comes on. I was about to do my crossword during it as usual, but I noticed it was a new one, so I figured I'd listen to see what bullshit he was spouting this time. It opened with an aerial shot of the wall, his crowning achievement. Mexicans were running up to it from their side, splatting against it like flies on a windshield. This was obviously a CGI effect. It had been a long time since I'd seen a Mexican, but I didn't think they splattered like that. Plus, I don't remember any of them having horns and a tail. Some had pitchforks, though.

Then it pans in on the prez's smiling mug. "Hey America, it's me again. Uncle Mel. I'll tell ya, I'll never tire of looking at that wall. What a fine job our craftsmen and craftswomen did constructing that beauty." Never once thanking the tax payers for funding the thing against their will. He then looked directly at the camera. "And what a fine job we did getting out those that don't belong here, and back to where they need to be. Their homelands. And they're much, much happier. They were not true citizens. Have you ever felt like you don't belong somewhere? Like at school, maybe you get picked on for being fat. Or at work, maybe they pick on you for having mustard on your shirt. You know, because you're fat. Well, these folks didn't belong here. Sure, they were chasing the American dream, but it wasn't really theirs to chase. Chase all you want, but in the long run, if deep down you know that you're never going to reach your goal, it's depressing. And it's a selfish person who allows someone to go off chasing rainbows. But now they're back where they belong. Just look at these smiling Jew faces." A photo flashed across the screen of a Bar Mitzvah or wedding that appeared to have been shot sometime around 1986, everyone all smiles. Someone crowd surfing in a chair or some such. "Well, it's about that time again for me to remind you fine people that I need your help. Uncle Mel can't do this alone. He's far too busy doing other, more presidential stuff. Like, um… like… well, it's top secret. Yeah, real top secret stuff. Being

28

president is no picnic, but if it were a picnic, let's just say I wouldn't be able to tell you what was in the sandwiches. There is something you can do, however. Something that is your responsibility as American citizens. Everyone must play their part. If you, or someone you know, know of anyone who you even remotely suspect of being one who doesn't belong here, please, do your civil duty and pick up the phone. Do not take matters into your own hands. Just call the number on the screen. Or you can email us, strictly anonymously, at getout@us.gov. Or if you're watching, and happen to be one of those that don't belong here, you know who you are, you may call the same number and turn yourself in. Believe me, you'll be glad you did. Don't you wanna go home? Just look at these happy Muslims." A photo flashed across the screen of a group of people that were clearly Isis. Who edited this thing? "Please, remember 9/11, and do your part. As the late, great Woodsy Owl said, 'In the city, or in the woods. Please keep America lookin' good. And safe.' And please, America, pick up your trash. This place is starting to look like a shithole."

The phone rang. I muted the TV and picked it up. It was Ray. Talking a thousand miles an hour. Hitting the Adderall again. We're all on Adderall, but some of us clearly don't need it. Like Ray.

"Doooood, can you believe this guy? Did you just see that? On TV? Hoooolyshit, man."

"Yeah, I know, but he's always full of it."

"Nonono not that. Imean, that's fucked up too b-b-but man did you see his face man?"

"Yeah," I replied. "He's a smug asshole."

"Nononono not that either. It slipped. His face slipped manjesus."

"His face slipped? What the hell are you talking about?"

"It slipped," he clarified. "His fucking faceman." He further clarified.

"I really don't know what the hell you're talking about. Ray, slow down, man. Breathe."

DAVE!

"Dude I can't believe you didn't see that." He wasn't slowing down. "Plus what the fuck is he talking about? He is literally making no sense right now. In fact, he's making less than that. Can you make negative sense? Because that's what he is making. Negative sense. Whoo. Is it hot in here? Who is this?"

"It's Eric."

"Oh hey, Eric. What do you want?"

"You called me, asshole."

"Ohyeahthatsright.   Dudelistentomeigottabebrief.   Shitsgoingdown. Soyoubettergetyourassto…" big breath, "Ourusualspotattheborder. ASAP."

"Where are you?" I asked.

"I'M THERE NOW! COME ON, WE NEED YOU! LATERS."

Click.

I had no clue what the hell he was talking about. But I packed my stuff and went off to our protest spot anyway. I'll be anywhere that shit's going down.

I stepped out of my gray Ford Libido, a stupid smile on my face. I waved to the crew over at the wall, still smiling like some sort of leprotic clown. My brown Bean boots tied up in knots only I knew how to tie. These were the type of knots that didn't loosen and untie by themselves (hint: the rabbit goes around the tree backwards. Try it, it works.), so I wouldn't trip and fall.

How ironic, I thought, as my face was speeding toward the dirt after tripping over a rock.   The gang stopped what they were doing, any sort of moroseness dropping off their faces, and they all busted out laughing. Laughing and pointing. Pointing and laughing. I pointed at them, too. With my finger straight up in the air. "Fuck you guys," I shouted, but I couldn't help but chuckle at myself as I got up and brushed the dirt off my jeans.

Ray, the only one who wasn't laughing, walked over to me like a zombie somnambulist. "Ok, what's so important I had to leave Mr. Bean to come all the way out here?" I asked him.

Ray looked like he was crashing off a six-day coke binge, his eyes rolled slowly up to regard my visage. "Huuhh?" he replied, drooling.

"Adderall wearing off, Ray?" I asked.

"I'mm ouutt," he said.

"Here," I said, reaching into my pocket. "Have a few of…"

His eyes lit up like a fucking slot machine. He snatched the pills out of my hand before I could say "mine". He scarfed them down with no delay.

A few minutes later, after me trying to understand what he was mumbling on about, he was back to normal. The words started to form, and I decided it may be time to listen; that whatever it is he had to say was probably important, since he felt the need to have me drag my ass down here.

"Start over," I said.

"Dude, remember what I said about Uncle Mel's face? About the slippage? It really happened! I'M NOT THE ONLY ONE WHO SAW IT HOLY SHIT!"

"Jesus Christ, this again? Who cares? Maybe it was a facial tic. Big deal. Lots of people have those. Your dad has a major one."

He slapped me across my face like a bitchy little girl. His dad had muscle spasms in his eye that he was quite sensitive about, brought on by extreme Adderall intake as well as a severe case of enjoying bourbon way too much.

"How dare you," I said, which actually came across as sounding way more girly than the slap in the face was.

"Dude, you gotta listen to me. Just, would you come over here?" He all but carried me to the group standing over by the wall. A few of them were talking about Mel's face. The others were talking about something more important. I tried to decipher through the cross-talk what the important group was saying, but somehow I got roped into the face conversation.

"I know, right?" Ray answered somebody. "Nick, Nick, Nicknicknick, show Eric the video."

31

"Hey Nick," I greeted the Resident Idiot.. I liked Nick and all, but every group had to have a Resident Idiot, and Nick volunteered one day. And lo and behold, he fit the suit. I thought for sure Ray was going to get nominated. Or at the very least get an Honorable Mention or an Also-ran.

"Hey Eric,"Nick said. So ok, so I'm sitting home reading, right?" See what I mean? I don't even think Ray could read. Which, in my opinion, made him way more of an idiot. But I digress.

"Are you done?" Nick asked me, as though he could read my thought processes.

"Continue," I said.

"Ok, so I'm sitting home reading. And I get this text from Mary. She and Drew had been watching TV, and Uncle Mel comes on, spouting his shit. So they started filming. I guess Drew has it in his mind that he's going to make some sort of documentary about the end of the world or some shit. So anyway, they're filming the PSA with their phone when they see this."

He shows me the video on his phone. And I watch Uncle Mel give his dumb spiel again. Or was it a rigmarole? Only this time, it was a lot grainier, being shot with a cheap-ass Walmart Tracfone. The sound was all right, but I could barely make out what was going on on the screen. Drew seemed to be shaking the camera a lot, either to lend the film some authenticity, or maybe he had the D.T.'s. Mary and Drew were going to film their documentary like this? Cloverfield had better picture quality and camera work.

Nick had been staring at me the entire time, with a dumb fucking expression, mouth agape, apparently waiting for some sort of reaction.

The video ended. "Didja see it? Didja see it?"

"Did I see what?" I asked.

"Uncle Mel's face. It slipped."

"Oh come on, not this again. I couldn't see shit from that video."

"Hold on, let me rewind it."

32

"I don't think it's gonna make any difference, Nick." I could barely make out the animated French Canadians with their little cartoon berets splattering themselves on the wall. How was I going to make out Mel's supposed face slip?

But Nick didn't listen to a word I said. He shoved the phone in my face, and played the second half of the video. "Ok, right….there." He paused it at the point when Uncle Mel was going on about Woodsy Owl. "You see it? You see it?"

"Guy, I can barely see anything in this video. What is it I'm supposed to be looking at?

He zoomed in, which made the picture even worse, and pointed at the lower corner of Mel's face. Or I guess it was Mel's face.

"You see that shit, yo? His chin just about hit his chest. That face be slippin'. It ain't real, homie. That's some straight alien shit. Uncle Mel ain't from this world, dude."

I wasn't sure why the 1990's Ebonics suddenly, and frankly I didn't care.

"Seriously?" I said. "An alien? How could an alien make such cool movies as Mad Max, or Braveheart? BRAVEHEART, FOR CHRIST'S SAKE!"

"That ain't Mel Gibson yo, is what I'm sayin'. That's an impostor. Trump was an impostor, too. They ain't the real ones. The real Gibsons and Trumps of this world got abducted. These dudes cut off their faces and is wearing them. They's aliens."

"Bye Nick. Nice talking to you,"

I excused myself and headed over to the other group, who I'd hoped were talking about more productive things.

"Hey, Eric," Carlton said. I like Carlton.

"Hey. Sorry for laughing at you. But that was some funny shit."

"I tripped, Carlton. People trip."

33

"It was the expression on your face. You were all like Whaaaahhaa," he said, and made a dumb face, which I don't think I was even capable of making. I was starting to not like Carlton.

"Okay, yep, well I hope you took a picture," I responded. "So, what are you guys talking about?"

"Here goes. I have one word for you. Topple," he said

"Topple?" I asked.

"Topple." He clarified

"Topple," I said.

"Topple," he echoed back.

"What do you mean topple?"

"We're going to topple the wall."

"We're going to topple the wall?"

"What did I just say?"

"We're going to topple the wall."

"That's right."

"I don't understand. How can we topple the wall? I mean, it has some engineering flaws, being that some of it is made of wood and all, but I don't think we can actually topple it."

"Eric, do you know how many protesters there actually are?"

"Millions, I think."

"Yes, Eric. Millions. Many many millions. We can all topple this wall if we put our backs into it." He pounded on the wall in front of him, for emphasis. It didn't budge one bit, and even seemed to have hurt his hand a little. The emphasis was lost in this pitiful display. "We have chainsaws, hydrochloric acid, and little inflatable pigs. We even have heavy equipment like bulldozers that are being towed there as we speak."

"No shit," I said.

"Shit," he answered.

"Seems like a huge project. Like, wow. I can't believe we're going to finally topple the wall."

"We're not gonna topple the wall," Carlton looked at me like I was a fifth grader trying to comprehend calculus. Which was actually pretty spot on.

"Wha…?" I articulated.

"I think this will explain it all," he said, and handed me a flier.

Greetings, fellow Topplers!

Are you tired of the government's tyranny? Are you tired of protesting and getting nowhere fast? Well, the time has come to DO SOMETHING! Grab your baseball bats, brooms, chisels, get back to the wall and start BANGING! Let's DESTROY THIS WALL and bring to end the TYRANNIC RULE that we have lived with for many years now! GATHER AT THE WALL! FUCK SHIT UP! Toppling will commence on June 3rd at 12:00 p.m. E.S.T. (That's noon, dummies.) Bring your BRUTE STRENGTH and put on your best worst clothes, because shit is going to get MESSY! This WALL IS COMING DOWN NOW!

Details will be given to you when you get to the border.

A light lunch will be served.

***

"So, we are gonna topple the wall," I said to Carlton.

"No," he answered. "We are not gonna topple the wall."

I sighed. "Explain this to me like I'm Ray."

"I've made so many of these, dude. This flier has gone out nationwide."

DAVE!

The flier itself seemed familiar and unprofessional. I wish he'd have given it to me or someone else to proofread before sending the thing out nationwide.

"I even sent a copy to the Huffington Post, so that they would post it online. Plenty of people will be in attendance."

"Fliers?" I asked. "Huffington Post? Don't you think the government's going to get wind of this right quick?"

He grinned like the Cheshire Cat who had just smoked way too much Afghani opium with the caterpillar. A shame that we cold no longer get Afghani anything, since there is presently a wall between us and Afghanistan. We are forced to grow and farm all of our opiates and cocaine on our own turf. And its obviously not as good. Some really good Afghani or even Mexican shit would be fun. "That's the point," he said.

I forgot what we were talking about.

"What's the point?" I asked. Then I remembered. We were talking about the government getting wind of this whole Toppling thing. But still: "I don't get it."

"It would have been so much easier if Ray would have explained this to you earlier."

"No," I answered. "No, it wouldn't"

Carlton giggled. "Yeah, I guess you're right about that. I guess you're right."

He looked over at Ray, and shook his head. "Boy, that Ray, huh?" I tried my best to look as annoyed as I felt. "Soooo…"

"The whole point is for the government to get wind of this. When they hear about it, they'll send their troops and most, if not all, of their resources to the border. The one thing Uncle Mel is scared of the most is something happening to his precious wall. It's a big wall. He'll need all the military aid he has at his disposal at the border. Which leaves a huge hole in the coverage in D.C. It's a cover, man. It's a straw man for what the true plan is."

"Which is…"

"We're taking over the Capitol."

"Nothing like aiming for the moon," I said. "How are we going to take over the Capitol?"

"This is bigger than you think, my friend. Much bigger. We've been planning this for years. We're a covert operation. We call ourselves the Invaders."

"The Invaders?"

"We think it has an ominous sound," Carlton answered. "Would you like to be an Invader, Eric?"

"Woah, woah, woah. Hold up. Slow down. This is all too much. So let me get this straight."

"Shoot."

"So you put out word nationwide that there is going to be some sort of secret operation, which is not so secret after all, to topple the wall. You call the group the "Topplers", a group which doesn't even exist, so that the Invaders, a group that does exist, can infiltrate D.C."

"You didn't really put it any differently than I did, but yeah."

"And you think this little group can pull this off?" I asked.

"We have just shy of a million members. We are all heavily armed. Yeah, I think we can pull this off."

"And this has been going on for years? How come I'm just now getting wind of it?"

"Well, Eric, despite the size of our organization, we're a tight-knit network. It's very hard to get in. There's a circle of trust. Ray vouched for you, though, so I just assumed he would tell you when the time was right. But, well, Ray's an idiot. Not the Resident Idiot, but a trustworthy idiot, and an idiot of Honorable Mention." I knew it. He was an idiot of Honorable Mention.

"Back to the Topplers, though, let me see the ad in HuffPo.

He showed me the post on his phone. There it was, in black and white, or whatever color you call an internet page. It was the same as the flier.

"How does the government even let sites like this exist? They're so anti-Republican."

"They won't for long," Carlton said. "But right now, they would cause more of a stir by taking it down than the Post is causing with their rhetoric. They hate making a stir. Gives the American people a rash. It's a setback for them. And you have to stop thinking of things in terms of Democrats, Republicans, right wing, left wing. They're all on the same side. The dichotomy of government is an illusion. It's the Government vs. the people now. It's been that way for a long time, but most of us are too dumb to see it. And they like it that way."

"Carl," I said.

"Carlton," he corrected.

"Carlton. Aren't our people going to read this in the Post, or get the flier, and believe this is real? The ones who don't know about the Invaders?"

"Most definitely."

"So they're going to head to the wall and start hacking away, with all these axes and heavy equipment and little inflatable pigs, and, Jesus." The realization hit me of just what the hell was going to happen. "They're going to die, aren't they? The second someone gets caught with so much as a hatchet in their hands, they'll be shot on sight. No questions asked. You're sending people to their death."

He looked despondent. For just a second. Then he regained his composure. "Okay, first, I'm not sending people anywhere. I'm not the head of this operation. And yes, there will be casualties. But no great wars are won without them. It's the cost of battle. We'll lose a lot more once we get to D.C."

"But the people in D.C. know the risk."

Carlton sighed. "The people at the wall know the risk, too, Eric. Don't fool yourself into thinking any different."

"Shit, we're just as bad as them," I said. "We are knowingly killing our own people. We're murderers. There has to be another way."

"Don't you think they've thought of every other possibility? This is the most effective plan. The alternative is much, much worse. Look at where we are as a country. You, me, Ray, Nick, we're all poor. The only rich ones are in the government, or are in cahoots with the government."

"So that's it, then. This all comes down to money, as always," I said.

"No, man. This is about control. He who has the money has the control. Everyone knows that; it's pretty basic. When you keep people poor, you keep them in a cage so you can poke and prod them with sticks and make them dance around like little monkeys."

I thought of the visual and laughed. Monkeys are funny.

He continued: "This place is rapidly going to hell. We don't have much time left. We need to act now before shit gets worse."

He saw the look I was giving him.

"You know I'm right," he said.

Truth was, I did know he was right. I didn't like it, but putting all the future casualties aside for a minute, it was a good plan. I didn't know if it was going to work or not, but it was the best shot we had at making some real change.

"I'm just shocked Ray didn't tell you about any of this. I was beginning to think that maybe you were someone I couldn't trust after all, and you'd end up as a Toppler instead."

"What made you change your mind?" I asked.

"I don't know. Something in my gut. It's hardly ever wrong. You seem like real people. Like good people. Maybe I'm wrong. But I doubt it. Friggin Ray, though, he's a dumbass. I'm wondering why he didn't let you know. Is he that thick? Did he just forget?"

"I don't know," I said. "Lately he's been worried about stupid shit. Like tonight, for instance. All he's thinking about is the president's face."

He froze. "Oh, that."

"What?" I prodded.

"Well, I'm beginning to think there may be some truth to that after all."

"Jesus, not you too," I said.

"I watched the announcement tonight, and I knew something about Uncle Mel wasn't quite right. It never has been. Not since The Passion of the Christ. I'm thinking now that maybe I did see his face slip, a little."

"So you think he's from outer space or some shit."

He shrugged. "Outer space, inner space, Mars, Pluto, Uranus, my anus. It's not that far-fetched. This shit happens all the time."

I looked at him. If my face were an emoticon, it would be the one with the squiggly mouth.

"What, you don't believe in extraterrestrial life?"

"Not really," I answered.

"Dude, that's like saying you don't believe in gravity, or you think the moon landing was a hoax. What, next you're probably gonna tell me you're a member of the Flat Earth Society, too. Just because you can't see it from where you stand, doesn't mean it doesn't exist."

If I were an emoji at that moment, I would probably be the little snowman dude. That's just how I was feeling today. Maybe it doesn't make sense to you, but this whole conversation wasn't making sense to me.

"Haha, you look like a snowman, dude," he said. "Look, I'm freaked out about this whole alien bullshit, too. But we have some serious ass kicking to do regardless."

"So assuming this coup is successful, what then?"

"I'm glad you asked, my boy. Come on, I got someone I want you to meet."

I got into my car and followed him. We pulled onto the Pacific Coast Highway and headed north for a few miles. It was about eight or nine at night at this point, and the highway seemed oddly dead for this time of day. Something seemed unsettling, but it may have just been the Chipotle I'd had for lunch. We turned off the highway and onto a fairly well-lit side road, through a gorgeous suburban development, which was mostly vacant at this point, since no one could afford to live there. All the rich people lived in places much nicer than this, and most of the people that had been living here had defaulted on their mortgage payments and evacuated the area. There were a few lights on in some windows, I assumed those belonged to families whose houses were already bought and paid for when the economy collapsed. Ironic. Or maybe tragic. Living in these nice million-dollar homes and barely able to put food on their expensive china. Their lawns, which were probably once nicely manicured, all grown over like a Rastafarian hairdo because they couldn't afford the gas for their riding lawn mowers. The more I looked at these houses, the more I understood. The Invaders were important. We were going to try and put a stop to it. Whether we were successful or not was sort of not the point for me. I was starting to get excited about being an important part of history. Hopefully it was a major turning point for the world, but I was just excited that I was chosen. Here we were. Driving down this road felt akin to George Washington crossing the Delaware. If that makes any sense. I used that analogy, and I don't really even know if that was a major event in history. But someone painted it, so it must have been. Yes, folks, he stood up in that boat and didn't fall over. Much like I will stand against the tyranny of this regime without falling over, sailing through the choppy waters of

Fuck. I lost it. Anyway, we pulled into a driveway of a house with the porch light on. Carlton got out of his vehicle and I got out of mine.

"Whose house is this?" I asked him.

"Mine," he said with very little enthusiasm.

41

"You don't sound thrilled," I said.

"What's the point in living in a house like this when I can't afford to live? I'd sell it for extra cash, but since the taxes are so high on real estate sales, I would only be left with about a quarter of what this house is actually worth. And I'll be goddamned if I'm going to let those cocksuckers take any more of my money."

We entered the house, and the very first thing that struck me when he flicked the light on was the emptiness of it. Such a big, nice house with nothing in it. We were standing in his living room, and there was no furniture. save for one recliner. And one tiny flat screen on the wall.

"Here it is," Carlton said. "Come on, I'll give you the grand tour." I could hear the sarcasm in his words.

"We are now in the living room. This is my recliner. Only I sit here. This over here is my TV. And over here," he scooched down and pointed at a moving spot on the rug, "this is my spider. Yeah, I got pets."

I was unimpressed. Most people had cockroaches.

"Come on, let's go upstairs."

He led me up the stairs. The landing went in two directions. There was a bathroom straight ahead, which was incredibly clean, and off to either side were what I assumed were rooms. Two of them were completely barren. I assumed they were bedrooms at one point. One of the rooms did have a bed in it, so it could be safely called as such. There was not much else in there. A meager book collection, no TV, no dresser; his clothes stacked in neat little piles on the floor. There was an en suite attached to the room, which glistened like the previous bathroom. Another room housed a desk with a laptop on it, and nothing else. Wait! Hold on a minute! There was a pencil.

"What happened to all your shit?" I asked.

"Liquidated. I pawned most of it for extra cash. Also donated a lot of it to the Salvation Army."

"Why?" I asked.

"Eric, there are people out there a lot worse off than you and me," he said. "There always will be. They need the stuff more than I do. Besides, I won't be here long, if all goes according to plan."

"So, where is this person you wanted me to meet?" I inquired.

"Oh, we're not there yet. I just wanted to stop by here to pick up some beer. I'm parched."

I felt something crawling on my shoulder, and reached up and squashed that fucker.

"Eric Junior!" Carlton screamed.

"Oh, sorry man. You named your spider Eric Junior?"

"Yeah, I thought it would be a nice tribute. I never thought you would kill him. Come on, let's get a beer."

He held one out and I shook my head no. I had no idea where we were going or if I had to drive there.

"Suit yourself." I followed him into the kitchen, which was furnished with nothing more than a card table and a couple folding chairs.

He opened the fridge, and I noticed that there was nothing in there either, save for an over-sized bottle of ketchup and lots and lots of beer. Typical bachelor. Typical poor bachelor.

He grabbed a beer out of the fridge. "One for me..." he said, poked a hole in the side, and shotgunned the first one. I hadn't seen anyone do that since college. The refrigerator door didn't even have time to swing fully shut before he slammed his empty can down on the counter. "And some for the road," he said, and took a thirty-rack out.

"Come on," he said. "Let's go."

We left the house and got in our respective cars. He got out of his, and knocked on my window. I rolled it down.

"Your little Libido isn't going to make it where we're going."

I laughed. "Boy, if I had a nickel for every time I heard that."

"I mean your car, dammit." Carlton laughed too.

"And your Honda Elephant will?"

"It hasn't not made it yet." Eric headed back to his car.

I got out of my Libido and into his Elephant. I have a real issue with getting in a vehicle where the driver has been drinking. But he assured me we weren't going too far.

This was the first time I'd ridden in a Honda Elephant. The seats were quite comfortable. After being made fun of for years regarding the status of the Element as an off-road vehicle, not to mention its sheer pathetic look, Honda beefed it up with better tires and gave it more of an SUV-style body. They called it the Elephant. The seats had the texture of wrinkled elephant skin, hence why they were so comfy. Everything, the radio, the seats, the mirrors, the internal temperature settings, had a memory like an elephant for each driver, and it was big and slow as fuck. Much like an elephant. I think Honda took the word a little too literally, but whatever. I wasn't driving it. My Ford Libido did nothing to attract anyone's attention sexually, in fact it was an ugly pile of shit. There were certainly never any excited people ever riding in my passenger seat. So perhaps Ford needed to be a little more literal with their branding.

We exited Carlton's development and he quickly pulled into a small turnout about a quarter of a mile down. "Lend a hand," he said as he got out.

We headed to the front of the Elephant and I saw that there was a dirt road there, as overgrown as Carlton's lawn, so it wasn't visible at all from the road. Also, there was a giant felled tree blocking its entrance. He looked at it and shook his head.

"Fucking Drew," he said. "He never puts it back the right way. Here," he said. "Get the other end."

"What the hell are we gonna do with this tree?" I asked.

"We're gonna move it."

"How the fuck…?"

"Just grab an end," he said. "You'll see."

I went to the opposite end of the tree, and realized as soon as I touched it that it was not a tree. It appeared to be made of papier mâché, covered with a weatherproof epoxy. We lifted it quite easily, and tossed it aside. Carlton got back in his vehicle and once he cleared the tree, we moved it back. We both got back in, my body sinking into the faux-elephant skin like a newborn baby sinking into a river.

"Well, it looks like Mary and Drew are here." He sounded disgusted. "Oh well, I guess you'll meet them eventually anyway."

"I know Mary and Drew," I said. "Nick's friends. Always throwing poop at each other. Making weird movies. Had that story written about them crashing into a moose in a plane."

"Yeah, that's them," Carlton said. "Can't fucking stand them."

A couple minutes went by, then he clarified. "I mean, they're good people."

A few more seconds went by, then he further clarified, "But I can't stand them."

He drove down the twisty road until he came to a fork. He took the left fork and drove into even thicker woods. A couple miles down and he turned again, down an even narrower road. It was all very spooky. I couldn't help but think of the horror novel Harm's Way, by Marc Richard. Some sick shit happens in that book, if you're into horror. You're welcome, Marc.

We stopped at what seemed to me to be a random spot in the road, as it seemed to end nowhere in particular. Carlton got out. "Come on," he said.

"Come where?" I asked. What the fuck were we doing?

"This way," he said, and he led me further into the woods, down some shitty footpath that was shittier than the shitty footpaths I'd been used to shitting on.

"How long do we have to walk down this shitty, shitty footpath?" I asked him.

"About a mile and half," he said.

"A mile and a half???" I asked, incredulously.

"About," he reiterated. Like that made me feel any better.

We walked for goddammit about an hour or three, tripping over bramble and brumble, and finally I said, "About?"

A stick had the nerve to poke my arm. I think it ripped a big gash in it, and I was bleeding all the fuck over the place.

"Doooood, how much farther," I had the nerve to ask.

"We're about halfway there," he answered. Trailblazing like he knew what the fuck.

"About?" I asked again.

"What is your issue, man? We're saving the world here."

For a second, it put everything in perspective. For a second. But then, a second later, it didn't.

"Can we…" I started, then he said "Hey look, there's Mary and Drew."

He pointed up at the sky, which was well-lit from the moon, and there I saw Mary and Drew hanging up in the trees like a couple of orangutans, throwing what looked and smelled like poo at each other.

"Oh, for fuck sake," Carlton said, cracking one of the beers he was carrying.

"Want one?" he asked.

"No thanks," I said. "But I will have a few hits off my weed vape, if you don't mind."

"Mind?" he said. "Of course not. Have at it."

I took a couple hits, thinking it would prepare me for the shit show that was Mary and Drew.

Alas, it didn't, and we waved them a fond goodbye as we kept on our trek.

"Bye, guys," I shouted over my shoulder.

They waved with poo-filled hands. "Bye, guys!" Drew shouted. And we left.

"Have fun!" Mary added, which I thought was too many words.

I realized through this whole ordeal, that Carlton had nothing to say to them.

"Wow, you really don't like them, do you?" I inquired.

"Can't fucking stand them."

A couple minutes went by, then he clarified. "I mean, they're good people."

A few more seconds went by, then he further clarified, "But I can't stand them."

"Right."

Finally, Carlton announced, "Well, here we are."

Nothing about this spot alluded to the fact that we were, in fact, anywhere. I saw nothing different in this particular location than I'd seen during the whole walk here.

He walked a couple feet into the woods, kicked aside some brush, and there it was: A wooden frame, which looked an awful lot like a child's sandbox.

"Where we are?" I asked.

He moved a rock, and revealed a pull-ring, much like you would see on the underside of an attic staircase. He pulled on the ring, and a 4x4 plywood panel swung up on hinges.

47

"Come on," he said, and climbed down a ladder anchored into the dirt. I followed suit.

He led me down this long dark hallway. Dark, yet somehow illuminated. By what, I don't know. I felt like my head was spinning. This was all too much. Suddenly, I felt weird. I felt like my soul was leaving my body. Or something. I'm not sure. I felt faded somehow.

The feeling passed very quickly as he opened the door to the main room.

He turned the light on, and it lit up a room, approximately twenty by thirty feet, bigger than I was expecting for an underground hideout to be. There were shelves lining the walls with very little on them.

"This was actually built as a fallout shelter originally," Carlton explained. "It was a stroke of luck how we found it, really. If we hadn't let our old buddy Nick into our little secret group, not only would be missing a Resident Idiot, but we would never have heard about this shelter. It seems Nick was a Doomsday Prepper a few years back, and built this here shelter with the help of a few friends. It must have taken a lot of time and effort to build such a massive structure. Being the decent person he is, he gave his shelter up for the cause. There are hundreds of these secret spots all over the country where the Invaders meet up. Most not as nice as this, but they're secret, and that's all that really matters. Here, let me give you the grand tour."

He escorted me around the room. Oddly, it seemed less sparse than his house.

"Over here are the shelves. This is where there is sometimes food, but nobody keeps it stocked but me. Over here is a box of crackers, here's a jar of peanut butter, hope you don't have allergies. And here's a knife for spreading the peanut butter on the crackers."

I was intrigued. I wanted to know more about the crackers, but he was off to something else.

"There's a sofa for sitting and/or napping." He pointed to a thing that didn't look so much like a sofa as it did a giant mass of foam and stains. But it did have a nice looking chenille throw on it.

"Through the door there is the bathroom. The ventilation in here is awesome, so you can shit all you want in there. Go ahead. Shit away."

"I don't have to at the moment," I replied.

"Suit yourself. Anyway, over here's a table and a chair. Here's another chair. We're standing on a floor right now. Above us is the ceiling, of course. We take great pride in our overhead lighting. And over here is a desk with a laptop."

He opened the fridge, which was loaded with mostly cheap beer, and a few bottles of water. "Ready for a beer now?" he asked. I was beginning to think he had a drinking problem. But whatever; so did I.

"Yeah, I'll have one," I replied.

We each cracked a beer, and he sat down on the chair at the desk and fired up the laptop.

"Come on over, grab a chair," he said.

He entered the password, which seemed to me to be an incredibly long series of random characters, but Carlton typed it all in, every once in a while hitting the shift key.

"Eric, you're about to meet the man who started it all. The Grand Poobah of the Invaders."

"Me?"

"Yeah I usually don't do this. There are just too many of us for him to meet personally. He usually only talks to the leaders, and he never talks to Nick, Mary, or Drew. Or Ray. But there's something about you I think he'd really like. I think you'd get a kick out of him. If he's available."

He clicked on Skype and logged on, with a password that was even more ridiculously long and complicated.

"How do you remember these strings of letters, numbers, and symbols that comprise your password?" I asked him, shortly realizing it was the first time I'd ever used the word "comprise" in conversation. I should use it more often. It's a fine word.

"Well, Eric, in the words of my late mother, 'In the end, son, they'll come and they'll take everything you own. Your shoes, your hat, and your pet roller skate. Your health will fail and your back will ache and all your insides will slowly rot away from cancer. Your hair will fall out, and your teeth, and you'll get wrinkled and old and you won't believe the person you see in the mirror. Where did my youth go? You'll ask. You'll have bad breath and just an overall stink that you can't pinpoint, and people will forget all about you and you'll be lonely and miserable. Water will start to taste funny. You'll find yourself talking out loud but it will sound like it's coming from somebody else. You'll lose control of your bodily functions, and you'll just start excreting stuff all over the place. Your neighbors will prank call you in the middle of the night, asking if your refrigerator is running. Then, when you tell them you know that joke, they'll call you "Cunt" and hang up rudely. You won't be able to find the right size pan to cook your eggs in. Then you'll realize that your eggs expired months ago and you'll wonder where all the time went. All your friends will die, and your relatives won't give a shit. They'll toss you in a nursing home and forget about you. Maybe they'll come around during Christmastime, but then they'll stop coming and they'll send cards instead. Then those will stop. You'll run out of money. And time. But one thing you'll be left with is your memories.' The sad thing is, none of those other things happened to her, and her memory was the first thing to go."

"Christ, Carlton. She seemed like an optimist. Sorry to hear about your mom dying and all, though."

"She's not dead," he answered.

"Oh? I thought you said she was dead," I said.

"No. I said she was late. On account of her memory being so poor, she can never remember to show up to her appointments. Now," Carlton said, "let's see if he's on."

He looked over at me with a smirk. "He's on," he said. He clicked on a name.

Within the darkened archway of a bridge an even darker figure stood, facing away from us. The archway was massive, but somehow this figure was more massive. And looming. The figure turned slowly toward the screen. I could tell he was wearing some cold weather gear, like a jacket and hat, and maybe gloves. It must have been cold where he was. I couldn't make out his face, though.

Carlton turned to me, smiling. "This is his intro. This plays every time he answers his Skype. I think it's kind of portentous and over the top, but it does well to enhance his image, doesn't it?"

"This is whose intro?" I asked.

He looked at me again and gave a creepy smirk, trying to add to the foreboding tone of the video clip. "You'll see."

The figure got closer and closer. This whole intro was running a little too long, and it was also really freaking me out, man. He got right up on the screen and slowly crouched down, but before we could see his face, the screen faded.

When the screen came back into focus, there appeared one of the most handsome men I'd ever seen in my life. Dark hair, blue eyes, a face of a god. Somewhere in between Ryan Gosling and Adam Levine. Please let him be gay, I silently prayed, then added, and single. Right. Like I actually stood a chance with this guy even if he was. This was the leader of a revolution. Like Che Guevara, but with less Del Toro. If this adventure we were on was a movie, he would be exactly the man they would have picked for his role.

"Carlton!" he said when he saw my companion's face. "Did you fucking see it? Did you see Uncle Mel's face tonight? Holy shit. What did I tell you? What did I fucking tell you?"

Carlton shook his head. "No, I didn't see it. But some of the others did. They said his face slipped?"

"Yes, it slipped. Yes it fucking slipped. Like he was wearing a mask. I knew it. Haha! I knew it!"

DAVE!

"Um," Carlton changed the subject. "I just wanted you to meet a friend of mine, and the newest member of the Invaders. This is Eric." I never actually told Carlton that I was going to be one of the Invaders. But when the man on the screen turned to me and smiled, I thought, Fuck it. I'm one of the Invaders.

"Hi," that gorgeous piece of mankind looked at me, a twinkle in his eye shining brighter than the North Star. "I'm Dave."

CHAPTER THREE

Um." My mouth was dry. I took a swig of beer so that I could actually move my mouth around enough to make sounds. "Hello sir," I uttered sheepishly

"Sir? He laughed. "No need for formalities here. Any friend of Carlton's is a friend of... well, Carlton's. Haha. Just kidding. You can call me Dave. Nice to meet you Erix."

"It's Eric, sir," I corrected.

"Eric?" He looked at me, his beautiful eyebrow raised slightly. "What a weird name. Eric. I'll have to remember that one. Did you see the president's face slip tonight, Eric?" He put air quotes around the word "president".

"Uh, no. No, I didn't. But a lot of people did, from what I gather."

"Yes, Eric. Yes. A lot of people did," Dave said.

"So the president wears a mask."Carlton looked away, scared perhaps that he was talking out of turn. "To play the devil's advocate here, that could mean anything."

"No," the leader said. "Not just a mask, Carlton. He's wearing Mel Gibson's face. Mel fucking Gibson. I had an inkling. I had an inkling he wasn't really Mel Gibson. Remember, Carlton? Remember when there were talks of there being another Apocalypto? And another Mad Max movie? He was going to be in it this time? And then poof, suddenly all those projects get dropped and Mel runs for president? The projects weren't dropped because it suddenly occurred to him he should be running for president. The projects were dropped because Mel fucking disappeared. They got him. They got him, and they are wearing his face now. Just like they wore Trump's face."

"So you're saying Trump wasn't Trump either?"

"That's exactly what I'm saying. Who in their right mind would say some of the stupid shit he said, and think they could get into office? 'The only kind of people I want counting my money are little short guys that wear yarmulkes every day'? 'Rosie O'Donnell is a slob who talks like a truck driver'?"

Carlton nodded. "But Rosie O'Donnell is a slob who talks like a truck driver."

Dave threw up his hands. "That's not the point. People, especially those running for office, aren't supposed to say what they mean. Yes, political correctness has gone too far, but there has to be some. If we all walked around saying what we meant all the time, there would be a lot more shootings and missing limbs and whatnot."

I interjected. "So, let me get this straight, Dave." I was already talking to him like I'd known him for years. "You're saying the White House has been infiltrated by an alien race?"

"At the very least, the president has. But I find it hard to believe that there aren't others who share work space with it and not know something is a little off about him. So yeah, I think there are more of them." Dave sighed, and thought for a moment. "But none of this really matters in the long run."

Carlton stood up, his chair rolling back. "Doesn't matter? Doesn't matter? What do you mean it doesn't matter? This changes everything."

"How?" Dave asked.

"If they are from another world, we don't know anything about them. We don't know what kind of weapons they have access to, we don't know how their minds work. Maybe they operate in another dimension, by another set of cosmic principles. We have no clue what they're capable of or how dangerous this is going to be."

"Did we before?" Dave asked. "Have we ever really known what the government was capable of? We know they can listen in to our conversations anytime they want, and check our browsing histories and so on. They somehow can know everything we're up to. Even before the age of the Internet, they have been spying on people. Sure, it's more prevalent now, because everything we say and do is out there if you want to find it badly enough. But throughout history there has never really been complete privacy. They listen in. And people have just ended up missing from time to time, victims of one conspiracy or another. This is no different."

"This freaks me out," Carlton said. "The human race is evil, sure. But we know what people can do. We know our limitations. Maybe these aliens could just wipe us off the face of the earth just by thinking about it."

"If they could have just wiped us off the face of the earth, they would have by now," Dave said. "No, I think their plans are a little more devious than that. They take over government, amass huge amounts of wealth, which they know we humans value above most other things, divide us up by building walls, increasing tension, and get us to kill each other. That's what I think."

"Wouldn't there be more tension leaving us together, rather than putting up walls and separating us?" I asked. "I remember when my brother and I would get in fights, my mom used to separate us till we promised to behave."

"And also keeping you from communicating, from working out your differences." Dave looked at me. "No, separating increases tension."

"But why us?" I asked. Why America?"

"Think about that for a moment," Dave said. "Do you really need to ask?"

I guess I didn't. Our country was so naive. So easy to infiltrate by spewing rhetoric. So easy to build wealth very quickly. There were lots of reasons. Still, it sounded like bullshit to me.

"Sounds like bullshit to me," I said.

"Doesn't matter," Dave answered. "Maybe I'm wrong. Doesn't change anything. We still need to do something about our situation. I've been thinking for a while now that something was weird about Uncle Mel, but I also came to the conclusion that we have to get things back the way they were, regardless. Our country, and our world, has been going to shit for a long time now. We should have done this years ago."

"I agree," I said. "Really I do. But holy fuck. This is a lot to take in."

"I know," Dave said. "Take your time. If you think this is too much for you, you don't have to do this. But I would really like you to be a part of it. Carlton vouches for you, and that's enough of a recommendation for me. The more the merrier, and all that. Of course," he added, "either way, you can't say anything about this. Ever."

I looked over at Carlton, and he dragged his thumb across his neck. I think if I refused to be an Invader, things would not go so well for me. Either you're in, or you're ignorant of the plan. And since I knew the plan, I guess I was in. All of this gesturing was unnecessary, though, because I'd already decided. I was in. What else was I going to do? Sit around the house and watch the world fall apart? No, there were far too many of us doing that as it was. We needed more people to actually get off their asses and do something; Topplers, Invaders, whatever.

"No, I'm in. What's the plan?"

"Carlton will fill you in on all the details. I gotta get going. Cake's in the oven. Take care, guys. See you around."

"WAIT!" I screamed. "DON'T GO! WHAT KIND OF CAKE????"

But it was too late; the connection was already broken.

"What kind of cake do you think he's having?" I asked Carlton.

"I don't really know," he answered. "I think maybe cheese."

I was thinking a flour-less chocolate torte.

"Well, that was a lot to take in," I said. Dave himself was a lot to take in. Goosebumps.

"If you need time to process this, I totally understand. It is a lot to take in." He turned to me, and looked me directly in the eye. "Of course, if you say no, I'll have to kill you. No offense."

"None taken. But regardless of your pitiful threats, I'm down. I want to be a part of this. Don't you find it dangerous to chat on Skype, by the way?" I gave Carlton the stinky eyeball.

"Not really," he said. "The risk is very minimal. We have the best hackers in the nation working for us, and not only is everything so encrypted and protected that it is damn near impossible to hack into, but everything also runs through its own server. We're not even on the web."

"You're not?" I asked.

"No. We can get on the web if we need to, but even our web connection is very hard to hack into. Watch," he said, and double-clicked on Chrome. It seemed like forever (like ten whole seconds) for it to load up the Google search engine.

"Notice how it took so long?"

I nodded.

"That's because the connection goes one place, relays to another place, relays to yet another place, then to our server. It's slow, but that extra time it took to load a page is the price we have to pay for having a virtually untraceable IP address. I thinks that's how it works, anyway. I'm not a techie. I'm the type of guy who Googles everything to figure out how to get my computer to do what I want it to do, but when I lose my connection, then I can't Google how to fix my connection, and I'm caught in a weird vortex. And anyway, we don't really go on any sites that raise any red flags. We mostly sit in here and watch Youtube videos like the Weird Arby's Guy or Die Antwoord music videos. And Skype? That's a whole other thing altogether. Ever hear of the Dark Web?"

"Yeah," I said.

"Well, our version of Skype is kind of like that. Except harder for the government to hack. Think of it as closed circuit T.V. Plus," he added, "they're much too busy watching shit like this."

He went to Youtube and typed in "Toppler video", and clicked on "Toppler Video #1". This particular video had over three million hits.

After an excruciating fifteen seconds of buffering, the video played.

A beautiful, familiar face showed up on the screen. And he began speaking.

"Hello America. Most of you don't know me yet, but you will soon enough. My name is Dave. I've had years of experience working both for and against the government, as well as heavy training in the United States Marine Corps. I've come to you today, because I want to tell you about this cool new group. We call ourselves the Topplers. And this is a call for all of my fellow Americans to come and join me in the fight against our cruel and oppressive rulers. In the words of the late, great Ronald Reagan to Mr. Gorbachev, 'Tear down this wall'.

"It's time to put down our picket signs and Pink Floyd memorabilia, and actually do something rather than shouting for a change. I ask you to simply go through your garages and basements, grab any sharp implements you can, and on the third of June, 2031, we shall all gather at the wall, and tear this sonofabitch down."

An image of the wall flashed across the screen. The picture was of one of the less reinforced sections, held together by planks and bubblegum. As if to show that it would be quite an easy job.

"Now, I know what you're thinking," Dave continued. "This will not be an easy job. And you're right. It won't be. We've been trying for years to hack away at this monstrosity to no avail. But never have we all gathered at the wall at once. Never have we had access to such heavy equipment. This may take weeks, or months, or I don't know, maybe even a year, but gathered together we will stand up and fight. We will show Capitol Hill that we will not take this separatism. We will no longer keep our Muslim friends, our Jewish friends, our friends of any race, creed, or color trapped out in the cold. We will no longer keep ourselves trapped in. It has been years since America has seen the ocean, for godsake. I mean, look at this lovely ocean."

An image of the ocean filled the screen.

"Isn't she beautiful, guys? Show the government we want this back. We want our freedom back. We want to be able to go swimming in the ocean, or set sail on the seas. We want to take a cruise. We want to see our Canadian and Mexican friends again. We are tired of living under this regime. It's time for a change. Please stay tuned for more installments in this series of videos for further details. Thank you."

I couldn't believe what I had just witnessed.

"How does this even exist? Why doesn't the government just pull this video down? It would be easy enough to do. They fund the site, for the love of Pete."

"Come on, man. You're not stupid. Think."

I did. I knew the answer even before I asked the question. They wanted the video up. They wanted the Topplers to gather at the wall. It never occurred before, having them all gather in one location. They would be easy targets. Yes, the wall was big, but the military was bigger. We killed as many in Vietnam, and they were all hiding in the jungle. This would be lining them up execution-style.

"Jesus Christ, What was that, Carlton? What the fuck was that?"

"What was what?"

"All that bullshit. How can Dave keep a straight face, knowing that this is all a ruse? He's setting millions of Americans up, and sending them to their deaths. It's unconscionable. It's morally reprehensible. It's…"

"It's something that has to be done in order for us to do what we need to do," Carlton finished my sentence for me. That was not what I was going to say.

"These people, these innocent people, are going to get killed. And they don't even know it."

"That's where you're wrong, dude. They do know the danger. They do know the risk. If they don't want to be a part of it, they don't have to be. They can just stay the hell home."

"But Dave, with all his charm and stunningly good looks, is going to make people feel riddled with guilt if they don't do something," I said.

"Yep. You should see the rest of the videos, when you have time. He certainly does a good job at shaming without shaming."

"It's wrong," I said for the umpteenth time.

"I don't know why you're so concerned about the Topplers. The Invaders, us, we'll be in just as much danger doing what we're doing. If not more danger. I don't see what the big deal is."

"You're right, I guess." I couldn't argue with that. Except to add, "I just wish they didn't have to be kept in the dark. I mean, why can't they just know about the Invaders? Why can't there be two camps? The Invaders and the Topplers, the Topplers go to work on the wall and the Invaders take over D.C.?"

"They can't know about it because we don't know who we can trust. If word gets back to the capitol our plan is fucked."

Just then I thought about Starlet. She was going to be one of the Topplers. Jesus. I started to cry.

"What's wrong?" Carlton said, as he cracked another beer.

"I'm just thinking about my friend. In a few months she'll be heading to the wall, not knowing what she's getting herself into."

"For fuck sake, she knows what she's getting herself into."

"I don't think she does. She lives in this kind of fantasy world. I don't know if she understands the danger she's putting herself in."

"Then that's her problem, Eric. You can't change that."

"I can call her and see if maybe she wants to join our team."

"No," Carlton said. "I don't know her, and if she hasn't been chosen by now, chances are she won't be. And if that's the case, if she knows anything about the real plan, she will have to be executed. And so will you, for telling her. Because then you can't be trusted. Did I make the wrong decision, having you here?"

"No!" I said. "No, you didn't. I want to go kick some ass just as badly as you do. I just wish things were different."

"Don't you think I do, too? I have friends that are going to be at the wall on June third. I'm just as scared for them as you are for your friend. I'm also scared for us. But I'm more scared of what will happen to this country if we don't do something now. It sucks, the whole Toppler thing, but when history is written about this, they will be seen as some of the biggest heroes ever."

"Or biggest chumps," I retorted.

"Tomato, tomahto."

Oh, Starlet, if you make it through and somehow find this letter, please know that I didn't want this for you. I had no choice. I had to keep you in the dark to keep you the safest I could. I hope you realize that, and if you hate me for this, I totally understand.

I fidgeted in my seat. "So, what's the plan?"

Carlton grinned. "I thought you'd never ask."

Carlton went to the fridge and got two beers. "You want one?" he asked. When I nodded, he reached back in the fridge and got a third one.

He pulled out a neatly folded DeLorme map. I had always been secretly envious of anyone who could fold a map back up properly. All of mine were crumpled in little balls in my glove compartment. When he unfolded it, I saw that it depicted the Washington, D.C. area.

So, we start out on June fourth, the day after the toppling begins. We head across country, and land in D.C. on June eleventh."

"You think it will take a week to get across?"

"No, but we are all scheduled to meet around D.C. on the eighth. That will give the military plenty of time to evacuate the area and head to the wall to deal with the Topplers. We'll make our way slowly across country in my Elephant."

"Who's riding with us?" I asked.

"I figured we'd take Ray and Nick."

"Those idiots? Why them?"

"Because I'm the only one that can deal with them. Plus, you know Ray, so I figured you'd be okay riding with them. And," he continued, "I think it would make for a great adventure, and we'd have some really fun scenes to add to the next book."

Next book? What the hell was he talking about?

"Shit, man. Okay, so then what? What are all these little pen marks all around the capitol?"

"Those are where we have our caches of weapons stored. Wait till you see. Man, we have all kinds of shit. Guns, explosives, everything we need. Everyone has their own place to go." He pointed to one of the dots. "Ours is right here, in Annapolis."

"How do you keep all of this a secret?"

"They're hidden very well, and are guarded very nonchalantly by some very inconspicuous guards. We need to have these caches. We can't very well travel with these weapons. Even if I drive like a grandma, which I fully intend on doing, I'm sure to get pulled over a couple times. It's just the way things are now. If we're caught with so much as a pocket knife, we could be detained, which would cause a delay, and fuck up the whole plan. Now, I'm not saying I'm the most important piece of the puzzle, but every piece counts. The combination to the vault is very long and very hard to remember, and as you can see, I have a good memory for that kind of shit. So I'm the only one who knows the pass code. If I'm not there on the eighth, they lose not only me, but all the weapons we have stored will just sit there. And, like I said, we have some very cool shit. There are about a thousand of us, and although it's impossible to get an exact head count of all of those in the White House on any given day, a thousand employees is not an unreasonable estimate. So as you can see, we need every person and every weapon we have available."

"So we get the weapons, and then what?"

"Okay, here's where it gets interesting. The Invaders will split into two teams. First, there are the Distractors. Their job: High jinks and tomfoolery. They'll be running around the District, creating chaos. Sawing the head off Lincoln at the Memorial, skinny dipping in the reflecting pool, posing for pictures with the Washington Monument as though it were a big cock, et cetera. That will keep most of the police and whatever military is left busy trying to keep order. The rest of us, folks like you and me, are called the Inserters. Our job is to insert ourselves into the White House, and shoot to kill. We will take no prisoners, and we won't stop until Uncle Mel and every last soul in the building is dead."

"You're kidding me? The Distractors and the Inserters? Who came up with these titles?" I asked, purposely ignoring the part where Carlton told me I would have to kill a bunch of people.

"Probably the same guy who came up with the Topplers."

"Dave," I said.

"Yup."

He went on to tell me that once we had the White House empty, we would take it over and form a new government. Just like that?? I don't know the specifics of how the hell that was going to happen. When I asked Carlton, he said Dave had it all worked out. Ours was not to question how. I was beginning to think we were blindly putting an awful lot of faith in Dave, with no proof of his effectiveness. But there really wasn't an alternative. I just hoped this wasn't going to be another Jonestown, and that he really did have the world's best interests at heart.

Our first mission was to break down the wall, for real this time.

"What then?" I asked.

"Toppling the wall is the easy part. Our dreams are much, much bigger than that. The first thing we do is we form a new government. We can't have anarchy. Even something as simple as breaking down the wall needs to be done in an orderly fashion, and we need it done quickly. We want to be a government of peace and love, and most of all equality."

"Great! Wow, I can't believe nobody has ever thought of this before! A government of peace, love, and equality! Gosh."

"Oh, shut the fuck up," Carlton said.

"Okay, and then what?"

"Then we get the United Nations together. And we discuss. And we all agree to one world government. Just think of it: No more borders. No more countries. Just one planet. One mind. One love."

"And anarchy."

"Not at all. We'll have a leader. We'll have rules and laws that we have to abide by, and consequences if we don't."

"And who's going to be the leader of all this?" I asked. "Let me guess. Dave?"

"Maybe. Maybe they'll come up with an even better one."

"And then everything will be ducky. Of course. I'll gladly trade all of my Adderall for whatever the fuck it is you're on."

"I have high expectations and even higher hopes," he said, matter-of-factly.

"Cool."

"I have to have high hopes. What, do you want me to go in there with a shitty attitude? We're gonna win this thing, Dave will take over; it's gonna be great, really.

"What makes you think it won't be a case of meet the new boss, same as the old?"

64

"Who knows? I don't know everything, Eric. It may very well get to that point again, hundreds or thousands of years down the road. But we need a shakeup. We're heading down a very bad road, you don't need me to tell you this. You can't just sit at home while our country, and even the rest of the world, goes to shit."

"Why not?"

"Because then you'd be an asshole." He looked very serious suddenly. "Also, I'd have to kill you."

"Heh, I know, I know. I'm just kidding. I'm with ya, of course." Wow. We were really going to do this. It just hit me. This was it. No turning back now. Starlet popped in my head again. I wish she would stop doing that, so that I could keep focus on the task at hand.

Carlton noticed the somber look I must have had on my face.

"You're still thinking about that chick, aren't ya? What's the deal with her, anyway? You fuck her? Is she your girrrrlfrieeend?"

"No, no. Well, not anymore. She was once, when we were teenagers. For like five minutes. We're still pretty close though. Are you sure there's nothing I can do for her? I really can't let her know what's going on?"

He made another cutting gesture across his throat. I guess not.

"The fuck kind of a name is Starlet, anyway?"

"She chose it."

"No shit," he said. "She work in porn or something?"

"No."

"Stripper?"

"No."

"Chick with a dick?"

I paused.

65

"Hahaha I knew it! She's a chick with a dick! Oh, man. Priceless."

"Correction: Used to be. And fuck you, dude. It's 2031. You'd think people would be a little more understanding nowadays. What are you, a transphobe or something? You know what? You're really starting to get under my skin. I have very little tolerance for bigotry. Get me a beer."

"Yeah, all right. I'll get you a beer. Then we gotta have a talk. I'll show you who's a fucking bigot."

He went to the fridge and got out three more beers. One for me and two for him once again, I assumed.

He opened all three beers and placed two of them in front of me.

"Jesus, man. One at a time."

"Just drink up."

I took a couple sips and placed the beer down on the table. He picked it back up and raised it to my lips. "Come on, down the hatch. That's a good boy."

I guzzled the rest of the beer, to appease him.

"You better drink the other one. Fucking bigot, I'll show you."

I took a couple sips off the fresh beer as Carlton rose. "What, are you gonna fight me or something? I'm really not in the mood."

But he didn't fight me. Instead he dropped his pants. And I could see now why he thought it was funny that I called him a transphobe. He had a vagina.

"No fucking way," I said.

"Who's a bigot now?" he asked.

"Wow, dude. I had no idea."

"You wanna fuck me now, don't you?" He asked, his lady parts a little too close to my face.

"No, not really. I've been into dick lately. No offense."

"Yeah, see? This is the problem. Every time I drop my pants, I scare people away. This is why I've been celibate for years now."

"No, it's not that. I'm sure you'll find someone who enjoys what you have. You just gotta trim a little, is all."

"I hate this stupid thing."

"It's not stupid. But why don't you get yourself a dick if you're that upset about what you have now?"

"Who do you think I am? Trump or something? I don't have that kind of cash. There are a lot of things I would change about myself, if I had the money. My nose, my cheeks, my vagina. But I'm broke. Like everyone. I should have gotten the sex change when insurance actually covered the procedure. But now that it's considered cosmetic, I'll have to wait until the policies change. If they ever do. If not, I'm stuck with this."

He was right. Insurance used to cover it, as it was considered a birth defect. But then people started abusing the system. Getting a sex change became all the rage. It was almost as cool as getting a tattoo or piercing. Then, when people got bored with their new parts, sometimes they'd switch back. It became a real money loser for insurance companies. Soon, there was no telling who actually needed one and who just wanted one, so they had to shut that shit down.

"So, what was your birth name?" I asked.

"Carlton. I've always been Carlton. My parents really wanted a boy, and when I was born with an inny, it didn't change their minds any. I grew up a boy. I don't know if I was a product of my environment, or if I really am a dude trapped in someone else's body, but I suppose it doesn't really make any bit of difference. I am what I am."

"Sure, sure," I said, and added, "Now, could you put that away?" I downed the last of my can.

He pulled his pants back up and grabbed us both another brew.

"Hey, wanna wrestle?" he slurred. Why is it when dudes get drunk, they want to wrestle? "Come on, try to pin me."

"I'm all set. You can put that beer away. This has been a very enlightening evening, but I'm beat. I'm gonna go collapse on that thing you call a couch."

"Suit yourself," he said.

And so I reclined on the couch while Carlton surfed the web, my thoughts drifting to Starlet and Hawaii once more.

As I said, there I was, walking down the beach with my mug of delicious hot milk. I never started out as a hot milk drinker; back when I was eight or so I developed a pretty nasty coffee habit. My parents weren't like other cool parents, letting their kids sneak a beer here and there at family functions. They never allowed me to even be around alcohol. Maybe that's why I'm such a heavy drinker today, I don't know. They did, however, encourage me to drink plenty of coffee. They thought it a healthier alternative to Adderall or Ritalin. It started out with just one cup in the morning, before I went off to school. Soon, however, that one cup wasn't enough, and before I knew it I was up to five cups a day. As I got older, I drank more and more coffee till at the age of fourteen I had a pretty serious anxiety attack, which led to a full-on nervous breakdown, followed by a week stay in the hospital. When I was released, I still felt that I needed hot beverages in my life, and there was no way in hell I was going to drink tea. Ever. So I started drinking hot milk. All I had to do was pretend that I was drinking a very weak latte. If any of you have ever tried warm or hot milk before, it tastes like expired horse cum, but soon I got used to it.

Lost in my thoughts, I was startled by a beautiful sight. A girl of my age, sunbathing on the sand. I'm a leg guy, and hers were quite possibly the best set I had ever seen on a dame. Like they were sculpted out of whatever substance they would use to sculpt something really nice. Her hair, long and brown, with highlights of gold. She had that exotic look to her, almost like she came from a family that was Asian a few generations back. She was absolutely stunning in her one-piece bathing suit, although she didn't fill out the top part very well, and down below she had a bulge that looked suspiciously like a dick.

68

Neither of these aspects really bothered me all that much, but I did find myself silently thinking, please let her be into dudes. By her side was a frozen daiquiri , which I'm sure was virgin, since she didn't look to be much older than sixteen. Her eyes were closed; she must have been asleep. I got even closer, and slowly I reached out my foot and tipped her drink over, spilling a little on her arm. Which also looked like it was sculpted out of that stuff I just mentioned.

"Oops, I'm so sorry," I grabbed the towel that was laying by her side, and blotted her arm off.

She looked at me and cocked her arm back, about to throw a punch, but then her look softened a bit. Her eyes were the coolest shade of blue, almost gray, and they saw right through me into my soul, and knew that I meant no harm, and that look felt good. I thought then, this is the girl I want to spend the rest of my life with.

"It's okay," she said, her voice that of a young Thai ladyboy. "Come. Sit."

I laid out the towel I had been blotting her with and plopped down next to her. I thought there was no way in hell I was going to have a chance with this vixen.

"Let me get you another drink," I said, and signaled the waiter over. All-inclusive resorts were awesome back when they still existed. You could just sit all day and have everything brought to you, like you were rich or something.

"Waiter, another daiquiri for my lady friend, and I'll have a glass of hot milk, please."

The waiter looked at me like he wanted to kick my teeth in for ordering such a preposterous drink. Especially on a beach in Hawaii, but he said, "Very good, sir," and turned to walk away.

"Actually," the girl said, "I'll have a glass of hot milk too."

My jaw gaped. This was the moment of a lifetime. A hot girl who liked hot milk? What were the odds? I don't know if I believe in fate, especially with the way the world is now, but I believed in it right then.

I introduced myself. "I'm Eric."

"Starlet," she said, and held out a hand for me to shake.

"A beautiful name for a beautiful girl," I said, sounding cliché as all hell.

"Thank you," she said.

"I can't believe you like hot milk too!" I exclaimed.

"I most certainly do. See, I used to have a very bad caffeine habit, but then I went to rehab. Someone in there turned me onto the beverage. It's my favorite. Even though it tastes a little like hyena cum."

"I think it tastes like horse cum!" I said. We started laughing.

"So, what's your story?" I asked. I knew with the bulge she had between her legs, she had to have had a pretty good story.

"Well, my name's Starlet. I'm from Blackburn, Ohio. I like hot milk and stale chocolate chip cookies. Um, I like reading, fashion, reality shows, and I was born a dude."

"Wow. A dude? I hadn't noticed."

"Thanks, but I know I have a pretty decent package. You don't have to pretend you don't see it. I can't hide it. Especially in this bathing suit. Anyway, what about you?"

"Um, I'm Eric," I said.

"Well, now that that's out in the open, you being Eric and everything, wanna go shoot a game of pool or something?"

"Sure thing," I said. "But I have to warn you, I'm pretty good."

We grabbed our hot milks and headed to the activity center. Starlet got a pretty good chuckle out of the activities director when she asked for some balls, but other than that, the date went off without a hitch. Sure it was just pool, but it felt like a date to me.

"Come on," she said. "I want you to meet my dad. He's a fluffer."

"A what now?" I asked.

" A fluffer, you know." She made a jerkoff motion with her hand.

"Ohhh." The realization hit my face, as did seagull shit. Goddammit! Just a minute," I said, and ran to the ocean to rinse it off. Them dirty fucking seagulls. That's why I don't feel the least bit bad eating them.

Introducing me to her father? So soon? Were we a thing already and I didn't know it?

We entered a cabana, and there were two gentlemen sitting in lounge chairs, each nursing a cocktail.

"Dad, I would like you to meet my new boyfriend, Eric."

Boyfriend?

Her father held out his hand. I shook it. "Nice to meet you, Eric. Boy, Starlet has told me nothing about you." He glared at her.

"And this is my brother, Glenn," she said dismissively.

"Nice to meet you Glenn," I said, and held out my hand.

"Yuh," he said, and looked away. I put my hand in my pocket.

"Sweetie," her father said, "we were just thinking about going to grab something to eat. Would you care to join us?"

"Nope," Starlet said, and led me away.

"It was nice meeting you," I called over my shoulder.

"You too, Eric!" her dad shouted. "Stay well, my friend!"

Then I says to Starlet, I says, "Your family seems nice."

"Yuh," she says.

We spent the entire day together, enjoying each other's company. Before we knew it, night had fallen.

There we were, Starlet and I, in Hawaii; she chomping on her cheeseburger and me nervously picking at my roasted seagull leg that we had gotten from the all-night snack bar on the beach at the resort. You see seagulls all the time in the wild, and they're all the size you think seagulls should be.

71

But these legs they sell are enormous. They must keep them in captivity and pump them full of steroids and protein supplements to get legs as big as that. I'd hate to see what the rest of the bird looked like. It would be funny if the top of the bird was normal-sized, though, wouldn't it? This little ugly bird walking around with the legs of a bodybuilder? We were sitting under the clear starlit sky, she with mustard smears all over her hot little face. I kissed her, right then and there, getting the yellow mustard and maybe even a little ketchup on my face, bits of ground beef mixing with seagull in my mouth. Skyrockets shot off like they did when Bobby Brady kissed Millicent. That had been our first kiss, and it would not be our last.

Later on, we found ourselves making love under a palm tree, every star in the night sky calling our names. Or some shit. I had only had one other partner in my life, which was my culty ex-girlfriend. I said "culty", dammit. This was nothing like anything I had ever experienced before. It was wild, it was insane. The dick thing didn't even bother me. In fact, later in life, I'd grown to develop a fondness for them. It wasn't her anatomy that did it. Something about how it felt emotionally. I had never felt such a deep connection while making love before. This was something new. So this is how it's supposed to feel, I thought. This is love.

Just then, our session got interrupted when Starlet got hit in the face with something that seemed to have fallen from the sky. I wondered if it was more seagull shit. I tasted it. Cream pie.

"Hoo-hoo-hoo," a laugh followed the pie. I looked up, staring into the heavily made-up eyes of a clown.

Jesus Christ, I thought. Fucking clowns are everywhere. Why don't they go back to where they came from? Now they're on our beaches. Throwing pies.

"You'll never catch me!" he shouted, and started to run. Starlet and I both got up and, without bothering to put our clothes back on, started chasing the clown down the beach. What a sight that must have been to passersby! Despite his floppy shoes, we couldn't catch up to him. We kept up the chase, however. Sometimes you just have to humor them, or they'll never go away. We chased him through a fancy restaurant, disgusting the patrons, through the kitchen, and out the back door. "I can't swim!" he yelled, which I didn't understand, since he was nowhere near the water. He changed direction suddenly and headed back up toward the hotels. One hotel after another we ran through, disturbing the guests. The pursuit attracted more clowns, and we attracted more naked people. Soon there were hundreds of nudists chasing hundreds of clowns down the garden paths, as if in some bizarro foot race.

When we finally called it quits, we collapsed, still naked, on the beach, too tired to make love again, but not too tired to do a little more stargazing. That was one of the best nights of my life.

Starlet and her family flew back to Kentucky the next day, and we never hooked up again. We still keep in touch, and I will never forget the time I had with her in Hawaii.

CHAPTER FOUR

May 30, 2031

I Walked into the flower shop, my sunglasses still inexplicably perched on my face.

"Hai," I said.

I no sooner could get the word out of my mouth, when I was cut off by a very impatient, "Can I help you?"

"Yeah, can I have a dozen red roses please?" I asked the florist, while simultaneously moving my sunglasses up so that they instead rested comfortably on my forehead.

"Oh hi, Eric, I didn't know it was you," the florist said. She was obviously a lesbian.

She reached over to her left, and pulled out what appeared to be twelve long-stem roses, already packaged up for me, like they just knew I was coming for them.

"Here you go," she said, as she pulled the roses out from whatever was holding them.

"That's me," I said, not quite sure if I meant It is I who have come to pick up the roses that must have already been waiting with my name on them, or if I meant, The roses are me.

"How much is it?" I asked, to which her ever-quick response was:

"It'll be eighteen dollars."

Was there some contest going on that I was unaware of? See who was the quickest draw with words? Well, I'll show her who's boss.

"Here you go, keep the change," I said, slamming a twenty down on the counter. I didn't care how much the roses cost, I came in there to spend exactly twenty dollars, and that was all I was going to spend. Try to best me with your quick words. I'll spit out words so fast they'll make your head spin. And I'll throw money down on top of it.

"Hi Doggy," I said, and pet the ugly dog on the counter on its head. I don't know how I didn't realize it was there before, with all the whining it was doing.

"You're my favorite customer," she said, as my words that were directed at the canine were still leaving my mouth.

I quickly turned. I'd had enough of this fiasco.

"Thanks a lot baii," I said, hoping to God she wasn't going to utter any more language. I was going to get the last word this time.

"Buh-bye," she shouted to me as I exited. Whore.

What a whirlwind that was, and yet, the whole exchange seemed somehow familiar to me.

I got in my car and left. I very badly needed a drink.

I sat at the bar, peeling off the label from my bottle. "Another one, Charlie," I said to the bartender.

"Sure thing, Mac," he called over. "But could you not peel the labels off the bottles? We recycle here, and you can't get the fifteen cents back if there ain't no labels on the bottles."

"Okkayy,." I slurred. I was starting to feel good. I have a tendency to drink too much once I start; I don't know if that makes me an alcoholic or what, but it is what it is. Ordinarily I don't really drink too often, perhaps once a week or so, but I do come to this bar quite a bit, normally to shoot pool.

Andy's Pub is the oldest bar in Sunny Springs. Owned by none other than Todd, the bartender that stood in front of me. His name was Todd, but I'd always hated that name, plus it didn't suit a bartender of his caliber. I always thought that "Charlie" seemed a more appropriate name for a barkeep. Plus, he just looked like a Charlie. You know the look I'm talking about. In return, he called me "Mac". He called everyone "Mac", actually, which not only made things confusing, it also made me feel not very special. Nobody knew who the hell Andy was. Nobody but Charlie. I'm assuming he was the original owner, but every time I ask Charlie, "Please tell me who Andy was again," he always tells a different story. One time he was a Federal agent who had this little bar set up as a way to catch lowlifes and criminals. The next time he was a mafia don, who had this little bar set up as a way to clean his cash.

This time, though, he told a doozy. "Long time ago, just after the prohibition era, when speakeasies once again became shouteasies, or speakfreelys, or some such, there was this alien race that infiltrated our town. Came from a little planet called Remulak, that inhabited a galaxy not too far from our own."

"Watching Coneheads a little too much, Charlie?" I asked.

"Yessir. A fine documentary, if I do say so myself." Seriously with this guy? "Anyways, they all came over to earth and decided to settle in this very town. Nice people, them. Anyways the leader, or I guess he was the leader, looked just like one of us. I guess they worshiped him because he was the handsomest of the bunch. Called himself "Andy". Had this little bar set up as a way to study our customs. He left town sometime in the fifties, and I guess he left the planet, and took the rest of them with him, 'cause I ain't seen no aliens since."

"Did you happen to catch the latest message from Uncle Mel?" I asked, fearful of what the answer may be.

"Nope. Hate politics," he said. Good. Let's leave it at that, then. If he was one to so quickly believe in aliens, I think the rumor that our president may be one would give him a nervous breakdown. Or make him very excited. Either way, I didn't feel like getting into it.

"Hit me up with another, Charlie," I said.

"Sure thing. You're not driving tonight, are you, Mac?" He placed a fresh, cold beer in front of me.

"You know I don't drink and drive. I live just two blocks from here. I always walk here. Are you okay? Are you becoming forgetful in your old age? Do you even know who I am?"

"Sure do," he beamed. "You're Mac."

That didn't clarify shit. I liked Charlie, and I didn't want to see him losing his mind. Maybe he was just tired. As long as I'd been going to Andy's, Charlie was always behind the bar. I wonder if he had a home to go to? Wife? Grandkids? Sofa? Bag of potato chips? I wonder if he even slept. Maybe it was time for him to take a vacation. I thought of suggesting it to him, but then I realized I didn't really care much about Charlie.

Aa series of BLOOPs and BLEEPs and PINGs and CHUGGACHUGGACHUUGGACHAROOOBINGBIGBINGBINGDIN Gs came from over in the corner. Two young men were standing at the W.A.S.P. pinball machine, their eyes lighting up brighter than the machine itself every time the ball hit Blackie Lawless' codpiece. Time to go make some money. Usually I would hustle by getting in on a game that was already being played, one that I observed out of the corner of my eye to gauge the players' skill levels. It was getting late, however, and I didn't think that anyone would be showing up to play any pool tonight. I could only judge by the way the blond-haired one was leaning up against the table, disrespecting the felt, that these guys didn't know the first thing about the game. It would be easy to win against them, but it's difficult to make anyone throw money down when they have no confidence in their own game. Whatever, maybe I could squeeze a few bucks out of them.

"Toss me the pool balls, Charlie. It's time to make some cash."

"Sure thing, Mac." He got the balls out from behind the bar. Some places make you pay by the hour, some have those stupid coin-op tables that encourage people to bet quarters instead of dollars, but one thing about Andy's Pub, billiards were always free. As long as you were drinking.

"Here ya go, pal. Say, do you know that I have never once had a vacation from this place? I guess that don't mean shit since I have no home to go to. No wife, no grandkids, no sofa or bag of potato chips."

"Yeah, that sucks," I said dismissively as I headed over to the table. "Thanks, Charlie," I called over my shoulder.

I stood at the table with my balls in my hand, waiting for the two tourists to finish their pinball game. It didn't take long, because the one guy was kind of sucking. All he wanted to do was hit Blackie's codpiece, as if that was the whole object of the game. The codpiece was the largest object on the table, and therefore very difficult to miss. The real points were getting it in the "Fudge Tunnel" between Johnny Rod's legs.

Their last ball went down the chute, and I waited for the little "MATCH" thing at the end to disappoint them, but then I heard the familiar "CRACK!" which meant that they had miraculously scored a free game.

Sigh. "Another cold one, Charlie," I said. Fuckin' tourists. Whatever, it gave me time to slug down one more beer at least.

I could drink beers fast, but they could lose balls faster, apparently, because before I knew it, their game was over. The towhead was about to pop a couple more quarters in the machine when I ran up to him, yet another full, cold beer sloshing around in my hand and all over the floor. Whatever. I don't think Charlie had mopped the floor, ever. That's what gave it its bowling-alley-like gleam. Who needs floor polish when you have malt beverages?

"Waitwaitwait," I shouted at the two guys. "Hold up."

The blond moved away from the machine, and put his hands up like he was under arrest.

He turned to me, and when he saw I wasn't a cop, held his fifty cents out to me. "Cacamaa?" He questioned, which apparently meant, "Do you want to play this W.A.S.P. game with my quarters?"

"Nono," I answered, and motioned toward the table. "Billiards."

The dark-haired gent turned to his friend. "Billiard?" he asked him. The blond swept his hand in the direction of the table in a "be-my-guest" gesture. A be-my-guesture.

I pulled the rack out from under the table as the two tourists stood there, fascinated. Like they'd never in their lives seen a triangle. I arranged the balls in the rack, and removed it. The two dudes began clapping. Jesus, if they were that impressed by my racking skills, they would soon be very impressed with my money-making skills.

I handed the cue ball to the dark-haired one, and asked, "Break?"

He took the ball and threw it onto the floor as hard as he could, chips of resin flying through the air. "Break!" he shouted. "I win?"

I went to the bar and asked Charlie for another cue ball. "No, you don't win." I said, and put the ball down on the table. "Now, quit being a smartass and try again."

He bent down toward the table, grabbed the white ball and slid it toward the other balls, like he was pool-ball bowling. It was a fairly nice break, but I'm pretty sure it went against all league rules.

"Oh, for fuck sake," I said, and re-racked them. "If you're not going to play nice, then you're not gonna play." I handed him a pool cue. "I'll break."

I debated making a shitty break, but I wanted to score some cash as quickly as possible. Plus, I hated it when the balls stayed all bunched-up. It screwed up the flow of the game. So I broke, trying to get nothing in with my first hit. I got one in, however. I guess I was high ball.

"I'm stripes," I said, and aimed half-ass at a stripy one, deliberately missing the pocket. "Your turn."

79

He aimed for the same ball I just did. I couldn't believe that there was anyone on this planet who didn't at least get the very basics of pool. Either this guy was trying to out-shark me, or he came from a place where they had never played pool before. "No, dammit," I said, and pointed to a few solid balls. "You're solids. Aim for the solid ones."

"Blorg?" he asked.

"Yes! Yes! Blorg!" I agreed.

He aimed for the three ball and missed.

It was my turn. I missed my ball, once again on purpose. Then he missed his.

After about five minutes of this horse shit, I "accidentally" pocketed the eight ball, losing the game.

"Awww, I guess I suck," I said. "I lost." I chuckled a little, acting like this was all in fun, and seeing me laugh got my opponent to laugh even harder, "HAHAHAHA!" he said, and looked at his companion. "HAHAHA!" he continued.

Following his buddy's lead, the towhead starting laughing, too. It wasn't really that funny. "HAHAHAHA HEEHEEHEE BLEEEPBLOOP!"

Did he just say Bleeepbloop?

The Bleeepbloop was soon followed by the strangest sound I'd ever heard come out of a human mouth. A chuga-chuga, like a freight train, but somehow electronic sounding. These guys must be Albanian.

"Your turn to rack," I said. The dark-haired one gazed at the table, and one by one, the balls jumped out of their little holes and all congregated in the middle, in a perfect triangle. Something wasn't quite right, but I couldn't put my finger on it.

"How about we make it interesting," I said, and put a few dollars down on the table.

My opponent followed suit, and threw a handful of hundred dollar bills on top of it.

"No!" I shouted. "Too much. I don't have enough to cover it." I doubted I would lose, but the way he got the balls to jump out of the holes by themselves, I had an idea that maybe he wasn't going to play fair this time. That maybe he was trying to out-shark the shark.

"You may as well break, too." I handed him the stick.

He took his direction from the way I broke last time, aiming the stick very carefully.

I had never seen anyone do this before, and I don't think I ever will again. I swear to God that fucker hit the one ball in front, and every ball scattered, like the table was a town with a very strict curfew, and they tucked themselves neatly in their little homes. Every ball found a pocket. Every one. Which means even the eight ball. Which means I won! League rules may be different, but I didn't think these guys knew any better.

I scooped the money off the table and put it in my pocket. "Well, guys, it's been fun. Hope you enjoy your stay here in our little town." Then I thought about Uncle Mel and his rules against tourism. "And don't worry, I won't tell anyone you're here."

I reached out my hand for them to shake it, and they just stared at it like it was a dead cat laying on the side of the road.

"Good-bye!" the blond dude said, and quickly whisked down my trousers and stuck his finger in my bum.

"Good-bye!" said the brunette, and did the same before I could pull my pants back up. If I didn't know any better, I would say that I was being anally probed.

They both pulled their pants down and bent over, waiting for me to return the favor. This might be the way they shook hands in Albania, but I'd be damned if I was going to go home with stink finger.

Although, I thought as I left the bar, the two tourists waiting there with bare bottoms, if that's what it takes to get a thousand dollars nowadays, I'll gladly take a finger in the ass anytime.

81

I half-stumbled those few blocks home in the pitch dark. Aside from the moon shining, there were no street lamps. Well, let me clarify. There were street lamps, but in this section of town, they couldn't be bothered putting them on. Despite the town switching to very energy efficient bulbs, the taxpayers still decided against leaving them on past midnight. They were cutting corners left and right, and the way I felt tonight, I thought that that was a very bad move indeed. Although, walking home drunk at such a late hour was also a bad move, but really, who's keeping score?

The town was eerily quiet. No sound of car tires on the dewy pavement. No shuffle of the random homeless person's feet. No skittering of little squirrel paws, or other such animal noises. This wasn't normally a very busy street, even in broad daylight, but the total lack of sound made things feel not quite right. Like I was in a dream or something. There wasn't any wind; even the weather was dead.

I took the thousand dollars from my pocket and put it in the waistband of my underwear instead. I had a bad feeling about tonight, and I felt it safer if any potential muggers thought I didn't have anything to steal. Although the government was cracking down on crimes of all types, the rate of theft across the country was at an all time high. People are poor, people get desperate. And I'm not saying what I do for a living is a hundred percent honest, but to steal money right out of someone's wallet by force? I couldn't ever, and wouldn't ever stoop to that level.

Passing the closed-down shops, I caught a whiff of something. The scent of homemade bread permeated from somewhere unspecific. I remembered back to a day when those little shops used to be open. Wal-Mart had completely taken over the country. Although, the Wal-Mart that we all used to know a few years back isn't the Wal-Mart it is today. It used to be a one-stop shop for all your clothing, cereal, and beer needs. Now that it's government-run, it is the one-stop shop for all your clothing, cereal, beer, porn, marriage license, hot-air balloon rides, and party planning needs, and so much more. Some of them even have churches in the back, so that you could spend your entire Sunday there if you so chose. There were a few small shops still hanging on, such as the little flower shop I visited earlier, as Wal-Mart flowers tended to die the second you left the store, but the little shops that used to make pastries, little mom and pop music stores, neighborhood pharmacies, all of that was gone in the matter of a couple years. People no longer had the means to pay a little extra for quality; everything they needed was plentiful and cheap, all in one place.

I was staring into the window of an old bread store, the sign on the door still said OPEN. It didn't matter anymore; everyone knew the store wasn't OPEN, and it would never be OPEN again. The equipment, dusted in a light coating of flour, all stood at attention, ready to make some delicious pastries. But there would be no more delicious pastries. There would be no more work at all for them. They had become obsolete, and soon they would rust like everything else. I felt bad for them. They looked sad. Their one mission in life, stripped from them. I felt a kinship with them. Like so many Americans, these things had lost their jobs, too. My eyes started to well up. I probably had too much to drink.

This little touching moment didn't last long, however. From the reflection in the shop window, I noticed two men slowly creeping up on me. I didn't dare turn around. An arm reached around from behind and I felt something pressed against my throat. A knife. These guys had knives.

"Hey, vato. Hey, homes. Gimme your money and stuff. And turn around slowleee."

I did. I turned around slowleee. And I noticed something right away. These guys weren't Mexican at all. Especially not the Macklemore-looking asshole who had the knife against my throat, and was the one doing all the talking. Ever since Mexicans were banned from the country, it became all the rage to talk like them. I don't know if it was a mockery, or a tribute.

"All right, all right." I reached in my back pocket for my wallet. "Just don't hurt me."

"We'll churt you if we wanna churt you," the talking one said.

I opened my wallet, more for show than anything. I knew what was going to be in there. Not a fucking thing.

83

"Sorry, guys. I spent my last dollar on beers. Is there anything else you want? Hand job or something?"

"No, man, I don't want no steenking handjob." He looked at his compadre. "Carlos here just blew me an hour ago."

I turned toward "Carlos". He looked no more like a "Carlos" than I did an Ahmed.

I reached into my front pocket and came up with seventy-nine cents.

"H-h-here you go," I said. "Here's seventy-nine cents. Go buy yourselves something nice."

Macklemore shook his head. "Dat's not gonna cut it, homes. We can't even divide that chit eeequalee."

He was right. As dumb as the white dude with the Mexican accent sounded, he sure knew math. This was an odd number. It occurred to me that these guys weren't messing around, and I was going to be shot if I didn't think of something quickly.

Just then, a light bulb went off in my head, which did little to illuminate the dark street. I took a penny and threw it down the street. It skipped off the tarmac like a flat stone on water. "There. Now it's seventy-eight cents. That's thirty-nine cents each. You can now divide it equally."

Carlos' eyes widened, and he spoke for the first time that evening. His breath reeked of Macklemore's spunk. "He's right, homes. We can divide that chit eeequalee."

Macklemore smiled. "Chit, man. Tanks a lot, honky."

Honky? Really?

"Glad to help a fella out." I turned to leave. "You gents have a nice evening. Don't spend it all in one place, now."

The knife once more appeared against my neck. "You didn't tink we was gonna letchoo off dat easy, didjoo?"

Fuck.

"What else you got, homes?"

Double fuck. They knew. Somehow, they knew about the thousand dollars in my underwear. Did they see me tuck it in there earlier? I weighed my options. I could run, and risk getting stabbed, or I could play dumb and risk getting stabbed, or I could fork over the cash. The win tonight was a fluke. It would take me months of hustling to win that much cash again. This was a tough call.

"Ummm," I said. It was as good a response as any.

But Macklemore didn't like it. His non-knife hand reached around my waist and grabbed my cock and balls, squeezing just hard enough for me to scream, but not hard enough for me to lose consciousness.

"Ummm," I said again.

"You know what we want, motherfucker. Fork it over, bitch."

Apparently I moved too quickly for him, because he pushed the blade even harder into my neck. I felt a slight pain, and a trickle of blood flowed down, staining my shirt. He grabbed my nuts even tighter. "Slowleee."

I slowed down my speed, and started to reach into my underwear. He let go of my balls.

"Woah, woah, wait. I already toldjoo I don't want none of your sex stuff. Leave dat in your pants. I'm talking about joor wallet."

"My wallet?" I asked. "It's empty. You saw that."

"No, it's not. Take it out. Slowleee."

This guy really liked using that word. I did as I was told, and handed the wallet over to Macklemore.

"Here. Take it. It's a piece of shit wallet, you know that, right? It's not even real leather."

"I don't want joor wallet. All I want is dis."

DAVE!

He took a picture out of its sleeve. My ex-girlfriend, Janet. I don't know why I still carried it around with me. Nostalgia or something. She is the only female I have slept with, Starlet aside, and I still sometimes looked at this picture to jerk off to.

"You want that picture?" I asked, incredulous.

"Fuck yeah, cheeze hot. I'm gonna go home and jerk off to her."

Really? I'd offered him a handy, and he'd rather go home and jerk off? Whatever floats, man.

"Shit, take it. Take all my pictures. My mom's in there somewhere."

He shook his head, "Nah, dis'll do." He handed me back my wallet. "Now get the fuck out of here before I change my mind and stab you."

He didn't need to tell me twice. "Sure thing, man." I walked away, and shouted over my shoulder, "You know, she's in a cult, right?"

"Ooh, dat's illegal," Macklemore said. "Dat's even hotter."

I walked quickly the rest of the way home, thanking Janet for saving my life.

I sat on my futon staring blankly at the whizzing images on the screen. The whizzing images happened to be a group of young Mexican boys, peeing on the wall. All was status quo in Mexico. Just a few feet away, on the other side of the border, utter chaos.

Bullets were flying, some skillfully aimed from the men and women in uniform, some stray shots obviously fired by people in street camo. Obviously amateurs. The military had a job to do, and they were doing it, regardless of the cost of innocent human lives. They could not betray their government lest they get executed themselves. I'm sure more than a few had tears in their eyes, and years down the road would all be treated for some form of post-traumatic stress disorder. I get it. Those who serve their country are doing it under the guise of fighting for freedom. It has been this way since the beginning of time. But I knew a lot of those brave people knew they were doing something wrong and wanted to just throw down their guns and go the fuck home.

It was the civilian warriors I had the problem with. I can't believe there were that many, and that not only did our government put their trust in these people, but these people put their trust in the government. They actually did believe in their cause, and they seemed to enjoy eliminating innocent lives. They didn't see these people as innocent protesters; they saw them as terrorists. They saw them as people who would stop at nothing to tear down the wall, letting the real terrorists on the other side in to ruin the country. Never mind the fact that this was the Mexican border, and the only terrorists over that way were those destined to steal our shitty jobs that we don't want, and send a little money back home to their families. The twenty dollars a day they made here would go a long way toward little tacos. (I'm talking actual tacos here, I'm not calling the children little tacos.) They were working for their own "greater good". Some actually were pretty good marksmen, no doubt republicans who had spent their entire lives advocating the deliciousness of guns. Others were firing their errant bullets into the dirt, sky, and the wall itself. Surprisingly, not much harm was being done to the wall; a little dust, perhaps, and a few random flying flakes, but no real structural damage. The military probably provided the firearms, and without a doubt they also provided the ammunition, something that would rip its way through flesh but do very little damage to concrete.

Come on, you idiots, I was thinking. Aim! I had never in my life shot a rifle, except maybe at a duck or an old piano player. On the midway in the carnival, of course. In the real world, I had never shot an old piano player. Or a duck. And those guns sucked. These people were using professional grade shit, and missing.

Then I realized what I was doing. I was rooting for them to hit their targets. What a dumb shit. This is what happens when you watch that much violence on T.V. The American people love that shit. They want people to get all fired up and join their cause. It seems like shooting fish in a barrel, and it is, but there are millions of citizens lined up against the wall, chipping away, minding their own business. This would take a couple years to kill them all. The more people the government gets to fight with them, the quicker it will all go. Showing this all day every day on T.V. was serving another purpose, too. It was keeping any of the other prospective Topplers away. Not all of them,

87

mind you; they still came rushing to the wall in droves. But it most likely slowed the onrush of people down a little.

The cameras are perched at the Mexican border, the Canadian border, and all along the coastline. I've been sitting here watching this shit for two days straight. I mean, I'm doing other things, like eating, going to the bathroom and getting drunk as fuck, because my eyeballs can only take so much. I can only look so long at the growing pile of bodies, lying there, some of them with dumbass hopeful looks on their faces, like they thought they were making a fucking difference. I suppose they are, in a way, if you want to believe what Carlton and Dave said. They are clearing out D.C. for us to move in. But not one of them dumb, stupid fucks knows anything about what's really going on. It's making me sick. I can't help but think about Starlet again. Is she going to be the next to go? Is she dead already?

I just threw up. The mixture of beer and thinking about Starlet's lifeless body sent me over the edge. I'm going to call Starlet's phone again. I tried calling her before earlier. I had to tell her about the Invaders. I didn't care about the consequences; she needed to know. She needed to get the fuck out of there and come join me in California. We could be a fighting machine. We could have our own weapons and actually be making a difference, and she wouldn't be just standing there, waiting to get shot like some piano player at the Midway shooting gallery. But I got no answer. I'm going to try her again. Come on, Starlet. Pick up!

No answer again. Voice mail. I'm starting to think the worst.

It's three a.m. Today's the day. In just three hours Carlton and Ray are going to pick me up and we're making the long journey to D.C. I should probably eat something, but I can't. Maybe we'll stop somewhere and get some breakfast. My stomach is in knots right now. I'm no fighter, and I know I may be going to my death, too. This is some scary shit. What the fuck am I thinking? But what's the alternative? Sit home and do nothing? At least folks like Starlet are doing something. No, sitting at home is not an option. Things are only going to get worse, and I'll be damned if I'm to blame for it by my inaction.

I'm crying. Jesus. These may be the very last words I write, ever.

It's six o'clock. They're here. I gotta run. It's go time.

PART II:
D.C.

CHAPTER ONE

June 4, 2031

The alarm on Starlet's phone goes off. She rolls over to look at it. 3:45 in the morning on June fourth. The day her life is going to change forever. She picks her phone up and scrolls through the missed calls. Seven from Eric, just from the night before. Looking at the signal strength, she sees there is one bar. Maybe enough to make a call. She hits the dial button, but there is no tone. Just a three beep indicator that lets her know her call can not go through. Starlet looks at the signal again and sees that the bar has disappeared. There is lousy reception up in the North Woods. Sometimes she can get a couple bars if she climbs a tree and stretches her arm up really high, but one time an owl absconded with it, thinking it was a mouse or something, and now the owl is probably making calls to his friends in Canada. Owls can probably get good reception, especially because they're high up in a tree most of the time. She hopes a hawk has stolen it from the owl, and the owl got a taste of his own medicine. She wonders why she even got a cell phone in the first place. And also, why she didn't get a land line. She never really has anyone to call, but texts once in a while with Eric. He usually gets her message days later, and by the time she gets a response back, sometimes three weeks have gone by. She's curious why he called her so many times last night. She hopes everything is all right. He's probably fine. He's probably out there with the rest of the Topplers in Sunny Springs, making shit happen.

DAVE!

She goes outside and lights herself a cigarette. She feels the warm smoke filling her lungs, and remembers back to the time when cigarettes almost fell out of fashion. Everyone was puffing on those stupid electronic things. Vaping, they called it. The only reason they did that, she thinks, is so they could smoke indoors. Those were originally invented for smokers to kick the nicotine habit, not to start one. She's glad those fell out of fashion and real smokes made a comeback, because this is nice.

She goes back inside and sits at her desk. Picking up a pen, she writes a letter to her boss.

Dear Framp, she writes. I am sorry to inform you that I will not be making it in today. I know that it means there is no one there to open up the store, but I can't worry about that right now. I have an appointment with a wall today at noon. I probably could have come in this morning, but I don't have it in me to stand at a cash register and ring people up for Cokes and camping supplies. Somehow, it just seems frivolous. I don't know when, or even if, I'll be returning, so if you need to find another person to fill my position, I totally understand. You can just mail me my last paycheck. Again, I am very very sorry. It has been a pleasure working for you. You are the coolest boss ever.

Best of luck,

Starlet.

She wonders if that's good enough, maybe she should include more words or something. But in reality, she could give a fuck less. She'll have to go to the store early and slip the note under the front door, but that's one of the reasons she woke up so early in the first place. She wants to avoid any sort of confrontation. There will be plenty of confrontation later on at the wall.

She gets in her car, not bothering to shower, and heads to the store. The streets are so dead. Of course, it's only 4:30 in the morning, but normally there would be at least a little traffic; lumberjacks headed to work and so forth. This used to be this a fairly booming town, for being in the middle of nowhere. The population was much bigger, home to Gagnons and Gauthiers and Belangers and Gallants, Gagnes and Lavoies and Fortins, Fourniers and Cloutiers, Leclercs and Greniers, Bedards and Lapointes, Ouelletts and Beaulieus, Pouriers and Poulins, Blouins, Simards and Desjardins. The names are still fairly prevalent around these parts, but most of the older Canadians, the ones who did all the work, the ones who weren't born in the United States, have been transfered back across the border. In turn, Northern Maine has lost a lot of its work force.

Now is probably not the time to be leaving the store, since it's one of the few stores open, and it's hopefully going to be busy with everyone stopping by to pick up some last minute supplies, and no one but Framp and his idiot son to run it. But this is not the time to be thinking of this crap. She doesn't know if anyone will be there to open the store, and although she does feel bad, she doesn't care enough to not slide the note under the door. Sorry Framp.

The streets are extra quiet. She hopes that later on, they won't be. Her hopes are that they will be packed with caravans of protesters and Topplers, headed to the wall. It's the second day of Toppling, and her first day up there. She wanted to see how day one went before she got up there. She thinks back to last night and the local news coverage that took place.

"Well, Jim, today is day one of the Topplers' destruction of the wall, and I'll tell you, they're doing a bang-up job. Pun fully intended, of course. We take you now to Chaz Mufflebeard, who is live at the wall in Frenchville. Chaz?"

"Thanks Marcia. As you can see, literally dozens of protesters are out here chipping away."

Chaz was right. There were about two dozen people out there. Two dozen! At this rate, they'd have the wall down in approximately thirty-eight years.

"The wall is sure coming down fast. At this rate, I expect they'll have the job done in just a few short days. I can barely hear myself think over the cacophony of machinery, as well as all the screaming and yelling going on."

The closest thing they had to machinery as far as Starlet could see was a twelve-volt Sawzall, which sounded like it was dying a slow, painful death. And the only screaming and yelling that she heard was when one guy shouted, "Hey Chaz, would you mind getting the fuck out of the way?"

Chaz laughed this off. "Well, you never know what you're going to hear on live television." He ducked as an invisible piece of something nearly hit his head. He reached down toward the ground and held up a lone wood chip, terror in his eyes. "My God," he said. "I could have been killed. Well, this is what you get when you put your life on the line to be in the thick of things. I should ask for a raise or something, heh heh. Thanks for saving my life!" he shouted to the asshole who asked him to move. "As you can see, Marcia, the men and women here are very brave."

"Chaz, it looks like at this time, there are no government authorities, am I right on that?"

"Yes, Marcia. You are correct. No authorities at this time. However," he knocked on the wall, "I'll knock on wood on that one. I don't think they'll be long in coming- OUCHMYEYE!"

"Chaz, what happened? Is everybody okay?"

"Yes, Marcia, everyone is fine. I just got a splinter in my eye. These are the dangers you subject yourself to when you want to be a field reporter. I suppose that's all for now. SOMEBODY GET ME SOME ICE!"

Starlet stared, incredulous. She wasn't sure if ice would be helpful for a splinter in the eye.

She had been shocked at such a low turnout. Frenchville literally had dozens of residents, and where were they all yesterday? Plus, with easy access to the border, she would have thought that the wall would be packed with folks who traveled hundreds of miles to be a part of history. At first she thought that there wouldn't be as many Topplers as predicted, but when she turned to the national news, she saw that there were so many in other areas that riots had broken out. People were getting killed. Holy shit.

People were getting killed? For a brief second she almost changed her mind. She supposed she hadn't fully thought about what this would entail. Maybe she was naive for thinking that they would all be left alone to destroy the wall. Maybe she thought there would be some arrests, but that it would mostly be quiet. She had no idea that the military would be out there, told to shoot to kill. So yeah, she almost changed her mind. But what else was she going to do? Chances are, they would leave those in Northern Maine alone, because of the lack of population. Most of the troops seemed to be focused on the Mexican border, so maybe they would be okay.

Okay, yes, but not very effective in their job. They need better tools. She scours the basement for anything that she can pack that would be better suited to wall-breaking. One would think that they would have all the tools that they needed up there for breaking down wooden barriers, being mostly woodsmen, like chainsaws and backhoes and bulldozers, and maybe they do, but from what the camera showed yesterday, they were all ill-prepared.

She doesn't have much in her basement. Some chisels and hammers and an old handheld egg beater. She doubts any portions of the wall are made of eggs, but she decides to pack it just in case. At the very least, she can whip them up a souffle or something. She curses the fact that she's so girly. Since she lives by herself, she should have some power tools in case something breaks. But nope. Resigned that she was going to be no great help tool-wise, she takes another sip of her coke-coffee concoction and figures it's time to head up. (Yes, she is back on the coffee. Lately she has been adding cocaine to the grounds for that extra boost that she so desperately needs first thing in the morning.)

She takes her sweet time getting there, even though she's cranked out on cocaine. She's able to keep enough wits about her to know that if she speeds, she'll most likely get pulled over, and this time she may get more than just a ticket. They need her at the wall. At the very least, she'll be one more person. But she's hoping today there will be a lot more than just one more person.

The lack of traffic makes her once again think back to the lost souls that were the French people of Frenchville. She sheds a tear for the Thibeaults and Thibodeaus, the Arsenaults and Audettes, the Lamberts, Legeres, Letourneaus, Lerouxs, the Picards, Paradises, and Perreaults, the Robichauds, the Robineaus, the Rossignols, the Messiers, the Mayeuxs, the Merciers, Moriers, Michauxs, Morreaus…

CHAPTER TWO

Eric opens the door, and there they are. Carlton and Ray and fucking Nick. Two idiots with their leader.

"Hey buddy," Nick says, which is a little presumptuous. "What have you got to eat in this place?" He shoulders past Eric and opens up his fridge. "Imitation butter and Yoplait? Seriously?"

"Hey Eric, do you mind if I go through your refrigerator?" Eric says facetiously. "Yes, Nick, you may. You are more than welcome to eat anything you find in there. I just cleared it out of food. But thanks for pointing out the old Yoplait in there. I haven't bought yogurt in years. That shit must be expired as hell by now."

"What did you say?" Nick comes out licking the foil top.

"I said, help yourself."

Eric hears voices coming from the kitchen. Which is weird, because everyone is in the living room.

"Who the hell?" he says, but when he walks into the kitchen, no one is there.

"Do you guys hear that?" he asks.

"Hear what?" Ray asks. "Some sort of distant chatter?"

96

"Yeah," Eric says. "It's coming from in here, but there's nobody in here." He wanders closer to the noise, and notices that it's coming from the area of the kitchen counter. Are there a group of little people hiding in the cupboard? He opens the tiny door. No. No little people hiding in the cupboard.

The noise gets louder and louder. He must be getting closer, but… wait… no way. Not possible. It's coming from the yogurt. There are little white specks crawling all around and through the gooey soup.

"Whoopee!" one of them shouts as it dives off the edge of the container into the yogurt.

"The active cultures have become mutant!" Eric screams, as Nick approaches the yogurt with his spoon.

He smacks the spoon out of Nick's hand. "Heyyyyyy!" Nick says. "I was gonna eat that."

"Dude, you can't eat that. It expired like…" He looks at the date stamp. "Four years ago. The active cultures are the size of ants!"

"Hey, they're supposed to be good for you," Nick says. "And the bigger they are, the more protein."

"There's no protein in bacteria!" Eric shouts, and throws the yogurt in the trash. "Sorry little fellas," he says.

"Well, great. Just great. I'm starving," Nick says.

"Here," Eric says and hands him a tub of Country Crock. "Eat this. Its still good."

"Gross," Nick says. "Let's just hurry up and get out of here so we can go get some breakfast."

"Yeah," Ray agrees.

Carlton looks at Eric. "Are you packed, man?"

"What?" Ray asks. "Am I Pac-Man?"

97

"Yes, Ray. Are you Pac-Man?" Irritated, he again repeats, "Eric, are you packed?"

"No, not yet. It'll only take me a minute, though. Mind coming up and giving me a hand?"

"A hand? What the hell are you packing?"

"Oh, just clothes and shit."

"Hmm. All right." Carlton follows Eric upstairs.

"Listen," Eric whispers. "Do you think those two are okay down there alone?"

"Haha, yeah. They're okay."

"Do you think, um, they're okay mentally? I mean, I've known Ray for some time now, but it seems that Nick is kind of bringing out the stupid in him a little. You don't think they're gonna fuck it up?"

"How are they gonna fuck it up?" Carlton asks.

He looks out his bedroom window and points. On the lawn are the two idiots, playing a game of soccer with a pretend ball. Nick raises his hands in victory. Apparently he scored a goal. "How are they not gonna fuck it up?"

"They can keep a secret; that's all that matters."

"Yeah but you're gonna trust them to shoot guns and shit?"

"Shoot guns?" He laughs. "Dude, I wouldn't trust either one of them to shoot heroin properly. Once we get to where we need to be, they're gonna split. You think I was going to have them on my team? Hell no. They're going to be Distractors. I'm just their ride, man."

"Oh, thank God. I thought…"

"Yeah, I know what you thought. You must not know me well enough."

"Must not."

"Think about it, though. Could there be any better Distractors?" He gestures out the window to Nick clearly kicking the ball out of bounds. Why

98

doesn't the ref call that? "All they have to do is be themselves in plain view and they're bound to get arrested. It's brilliant."

"I gotta say, it's an excellent plan."

Carlton opens the window and yells out. "Put your shit away, boys! It's time to roll."

Ray and Nick shake hands, say, "Good game," pick up their "ball" and head inside.

"All right, get packed. Let's get a move on."

Eric opens his bag and tosses some random clothes in.

"Hey, Weird Al," Carlton says, which was a very 1976-2016 thing to say. "Let's leave the Hawaiian shirts at home, huh? No sense calling more attention to ourselves than we have to."

"But the Hawaiian shirt is very popular," Eric says. And he's right. The Hawaiian shirt became extremely popular once Hawaii was kicked out of the Union. Much like talking like a Mexican stereotype became popular once the wall went up. "What should I wear, then? Black?"

"Yes, bring as much black as possible. I'm going to the car while you finish up. Remember, don't pack any drugs other than prescriptions in their original bottles, and nothing that could be regarded as a weapon. You got ten minutes."

Eric finishes packing, heads out the door, and locks it, although he's not sure why. He doesn't think he'll ever be returning.

"Shotgun!" he shouts. There's no way he's sitting in the back with either of the two Idiots.

CHAPTER THREE

Meanwhile...

In Colorado Springs a twelve-year-old boy sits in his history class, bored as usual. When it comes to boring subjects, nothing beats history. They say those who don't learn history are doomed to repeat it. This boy feels that by not learning history, perhaps things can go back to the way they used to be. That's his theory, anyway, which probably doesn't hold much water. Speaking of holding water, he has to go to the bathroom. Miss Krull is going on and on about how Kennedy was a communist, Obama was a racist, and how Uncle Mel is turning this country around. The boy raises his hand. Miss Krull stops her lecture and stares at the boy for an uncomfortable amount of time, a blank expression on her face.

"Yes, what is it you little shitmonkey?"

"Miss Krull, can I go to the bathroom?"

Sigh. "I suppose. But hurry back. Class can't go on without you."

He isn't sure if that was sarcasm or if she was being sincere. But the pee is just about coming out, so he doesn't really care.

He opens the door and steps out into the hallway.

"Hey, shitmonkey," Miss Krull says to him.

He turns around.

"You forgot your hall pass."

He steps toward her, and grabs the pass. Her claw-like hand grasps uncomfortably around his forearm. An intense pain shoots up his arm to his shoulder, through his neck and into his brain. The pain soon turns to pleasure, which soon turns back to pain, alternating back and forth. The room goes dark, and all he can see is Miss Krull. Her lips stretch out far past the rest of her face, and the skin slowly drips away like candle wax. The puddle of skin gets deeper and deeper, until he is standing chest deep in it. Her head twists around 180 degrees and a giant vagina-like mouth opens in the back. It continues twisting until it goes a full 360, and suddenly she lets go of his arm. The lights come back on, and he is standing there, the class laughing at him. He has pissed his pants.

Miss Krull huffs. "Well, I suppose you don't need to use the restroom anymore."

"I gotta poop, too," he says, and runs out, forgetting the hall pass once again.

The hallway is dark. The lights are on as always, but they seem dimmed somehow. He passes the restroom. He doesn't have to poop, but at this point he just needs to get out of the classroom, and away from Miss Krull.

Most of the classrooms are completely dark. He walks by one of the few lit rooms, its light casting itself through the little chicken-wired window and onto the hall floor. He peers in as he goes past. There is nobody in there but the teacher, Mr. Fudge. The man is staring blankly at the opposite wall, and when he senses the boy outside, his head turns, and he smiles. A smile as wide as Miss Krull's. He's not sure, but he thinks he sees teeth where Mr. Fudge's eyes should be. He needs to get out of here. And fast. He runs outside. The day's weather is bright and cheery, in stark contrast to inside the school. He reaches in his pocket to grab his phone to call his mother. There is no phone in his pocket with which to call his mother. His phone is in his backpack, back in his classroom. The way he sees it, he has two choices: He can either hoof it back home, which is about fifteen miles away, or he can go back in there and get his phone. It never occurs to him that there are really a myriad of other choices, because he's twelve.

101

DAVE!

"No guts no glory," his father used to tell him. His father died in a fishing accident. No, he didn't get eaten by a shark. If that was the case, maybe his death would have earned his memory a little glory. He was trolling from his boat, and his line got caught up in something at the bottom of the lake Rather than cut the line and lose the very expensive lure he had, he decided he would jump in and try to untangle the line from whatever it was caught in. He had had a difficult time getting the motor started that morning, and he didn't want to shut if off, for fear of not getting it started again. Sure, he knew he could get chopped up by the propeller, but he said to himself, "No guts, no glory." Those were his last words, as he jumped in and the propeller sliced his torso clean open, spilling his guts into the water. Now he had no guts and no glory.

So he goes back inside. Never once realizing that what can at first be mistaken for guts is actually just plain stupidity. He sprints down the hallway. He feels like he is being watched. Perhaps even followed. He gets to his classroom and throws the door open. Miss Krull once again stares at him with that wide-mouthed grin. But she isn't the only one. All the children at their desks are staring with that exact same expression. One by one, they rise from their desks, skin melting off their bodies. It soon fills the room as he feels the hands of the children dragging him under.

CHAPTER FOUR

Technically, the border between Frenchville and Canada cuts right down the middle of the St. John River. It follows this path, splitting the river amicably until it reaches Hamlin, where it then takes a drastic turn straight south, which is what gives Maine such a straight shape on the northeast side. Since building a wall in the middle of the St. John would be a total nightmare, the wall is built on the U.S. side, running along Route 1, and thus surrendering the St. John to Canada. Starlet is making the twenty-minute trek to the wall when a thought hits her. Check your cell. She hadn't missed any more calls from him as far as she could tell. And she'd have thought he would have texted her if he couldn't get through any other way. So maybe it wasn't so urgent after all. All the same, she thinks it's probably a good idea to send him a text, just to see if he's all right.

She gets her phone out of her purse and sends him a text: Everything ok? while keeping one eye on the road. She knows it's a danger to text and drive, and she doesn't really make a habit of it, especially since her phone never works anyway, but she figures since there's no traffic on the road, what is the worst that can happen? She hits send and watches as the little circle goes round and round, the short little message bouncing through the trees, trying to find a tower somewhere. Anywhere.

She looks up to see a squirrel in the middle of the road, and swerves to avoid it. Which sends her car bouncing through the trees. It doesn't find a tower, either, but it does find a rather large boulder, which crumples the front end of her car.

"Fuck!" she shouts. "Fuck fuck fuck fuck jezus oh blasted fuck!" She gets out of the car to assess the damage. It's undrivable. Awesome. What a predicament. She thinks about the time she had her sex reassignment surgery. Back then, she called it a deprickament. She chuckles despite the situation she's in. Her phone tells her that her message didn't go through. Awesome. Immobile car and immobile mobile. She laughs again. She just made a funny. Maybe she's cracking up. Maybe she's going looney tunes. Maybe some powerful force is trying to keep her from reaching the wall today. Maybe something bad will happen there.

Maybe that powerful force is stopping to take a breather, she thinks, as a truck approaches and slows down. It's Stone. "Hey gorgeous," he says out his window. "You all right?" Stone is an ugly sonofabitch who somehow looks like he had been born premature, and they left him in the incubator a little too long. So it makes her uncomfortable when he calls her "gorgeous", since she can't really say anything nice back.

"Yeah." She points to the wreck. "Car not so much, but I'm fine. You headed to the wall?"

"Sure am. Need a lift, obviously?"

"Wouldn't hurt."

She grabs the tools out of her trunk and gets in the passenger seat of his pickup.

"Welcome to my chariot," Stone says. He was always saying shit like that, trying to impress her or flirt or something. She thought it was pretty weak, and she thinks his attempt this time is also pretty weak.

"Thanks," she says.

"How the hell did you end up in the woods? Lemme guess. Texting and driving."

"Yeah," she says, ashamed.

"Wanna know how I know? Because women love to text and drive. They think nothing of it. It never occurs to them that they suck at driving in the first place, and adding not paying attention to the road makes them a total danger to themselves and others."

"Right," she says. Why bother arguing? He's being nice.

"I'll call you a tow as soon as we get somewhere I can get a signal."

"Don't bother. Car's a piece of shit anyway. Let it rust out there." She doesn't think she'll have much use for it anyway.

"Right on," he agrees. "Not at all like my ol' trusty pickup truck." He taps the dashboard lovingly and looks over at her. "This thing could hit a thousand rocks and keep right on going." Women may text and drive, but men have this tendency while they're driving to look at you when they are talking, even though you would be able to hear them perfectly fine if they kept their eyes straight ahead. But she doesn't say any of this. Instead she says, "Watch out!" as a squirrel runs out into the middle of the road and forces him to swerve, almost going off the road and into a boulder. She thinks it may be the same squirrel. Yes, something really wants to keep her from reaching the wall.

"Sorry 'bout that. I have a tendency to wildly swerve my vehicle to avoid wildlife. Gotta protect the little critters, you know. Could be that soon, they'll be the only ones left." She thinks there may be some truth to that statement.

"Did you go up yesterday?" he asks. She shakes her head.

"I assume by the question, that you didn't go up either?" she asks.

"No. Wish I had, but I had some business to take care of. I don't think there was that much of a turnout, though. Hope there's more people today. We really need to make an impact, you know? I hear they had some pretty good refreshments, though. Not that that's a deciding factor for me. I'd be there regardless. Of course, if they didn't have good refreshments, I'd make sure to pack some of my own. Like trail mix. You like trail mix?"

She nods.

"I like the one with the M&M's. Makes me forget about the raisins in there, having all them M&M's in there to offset the terrible taste and texture of the raisins. I don't like the trail mixes that are all nuts. Not a big fan of certain nuts, like cashews. I can't stand cashews. I know a lot of people like cashews, but me, I can't stand 'em. Peanuts are pretty good, but of course, they're not a nut, now are they? Are cashews nuts? Can we please come to a consensus on what are nuts and what aren't? Like how some vegetables are really fruits and vice versa? Maybe we need to reclassify stuff, you know?"

What the fuck is Stone talking about? He's a good guy and all, but one thing less attractive than his overdeveloped physical features is his ability to ramble.

"I mean, is it really wrong to call a tomato a vegetable? Or a squash? I think we should start classifying them by their tastes, you know? Fruits are sweet and vegetables are savory, and that's it. Of course, some people have very poor taste buds, and maybe a tomato tastes sweet to them. Maybe an apple tastes of umami. Umami. What a weird word. You know, we didn't have that word years ago, but we could taste things just fine without it. Does having that word really change our perception? Like how Eskimos have a thousand words for snow, so they can see different snowflakes or some shit? Do you know, that humans don't have different types of taste buds in different locations on their tongues? I wonder where that myth actually came from? Hey, look, we're here."

"Thanks for the lift," Starlet shouts as she bolts from the truck, tool bag already in hand. She needs to be far away from Stone. The loud banging on the wall today will probably be more quiet than that asshole.

CHAPTER FIVE

They pull into A Diner at 5:15. Eric thinks "A Diner" is either a very good name for a diner, or a very stupid one. He thinks about the logistics from a business angle. On the one hand, say you get someone looking for that exact diner. So they ask around, "Where can I find A Diner?" they may ask. And a local may point to another, totally different diner, because it is, in fact, a diner. But the tourist wants to go to A Diner because supposedly they have really good omelets. Instead, he has to settle for one where the eggs are runny, and when he calls the waiter's attention to it, they'll say, "Oh, that's just cheese." "Bullshit, it's cheese," the tourist will say. "Don't you think I know runny egg whites when I see them?" The waiter will take the eggs back and finish cooking them in the microwave, but not before the cook spits in them. Then, because the tourist ended up at the wrong diner, but was somehow unaware it was the wrong diner, he'll go on Yelp and write a shitty review for A Diner, when it wasn't their fault his eggs were runny; they always cook a perfect omelet. So their online ratings will go down, and the board of health will get notified, and being a government agency, they do everything in their power to make money, which includes fining establishments for health violations that don't even exist, and they'll have to close. On the other hand, it is a clever name.

"Excuse me," Eric asks his waitress. "Why do they call this A Diner?"

She sighs like she's totally annoyed. Like this is the thousandth time she's been asked this question. Which it totally was. "They call it A Diner because it's a clever name. For one thing, it comes up first in every alphabetical listing. All except the ones that list it as "Diner, A". For another, we feel we deserve an A, since that is, like, the highest grade you can get. Even the health department thinks so." She points to the plaque in the window, showing their health score. It won't be an A for long, though, if Eric's tourist scenario plays through. Before they close down for good, though, he decides to get a fucking omelet.

"I'll try your omelet. I hear it's the best in town," he says to the waitress.

"To tell you the truth," she says, "Sometimes the whites come out slightly undercooked."

"That's fine," says Eric.

The rest of the guys place their orders. Nick gets the seagull stew, which Eric actually contemplated getting, but maybe now he can just taste Nick's instead.

"Any of you want coffee?" the waitress asks.

"NO!" shouts Eric, then quickly apologizes. "Sorry, I mean, they'll have coffee. I'll have a hot milk, if you don't mind."

"Suit yourself, freak," the waitress says.

The food comes and the omelet is basically three uncooked eggs with some salsa and cheese on top. Eric eats it because he's starving. He thinks of writing a Yelp review, but he doesn't know if he'll have the time. Plus, he may end up reviewing the wrong restaurant.

"Hey Nick, I'll trade with ya," Eric says. But Nick is not interested.

"No way, man. I don't eat eggs. You know they're baby chickens, right?"

"Well, that's really a myth. Eggs are just eggs unless they're fertilized. What are you, twelve?"

"No way, dude. I heard one time some girl found a beak in hers. Tell me again how they're not fertilized."

"Well, some do sneak through," Eric says.

"Yeah, well, I'm perfectly fine with my stew. And why is it twelve is always the age people say when someone acts stupid or immature?"

Eric never thought of that, but Nick was right. It was always twelve.

"Can I at least have a bite?" Eric asks.

"Help yourself. But you gotta use your own spoon."

Eric doesn't have a spoon, because he didn't order coffee. And he doesn't dare use anyone's coffee spoon for fear of the residual caffeine lurking on it. He grabs his fork instead. All he really wants is a bite of seagull anyway. It is fucking delicious.

Carlton's phone rings. He looks at it. "Shit," he says.

"Who is it?" Ray asks.

"Shh-shh-shh. It's Dave."

Everyone at the table gasps simultaneously.

"A call from Dave?" Nick says. "Unheard of."

"Preposterous," Ray chimes in. It wasn't really preposterous.

"Preposterous?" Eric asks.

"Unheard of," Ray corrects himself.

"Toldja," Nick says.

"Will you clowns keep it down?" Carlton says, and excuses himself to head outside and take the call.

Eric watches Carlton out the window. Through his intense training in body language from an extracurricular class he took in junior high, he knows it's not good news.

"Bad news, guys," Carlton says as he resumes his seated position at the table and sips on his coffee. Slowly. Painfully so.

"Well?" Eric says.

DAVE!

Sigh. "That was Dave. He had some news that was not so good."

"Okay, yuh. We got that. What's the news?"

"Seems we're not the only ones with some tricks up our sleeves. Seems the government has infiltrators of their own."

"Infiltrators? What do you mean?" Eric asks.

"Like there have been some Topplers who have been killed by those passing themselves off as one of their own. Pretending to be on our side and burying axes and shit into innocent people. That's what I mean."

"Fuck," says Eric.

"Fuck is right. Dave is freaking the fuck out right now."

"Weren't they gonna probably end up dead anyways?" Nick asks, with a mouthful of bird. "What's the difference?"

"The difference is, this brings them one step closer to us. Let's say there are some Topplers who know of the Invaders. Even though there shouldn't be, I'm not that numb to think it couldn't happen. And let's just say that they happen to open their mouths to the wrong people. Our whole plan could be, theoretically, fucked."

"Fucked?" Ray asks.

"Theoretically. Also, if we can't trust all of the Topplers, who's to say we can trust all of the Invaders? Maybe they have infiltrated our group as well."

"Shit," Eric says.

"Ya. Shit."

"I feel sick," Eric says. "Must be the eggs."

"I'd leave a review," Nick says.

Eric throws a tubby down on the table. Twenty bucks ought to cover his meal. If it doesn't, fuck it, the other guys can figure out the bill. He excuses himself to the rest room and immediately calls Starlet. She needs to know. The chances of there being any infiltrators where she is is probably quite slim, but one never knows. The call probably won't go through anyway, but he has to at least try.

It's ringing.

"Hello?" comes her voice from the other end.

CHAPTER SIX

Starlet runs to the wall, getting as far away from Stone as possible. There's not a huge crowd, but it's still early. No one's even attacking the wall at the moment. Most of the faces she recognizes, but there are also a few new people who obviously traveled to get here. She heads over to Sarah and Greggg, who are setting up some tables, presumably for the food.

"Hey, guys," she says.

"Starlet! You made it." Sarah gives her a big hug, as does Greggg.

Greggg's a nice guy, but a bit of an oddball. His full name is Gregory. She remembers the time he explained the extra G in his name. "Extra G 'cause I like to keep things extra gangsta," he said. "In truth, it's because when your name is Greg, no one, not even your closest friends and family, can ever remember whether it's spelled with one G or two. My own mother was spelling it wrong half the time. So I added an extra G, because no one will forget 3 G's. Sarah has the same problem. H, no H. I keep telling her to change her name to Sarahh. But she says it won't work as well."

"Come, were just setting up the registration table. Then we gotta move on to the food."

"Registration table?" Starlet asks. "Register for what?"

Sarah puts a sign-up sheet, blank name tag stickers, and a Sharpie on the table. "Oh, it's just a formality, really. We just like to know where people are from, and give them a name tag. It makes us feel closer when we know who everyone is. Yesterday we had someone come up all the way from Jersey."

Starlet admires Sarah. She was so beautiful. Not that Starlet is bad-looking at all, but there's something about Sarah that's just gorgeous. Movie-star quality gorgeous. Greggg, on the other hand, is portly, bald, looking middle-aged but is probably no older than thirty. She wonders what she sees in him, and realizes that's a total guy way to think. He seems like a great person, and maybe that's all she needs. Still, eesh.

She's attacked from behind by something wet behind her knee. "Shaaboonga!" she shouts. She turns around and sees a very pretty black and white dog, smiling and jumping all over her, scratching the shit out of her legs, and waiting impatiently to be petted.

"Whose dog is this?" Starlet asks.

"That's ours," Greggg says. "Bella, down! Sorry, she gets excited when she sees people. She'll calm down in a second. She really is a good dog."

"No worries. I love dogs. I've always wanted one, but I don't think I have the time to give to it." She crouches down and pets her. "Here Bella. Good girl. I didn't know you had a dog."

"Sure do. We got her from the Greater Androscoggin Humane Society in Lewiston. Isn't she the prettiest?"

"Beautiful. What is she?"

"We're not sure," Sarah says. "She's a mutt of some kind. We thought she was a black lab, but Greggg got this DNA test on her that said she was a Golden/ German/ red bone coon hound mix. I don't get it. Waste of sixty bucks on the DNA kit if you ask me. So we don't really know. We got her as a puppy. I didn't want a puppy, but when we saw her sitting in the cage with her brothers and sisters, sitting there all quiet while the rest of them were busy yapping, we both fell in love with her. We usually leave her at home, but that," Greggg points to the old motor home thirty feet away, "is our home now."

"That's your home? Why? What happened to your house?"

"Sold it."

" Lost a fortune in taxes, I'll bet."

"We sure did," Sarah says. "But it gave us a little cash in the bank, and we had this motor home anyway, and it's in decent shape. And since no one really knows where the whole state of affairs is headed, we figured now would be the time to just bail."

"I hear ya," Starlet says. "I felt the same way as I was leaving my house today. Like it was the last time I would see it. Then on the way up, I crashed my car, and just left it. Like I didn't need it anymore. Like everything is changing."

"You okay?" Sarah asks.

"Yeah, I'm fine. Car is done, though. Rock crumpled it dead center in the middle. Kinda looks like a bum now."

"Well, I'm just glad you're fine. Come on, I'll show you the motor home," Sarah says.

Starlet's phone rings. "Just one minute, hun." She takes it out of her pocket. It's Eric. Holy shit, she has service!

"Hello?" she answers, excited to finally be able to talk to Eric.

"Starlet?" comes Eric's voice. Such a sweet sound.

"As far as I know," she jokes.

"Starlet, you're alive!"

"Well, of course I'm alive. I can't say too much for the scene here, though, as it's about as dead as it gets."

"Whew. That's good. ...isten I'm ...alling you bec... ay be in ....anger."

"Eric? You're cutting out."

"...arlet. Listen. It's ...safe for you ...ere. You need.... go now. I...D.C. Jus..... art ...iving ...eet you there, okay?"

"What?"

"…arlet. Listen. It's …safe for you …ere. You need…. go now. I…D.C. Jus.…. art …iving …eet you there, okay?"

"Yeah, I only got half of that. Hello?"

Her phone beeps. It's her dad calling. Shit, in all this excitement, she had forgotten all about her dad. Maybe she is a shitty daughter after all. "Hold on, Eric, my Dad's calling. I'll call you right back." She hits the talk button. "Daddy?"

"Starlet, you're alive!"

"Of course I'm alive, Daddy. Why does everyone worry that I'm not?"

"I've been trying to get a hold of you for two weeks now. You never return my calls."

"Your calls never go through, Dad. You know the shitty reception I get here."

"I still don't know why you won't get a land line."

"Who has a land line anymore?"

"…isten I'm …alling you bec… ay be in ….anger."

"I know, Eric said that. Although I don't know what those words mean."

"…arlet. Listen. It's …safe for you …ere. You need…. go now. I…D.C. Jus.…. art …iving …eet you there, okay?"

"Okay, Dad. But, what? What are those words? Are you in D.C.? Why are you there? Is Eric with you?"

Boop boop goes her phone, and it commences searching for a signal.

"Everything all right?" Sarah asks.

"I think so. I'm not sure. I didn't hear a word of what Eric or my dad just said. I think they said it's safe for me here."

"Safe as it gets," Greggg said. "Come on, let's go see the motor home."

DAVE!

CHAPTER SEVEN

Starlet's father Jake called himself a "pipe fitter". He thought it was a pretty clever description of what he did. He even belonged to the pipe fitter's union, before the union got wind that he was not, in fact, a pipe fitter, by standard definition. He was, in fact, a fluffer, in case you haven't been paying attention. When the union called to tell him his benefits had been revoked, he tried pleading his case. He actually did fit pipe. Just not the kind of pipe that most pipe fitters fit. For those of you who are anti-pornography first, get over yourselves, and second, you probably don't know what a fluffer is. And for those of you who don't have access to Google, I will define it for you. A fluffer is a man or woman who works behind the scenes at a porn shoot. You never see him on screen. No, he is not a cameraman. Once in a while Jake was called to operate the camera, when the cameraman called in sick, but he did shoddy work, and was much better suited to do what he did for a living. A fluffer is someone who preps the actors and actresses in a porn film. He was there to make sure the actresses were sufficiently lubed, and that the actors were standing at full attention for the scene. If, for some reason, an actor couldn't achieve full stiffness for whatever reason (e.g. the scene partner is Asian and they prefer Italian, the scene partner is a woman and they prefer men), and they cannot take care of the problem themselves (e.g. the actor doesn't know how to manually stimulate themselves, the actor has really rough hands and doesn't want to stimulate himself due to chafing hazards), the fluffer would prepare the actor by any means necessary be it oral or manual stimulation, or the use of various devices (e.g. you get my drift). And Jake was quite skilled at what he did, and he got paid rather handsomely for it. Porn was one of the few industries where you could make a decent buck.

So yeah, he got kicked out of the pipe fitter's union. They did refund him all the dues that he paid, but he was told to never contact them again unless he learned how to work black iron. When he argued that he did, in fact, know how to work black iron, they said not that kind of black iron, and to just not contact them again even if he learned how to work a threader. A threader sounded very painful, so he decided to just give up arguing. It didn't matter anyway, as unions became a thing of the past during Donald Trump's reign of terror. Republicans were scared of unions, as they reeked of communism, and their arguments were always, "It encourages workers to be lazy. Remember the Soviet Union?" Yes, he did remember the Soviet Union. They were some of the hardest-working people he knew. All except some of the workers in the Stolichnaya factory's taste testing department. Well, they did work hard at first, but by the end of the day, they were the only workers that were cut slack when they drunkenly spouted xuj, which pretty much means to go pound sand. All unions were quickly disbanded in 2018, falling under Mr. Trump's very broad definition of a cult. For some reason, Christianity was the only thing spared from this definition. Because, you know, it makes sense.

Although Jake's job was fulfilling, it did nothing for his sense of being. Sure, he was doing his part to help humanity, but he couldn't help but think that he needed more. That's when his friend Pherl called him up and told him they needed to meet secretly. And they did. It was as if God knew how Jake felt, how he needed to do his part for humanity and sent Pherl to talk to him. He told Jake all about the Invasion, and asked him to join with him and the rest of the Invaders to help put an end to the tyranny. It would be the start of a whole new planet, a new, better, more civilized, civilization.

He and Pherl were on their way to D.C. when Pherl got the call from Dave, regarding Toppler infiltrators. Quickly, he thought of Starlet, and the danger she may be in. He and Starlet rarely talked, since she didn't have a working phone, but he figured he'd give it a go this time and call her.

He picks up the phone and dials. It's ringing. A very familiar voice comes to him through the speaker thingy.

"Daddy?"

118

"Starlet, you're alive!"

"Of course I'm alive, Daddy. Why does everyone worry that I'm not?"

"I've been trying to get a hold of you for two weeks now. You never return my calls."

"Your calls never go through, Dad. You know the shitty reception I get here."

"I still don't know why you won't get a land line."

"Who …as a …andine any…ore?"

"Listen I'm calling you because you may be in danger."

"I… Eric …d tha… ough I don't …ow what those words mean."

"Starlet. Listen. It's not safe for you there. You need to leave. Go now. I'm heading to D.C. Just start driving. I'll meet you there, okay?"

"…kay, Dad. But, wha…? …t are …ose words? …in D.C.? Why are you …ere? Is Eric…you?"

The phone disconnects. He has the sudden urge to tell Pherl to turn the car around and head toward Maine, but he doesn't think that's the right move. He's doing the right thing. He loves both of his children very much, even though Glenn's kind of an asshole, and he has all the faith in the world in Starlet. He'll try calling her again later, but till then, she can take care of herself. She has to.

CHAPTER EIGHT

Meanwhile…

Another thirteen-year-old boy rides his skateboard down the hill, running over some bang snaps that he had placed at the bottom.

His mother drives by him in her car with a look of disdain. She unrolls her window.

"Adrock, I told you no riding your skateboard without a helmet."

"Then buy me a new one, Mawm. Damn."

"You watch your tone, mister. Get inside. Your father is bringing home a very important client tonight, and I want you to be cleaned up and ready for dinner by 5:30."

"But it's only 3:00."

"Don't you have homework to do?"

"Do I ever? I'm home-schooled. It's all homework. I don't have any extra, if that's what you're asking."

"Then come help me with dinner. And watch your back-talk, young man."

Adrock isn't sure what his mawm means by "client", as his da doesn't have a job that consists of clients. Wal-Mart shoppers are not clients. Yes, his da does work in the paint department, which is a more prestigious job than, say, stacking frozen fish into pyramids. Still, not clients. So he's bringing a customer home? For what? As far as Adrock could remember, his parents never brought anyone home. They have no friends, because they don't trust anyone. Well, whatever.

He helps his mawm chop carrots or something, then goes in his room to play video games.

"Dinner's at 5:30," his mother reminds him. Whatever.

The dining experience is kind of weird. So is the "client" his da brings home. He talks about Uncle Mel like the man is some sort of god or something, instead of just the president. Adrock likes Uncle Mel the same as anyone else, but he doesn't worship him or anything. His parents seem weird around this guy, too, and they talk just like him while they're around the dinner table. Like they, too, think Uncle Mel is a god. He's not sure what to make of it. They always liked everything Mel has ever said and done, but that's just because he's a republican, and so are they. They have to believe everything he does is great. If they disagree with one little thing, their brains might explode. But this, this is something altogether creepy.

"Have you enrolled for the Citizens' Army yet?" the guest asks.

"Not yet. Haven't had the time." Da says.

"How does that work, exactly?" Mawm asks.

"You just do it in your spare time. Go to the wall. Shoot a few Topplers. Log in your hours, and enter them online. It's all very simple. Good way to get extra cash, and you score major brownie points with the big guy."

Like Uncle Mel has enough brownies to give to everyone.

He eats his dinner as fast as possible. He doesn't even have any idea what it is, and he doesn't have time to ask. It's pretty awful; it tastes like some meat he's never had before. However, he knows if he doesn't eat it, he'll be forced to sit there until he does. Forced to listen to more of this stupid conversation.

"Where you going?" Mawm asks.

DAVE!

"To my room."

"Don't you want to stick around for dessert?"

"What is it?"

"Ice cream. Hood chocolate, your favorite."

"I'll pass. Nice to meet you, Mister…"

"Uh, Sanford. Fred Sanford."

"Mr. Sanford."

Later on, while Adrock is lying in his bed playing Fall of Booty VI, he hears noises coming from downstairs. It sounds like his parents and Mr. Sanford are playing video games as well. Which is odd, because there is only one gaming system in the house. Maybe Mr. Sanford brought his own for them to play. He's never seen his parents play video games before. Maybe that's just one of those things they keep secret.

He plays his game for a while longer. He looks at the clock. 8:30. The noises continue. They've been playing the game for a couple hours now. Maybe he should go down there to see what they're playing.

But when he tries to open his door, he can turn the knob, but the door opens no more than half an inch or so. Something is blocking it from the other side.

"Hello?" He shouts. "Somebody? Let me out!"

The electronic noises seem to be getting closer. They're not coming from a video game at all. The noises morph into what sounds like human speech, then back to noise again. He recognizes his parents' voices among the gibberish.

The voices are right outside. What's blocking the door? Then he sees it. A curved piece of metal. Someone had put a padlock on the door from the outside. "Shit," he says. Why would they lock him in?

Mawm's voice comes from the other side. "You watch your language young man. BOOOOOP."

122

Booooop? Something is definitely wrong. It can't possibly be his parents making those noises. Maybe they were once, but that, that is something else on the other side of that door.

The padlock starts rattling. They're coming in. Suddenly he realizes he doesn't want their help anymore. Whatever that is out there, he doesn't feel the need to find out.

There's only one other way out of his room. The window. It's not all that far of a drop from the second floor, and there are shrubs underneath his window which should cushion his fall a little.

He supposes the shrub probably did cushion his fall a little, but he can't really debate whether it did or didn't, because there is currently a large branch sticking into his neck. Other places as well, but the one in his neck seems to be causing him the most issue.

Footsteps on the front porch. Those voices again. They get closer and closer. Someone takes him down from the shrub and lays him on the grass. They all gather around, staring down at him. These three shapes resemble his parents and Mr. Sanford in general shape only. Their faces don't resemble those three people at all. Or any people. The sight, along with the branch in his neck, are enough to cause him to faint, An unconsciousness from which he only awakens once, as his body is being ripped apart.

CHAPTER NINE

Frustrated with the lack of any sort of intelligible conversation, Eric sends a quick text to Starlet. He hopes it gets to her at some point soon.

A knock on the bathroom door.

"Eric, you okay in there?"

He quickly stuffs the phone in his pocket. "Fine. Just bad eggs I guess."

The door opens. Carlton's footsteps approach and he opens the stall door. "Bad eggs, huh? Hmm."

"Yup, that's right, just bad eggs. Heh heh."

"You puke?"

"Mostly dry heaves. Mostly."

Carlton frowned. "Nobody dry heaves just after they ate, Eric."

"Okay, I threw up."

"Who were you talking to in here? Your vomit?"

"Well, yeah. There were little specks in there that looked like little creatures. I thought maybe I'd swallowed some alien bugs or something. They looked like they were trying to swim. I was trying to help them reach the surface. Funny thing about little alien bugs. They can't swim."

"Go on."

"I felt bad for them, so I flushed them down the drain. Mercy killing and all that."

"Go on."

"Well, as I was kneeling here by the toilet, a waiter came in to see if I was all right. He looked kindly enough. I mean, he had a lazy eye and an obvious comb-over, but the way he smiled at me was, well, just so darned friendly. I invited him to sit and have a chat with me, and when he did, he realized too late that I had left the seat up, and he got his bottom wet."

"And...?"

"And I helped him out of his pants and stuck them in front of the hand dryer. We talked the whole time while his pants were drying. Do you know he's a widower?"

"Is that so?"

"Oh yes. You see, his wife died in a tragic accident. He says her flight crashed when they were trampled by a moose."

"Hmm. Sounds familiar."

"Does it? I wouldn't know; I'm not much of a reader, really. Anyway, that's what happened."

Carlton holds out his hand. "Phone."

"Phone? I don't even think I have a phone. I wouldn't know how to talk on one if I did. I mean, how do you work those things, amirite, people?"

"Phone."

"You sound like E.T. Remember that movie? Man, I hope the aliens who have taken over this planet are friendly like he was. That's a weird word, if you say it enough. Phone. Phone. Phone. Weird, huh?"

"Give me your phone, please, Eric."

DAVE!
"I'm telling you, I don't have a..."

Carlton's hand reaches into Eric's front pocket. "Carlton! I don't really know you like that."

Carlton's hand emerges with the phone, and he scrolls through it. "I swear to God if you called...you motherfucker." He grabs Eric by the neck and pins him against the wall of the stall. "You motherfucker! You called her? Even when I specifically asked you not to?"

"You don't understand. I love her. Wow. Sounds weird when I say it out loud. I never knew I had these kinds of feelings for her. Perhaps I should look deeper into that," Was what he says, but since Carlton's hand is around his throat all that comes out is, "Grrahhahaehhghghhehrhhrhhhgh."

"You stupid fuck!" Carlton shouts, angry saliva flying from his mouth and hitting Eric on his cheek. "What did you tell her?"

"Grhrhegeghhregegrgegr."

Carlton loosens his grip a little on Eric's throat.

"Okay, I admit. I tried to tell her. I tried to tell her about the infiltrators. I tried to tell her about what our plans were. But I don't think she heard any of it. The connection was bad."

"The connection was bad? Doesn't matter! The fact is you tried. Whether or not your little girlfriend knows is the least of it. What if someone was listening to your phone conversation? You know they can do that, right? You're not that stupid, right? I will not have you jeopardize my mission. I can't fucking trust you now. I'm confiscating your phone. You're lucky I don't break the fucking thing."

"Sorry, man. You can trust me."

"Obviously not."

"No, no. This was just a one-time thing. Look, if it makes you feel better, you can smash my phone into a million bits right now."

Carlton's shoulders slump; resigned. "What's the point? The damage is done. I only hope this really was your one time."

126

"It was. I swear. The only reason I called her is because I really care about her. I don't want to see her in danger."

"For the last time, dude, and this time I hope you get it through your fat fucking head: We…are…all…in…danger!"

"All right, I get that. I get it."

"Do you?"

"I do."

"You're lucky I don't drown you in this fucking toilet right now."

"Yes, I suppose I am," Eric says. "Look, if it makes you feel better, you can give me a swirly."

"Forget it. Let's go. I left the two Idiots in the dining room. There's no telling what the hell they're doing in there by themselves."

They leave the bathroom to find Nick lying naked on the table, covered in food, and Ray eating it off of him, like at some elite sushi bar. Except it wasn't exotic raw fish; it was mostly corned beef hash.

"Jesus Christ, guys. I leave you alone for five minutes. Save this shit for D.C. Get your clothes on, Nick. Let's get the hell out of here before we get thrown out."

They throw a few more tubbies on the table and make their way toward the door.

"Have a nice day," Eric says to the cashier on their way out.

"Blooooorg," she says.

Eric looks at Nick and Ray. "Did you just hear that?"

"Hear what?" Nick says. "Her accent? Weird, huh? Probably of Albanian descent."

127

Carlton gives a serious look to Eric. "Just what I thought, man. They're everywhere. We gotta be careful. And you guys," he points to the Idiots. "Be on your best behavior."

Ray looks at Nick while pointing his thumb at Carlton, picks his nose, and scratches his left leg with his right foot. "He's right. We gotta be careful. Albanians are everywhere."

Albanians? Shit. "Carlton, I gotta tell ya, you may be right on this one. A few days ago I played pool with these fellas who sounded a lot like that lady in there. I thought they were Albanians too. Could they have been… you know… not of this world?"

"Depends. They could have very well been Albanians. Did they do anything weird?"

He thinks about that question. "Well, they didn't really seem to grasp pool all that well. And they had the ability to get the balls to move with their minds. Jesus. Carlton? Could it be? Am I… an Idiot?"

Carlton looks him up and down. "Hmm. Possibly."

"Oh no."

"Does it at least make you feel a little better that they're everywhere now? I told you we're in just as much danger as your little girlfriend."

"Somehow, that doesn't make me feel better, no."

"Me neither, dude. Me neither."

CHAPTER TEN

Starlet sends a mass text to her father and Eric. "What is going on?" The wind blows cold. A little too cold for June, but this is Northern Maine. The sky is starting to turn gray. Looks like rain, but who knows? She's pretty certain that it's harder to chip away at wet wood, but what does she know?

"Ayuh," Greggg said. "Looks like there's gonna be some weathah."

"Ayuh," Starlet agreed. Most folks who have never been to Maine think all Mainers talk like that. This couldn't be farther from the truth. There were two brothers who were a little slow in the head who were lobstermen out in Boothbay Harbor that talked like this. Unfortunately, quite a few years back they were hired as consultants on the set of a Stephen King made-for-TV movie. When asked if all Mainers talked that way, both brothers looked at each other, and at the same time said, "Ayuh." And thus, the "Maine accent" was born. Mainers found it both cute and annoying. And since weather is a big deal in Maine, because nothing else happens there, it had become tradition to talk about weather in that fake Maine accent. Any chance at all of precipitation was called, simply, "weathah". The reasoning behind this was that there was never any telling if it would be rain, snow, sleet, hail, or Italian sandwiches. Italian sandwiches, as every true Mainer knows, is Genoa salami, American cheese, onions, pickles, green peppers, tomatoes, black olives, oil, and salt and pepper on a hot dog-style roll. Anything else is not a Maine Italian. In Maine, it has never once rained Italian sandwiches. So I don't even know why I brought this up.

"We better get started," Greggg says. "It's much harder to chip away at wet wood, I think. But what do I know?"

A few more cars pull up. Starlet recognizes a couple of people, and some are new faces. And they are carrying food! Lots and lots of food. She was wondering when all the refreshments were going to get here.

"Patty!" She shouts to one of the people she knows, and runs up and gives her a big hug. "I haven't seen you in years. How's the family?"

"Well, you know. The same. Fuckin' kids. Am I right?"

"I know, I know." She doesn't know. She never had kids. As far as technology had advanced in gender reassignment, they have yet to figure out how to implant a uterus into someone. It seems that the insides of males were made up of... other stuff. She didn't know. Extra colon or something. Either way, there was no room for any birthing devices. Plus, she hated kids, anyway. Little brats.

"Here, let me help you with this," she said, and took a couple coolers from Patty's car. "What's in the coolers?"

"Ah, some beverages, and a few Italian sandwiches."

"Italian," she opens the cooler and beholds the wondrous little creatures; homemade, "sandwiches?"

"Sure thing. Who doesn't love a true Maine Italian sandwich?"

"Stupid people, that's who," Starlet says.

"Help yourself."

"Don't mind if I do," Starlet says, her mouth already full of sandwich.

"Starlet!" Greggg calls. "You gonna eat all day? We gotta get started. You know, weathah."

"Be right there," she says, stuffing the rest of the sandwich into her mouth.

130

"Gofff go," she says to Patty. "Ooo know. Werfer."

Patty looks at the sky. "Ayuh," she says. "Weathah comin'."

"You bring any decent tools?" Greggg asks Starlet.

"Not really. I thought I had some good stuff in my basement, but I got bupkes."

"Any good with a reciprocating saw?"

"I don't even know what that is."

"Well, it ain't bupkes, I'll tell ya that. What is bupkes, by the way?"

"I think it's a Greek hand tool," Starlet says.

"Well, here." Greggg hands Starlet the reciprocating saw.

"Oh. A Sawzall. I know what this is. Saw it in the Sex Machines store a while back." She pauses, then adds, "Although it had something other than a blade on the end."

"Believe it or not," Greggg says, "these had a function long before someone strapped dildos on the end of them."

"I know that, dummy. Well, come on. Go get Sarah. We got some toppling to do."

Starlet takes the reciprocating saw, complete with blade, and starts cutting away. She is soon joined by Greggg and Sarah, both with their own Sawzalls. Pretty soon the whole wall is bombarded with saws, axes, hatchets, and scratch awls. Someone even throws an inflatable pig at it, which does nothing but pop the pig.

Right around ten minutes later, the saw runs out of juice and slows to a crawl.

"I thought you charged these," she says loudly to Greggg, trying to raise her voice above the din.

"I did," he says, "but that's only a twelve volt. They die quickly. Go into the motor home. On the kitchen counter there's a charger with a spare battery on it. Go ahead and switch it out."

"Don't these things come corded?" She asks.

"Yeah, but these are all I have. I didn't have the funds to buy new saws."

"Who does?" she asks.

She goes into the motor home, switches batteries, and finds Bella fast asleep on the bed lying on her back, stretched out fully, her front legs straight up in the air. She pets her belly.

"Hey, girl. How can you sleep with all this racket?"

Bella's eyes roll over to acknowledge Starlet and she gives her a kiss out of the corner of her mouth. She rolls over and licks all over Starlet's face. Her breath carries with it the intoxicating fishy smell of dog ass, and it doesn't bother her in the least. Bella licks and licks until Starlet starts to laugh. She has never been kissed this much by a canine. She thinks that she should have gotten a dog when she wanted one, and if she makes it out of this alive, the first thing she's going to do is get one. Such love from such a simple creature.

Bella stops kissing, her eyes rolling once again, as if to say, Who's simple, bitch?

Starlet's eyes roll in response, as if to say Who's the bitch?

The door opens and Sarah comes in. "Isn't she the sweetest?"

"Friggin' adorable. So sweet."

"She just loves on everybody," Sarah said.

"Battery?" Starlet asks.

"No thanks, just had some. It's starting to rain. We're gonna pack it in till the weathah stops. Come help me take some food inside."

They go outside and she gets pelted by raindrops the size of her fist. Not unusual for Maine. They have really big raindrops there. She hears shouting coming from the wall. It's none of the Topplers; the shouts are coming from the other side.

"Hey dere!" shouts one voice in a French Canadian accent.

"Ya, you dere!" shouts another in the same accent.

Voice number one: "Wat all da racket is?"

Voice number two: "Ya?"

Starlet: "We're breaking down the wall."

Voice number one: "Ah."

Voice number two: "Ya."

Voice number one: "Hey t'row me over da wall your tools."

Voice number two: "Ya."

Starlet: "Why should we do that?"

Sarah: "Ya."

She gets a stern look from Starlet.

Voice number one: "All da noise."

Starlet: "We're trying to break down the wall. It's unsightly, and it's encroaching on our freedoms. And yours."

Voice number one: "Watt freedom?"

Starlet: "The freedom to get out of Canada. To come back to the States. You're trapped over there."

Voice number two: "Trap?"

Voice number one: "Like da bear?"

Starlet: "Yes. Exactly. Like the bear. No more will you be oppressed. When this wall comes down, you will finally be free!"

DAVE!

Voice one: "We fine over here."

Starlet: "Don't you want to come back to America?"

Voice one: "Nope. We like it 'ere. Dis is 'ome."

Voice two: "Ya."

Starlet: "Don't you miss coming down to Old Orchard Beach and swimming in the ice cold water, and walking along the beach with your Speedos?"

Voice two: "Ah, ya. Da Speedo."

Voice number one: "We will deal. Go 'way. Get outta da wedder. 'Merica ain't so good, ya."

Voice number two: "Ya."

Voice number one: "Oh, ya."

Starlet: "Okay, well fuck you guys." That's the best she can come up with? She's really off her game today.

"So," Starlet says, making herself comfy on the motor home's sofa, "tell me again why we're doing this?"

"What do you mean?" Greggg asks.

"Why are we chipping away at this wall, trying to break it down to open up the gates, when people don't want to come back?"

"Who doesn't want to come back? A couple of Frenchmen? Do you think a couple of Frenchmen are representative of the entire world?"

She thinks about it for a moment. French Canadians, with their dumb hats and bear traps, their stupid bathing suits and foul odors, their stupid accents that make them sound even dumber than they really are. "No, I suppose not."

"No, of course not. Look, if some people don't want to come back to America, that's fine. What we're giving them is a choice. Right now they have none. Some of these Canucks would like nothing more than to be able to drive

134

six hours south to Old Orchard Beach, wrap their balls really tight in a pair of Speedos, and jump into the icy cold water. Remember every year, they used to come in droves to Old Orchard, turning it into one giant shit hole? That's what makes America great. Little shit hole touristy crap like OOB. Right now, I bet the 'Dorch is like a total ghost town. None of the locals enjoy the shitty bars and rickety amusement rides. It's little shit like that, things we don't think of, that make the world a better place. Happy Canadians. That's what it's all about."

"Happy Canadians, huh?"

"Exactly. Plus, this wall is trapping us in as much as it's keeping them out. So if nothing else, we'd at least be doing it for our own freedom. This wall, these fucking Citizen Implants in our arms; we're prisoners. All of this needs to stop. We need things back the way they were."

A faint buzzing sensation on her thigh. Her first thought: OMG is this the onset of Parkinson's? Or Huntington's? Am I going to turn into a paraplegic? Am I going to end up a shitting, drooling mess in some hospital somewhere? Am I going to lose control of all my bodily functions? For the love of God, what's happening to my leg?

Her phone. It's her phone. Wow. The coke-laced coffee has worn off, leaving the residual paranoia with none of the fun. Plus, since her phone barely ever has any activity, it's forgivable she doesn't recognize the buzzing of an incoming text.

"Hold on, guys. I got a text." She opens the phone and reads the message. Her expression turns serious.

"Who is it?" Sarah says.

"Is everything all right?" Greggg asks.

"I need a cigarette." Starlet puts on her coat.

"It's pouring rain drops the size of babyheads out there," says Greggg.

"Fists," Sarah corrected.

135

DAVE!

"It's fine. I'll be right back. I just need a minute."

The text says, simply: INFILTRATORS IN THE TOPPLERS. PEOPLE DEAD. SOME ARE NOT WHO THEY SEEM. U OK?

The hell does that mean? Infiltrators?

She texts back: MORE SPECIFIC PLZ, hits send, and the little circle goes round and round, searching for a signal once again till it gives up.

She lights up the cigarette, even though she really doesn't want it. Thinking of the text is making her sick, but she said she was going out for one, and didn't want Greggg and Sarah to think something was up. She debates letting them know what the text said, but there are a couple of reasons why she decides against that idea. For one, she didn't want to worry them unnecessarily. If the text means what she thinks it means, there are people pretending to be Topplers that aren't. The chance of there being anyone like that in their little group is quite slim. Then again, since it was such a little group, maybe the chance is greater. Maybe that's how they took care of the smaller groups. They can't afford to send troops to every single little group all along the wall, so they send one or two people dressed for the part, unassuming, to kill people when they least expect it. She knows most of the people here. Most of them. But what about the couple of out-of-towners? The out-of-staters? What if it's someone she knows? What if it's Greggg and Sarah? Have they been on the other side all along? That's the other reason she can't tell them. If they are infiltrators, they'll kill her on the spot.

Calm down, she tells herself. It's not Greggg and Sarah. Most likely you're overthinking it. Maybe the text doesn't even mean what you think it means. Maybe it means…well, something else. Calm down, deep breaths, finish your cigarette, go inside, say nothing.

She takes another drag, and as she does, a raindrop the size of a fist comes down and hits her cigarette and snuffs it out. Oh well, it was starting to make her ill anyway.

She enters the motor home and is greeted by more love from Bella. Right then she decides that she can trust Greggg and Sarah. For some reason, them being horrible people doesn't jive with having a cute, loving doggy. Still, she can't tell them what the text said.

136

"You all right?" Sarah asks.

"Yeah, fine. Been a long day. I think I'm gonna hit the hay."

"Aww, really?" Sarah asks. "Greggg and I were just talking about playing a quick game of strip poker."

"Oh."

Greggg puts a hand on her knee. "Come on, it'll be fun."

"Gee, I don't know. I'm really bad at cards. I was playing strip poker a couple nights ago, actually. It was by myself, though. And I had my clothes on. Come to think of it, it was solitaire." She frowns. "And I lost."

"Good, then it'll be a quick game."

Why not? She thought. She had a great set of breasts, and her new pussy was amazing. Although, it isn't quite new. It was her gift to herself on her eighteenth birthday, so it's twelve years old. But it's hardly been used. She is very picky about who she chooses to sleep with. Up in Frenchville, the pickings are slim, anyway. But her pussy is like new. If she were to advertise it in Uncle Henry's, that's how she'd describe it: One pussy, like new. Although she would never sell herself, she was no whore, maybe there would be other uses for it. Rednecks can find uses for anything. Maybe make a plant pot or a gravy boat out of it.

"No creepy sex stuff?" she asks.

"God, no," Sarah answers.

"What about Bella?"

"She's already naked," Greggg says.

"I don't want her watching."

"She'll be sound asleep. We'll close the curtain."

"Sure. Fine. Whatever." It's better than sitting there, contemplating the possible terror to come. Maybe she can also get shitfaced. "You have any wine?"

DAVE!

Sarah smiles, just like Daryl Hall instructed her to. "Boy, do we ever."

MARC RICHARD

CHAPTER ELEVEN

They pull into the parking lot of the hotel they would be staying at for the evening. After much debating back and forth between motel, motor lodge, hotel, etc., they decided they would stay in a hotel. Why not splurge a little and live in the very lap of luxury that only a La Quinta could provide? Eric can always bring in more money by hustling pool if he has to.

They get out of the Honda Elephant, grab their shit, and head inside and to the front desk. The clerk appears friendly, as she had no doubt been trained to be. Her name is Debbie, and she is covered in sores that look quite painful. They are leaking a green residue, which turns insect-like and takes flight in midair as it drips. Perhaps she should have taken the day off.

"Room for four," Carlton told her.

"Two rooms for two each," Eric corrects, and gets no argument from Carlton.

"$89 please," Debbie says.

"Can't beat that," Nick says. Eric wishes he wouldn't speak sometimes. Well, most times.

Eric pays for the whole thing in cash, and Carlton agrees to run his credit card for incidentals.

"Stay out of the mini-bar," he tells the idiots. "And no soccer indoors."

"Football," Ray says.

"No football, either."

"No, the proper term for soccer is football."

"The proper term for fuck off is fuck off," Carlton says.

"We don't encourage sport of any kind in the rooms," Debbie says, the insects buzzing around her head like insects. "There is a pool around the back, however, if you care to take a swim." She scratches at one of her sores, and her face begins to lift off of her skull. Just a little. Eric nudges Carlton. Carlton nudges back, as if to say, I see it, now shut up.

"Your change, sir," the clerk said.

"Eww, keep it."

"Don't hesitate to ring if there is anything else I can do for you. My name is Mark."

"Oooookeeeey," Eric answers.

"Enjoy your stay!" Mark or Debbie shouts down the hall.

"Fat chance," Carlton says under his breath.

Before they get on the elevator, Nick stops at the vending machine. "Anybody got two dollars?"

"What for?" Carlton asks.

"I wanna get a Kit-Kat. We can split it four ways."

"What adult splits a Kit-Kat four ways?" Carlton says, as he gets out a couple bucks.

"Dude, get a Skybar. We can split that four ways," Ray says.

"Nobody's splitting anything four ways," Carlton says. "Plus, they don't make Skybars anymore. Outta the way. I'm gonna get something too. Hmm, let's see, I'll get a…"

The vending machine contains the weirdest assortment of goods. Sure, they have the usual Kit-Kats, Andy Capp's Hot Fries, soiled Japanese underwear, and powdered donuts. But in between them are what can only be described as "indescribable". Artifacts that look like talismans of some sort, some of them glowing red or purple. Those plastic bubble-gum machine eggs that usually contain mystery prizes, these containing something living. Carlton can't get a good visual, as these eggs are slightly opaque, but some are wriggling and some are thrashing. And they cost five bucks.

"You know what, fuck it, not hungry," Carlton says. "I'm gonna head upstairs. You coming?" he asks Eric, who notices that he doesn't ask Nick or Ray.

"Yeah. Maybe they have a minibar upstairs."

"Hate to see what's in that," Carlton replies.

When they get to their room, they collapse on their separate beds.

"Boy, I could sure use a nap right about now," Eric says.

This very comforting thought is interrupted by a very rude knock on the door.

"Who the hell is it?" Carlton shouts.

"It's us," says Nick.

"It's Ray and Nick," says Ray

"Go away," Carlton shouts.

"You guys wanna play strip poker?" Nick.

Carlton and Ray, simultaneously: "Go away!"

Nick: "Come on, guys. Let's do something. Meet you at the pool for a skinny dip?"

Eric thinks about it. A swim may be quite relaxing, after all. Why the clothes have to come off is beyond him, but whatever. He's not ashamed of his cock. He's had it from birth, and it really is quite pretty.

141

DAVE!

"Yeah, all right," he says. "Be right down. You coming?" he asks Carlton.

"Why not? I'm not skinny dipping, though. Because, you know, vagina."

"Oh, that's right." Eric had forgotten that Carlton is, in fact, a woman. Well, he has woman parts, anyway. He chastises himself for mentally saying that Carlton is a woman. How offensive.

They undress, and Carlton puts on a pair of brightly colored swim trunks. Eric throws on a robe. As they're changing, they hear voices in the hallway. Chamber maids.

"Clurrrg bog BEEEP BOOOP."

"Hahaha. GRREEEEEE!"

"Hahaha."

He looks through the peephole to see two creatures standing right outside his door. They do not have any recognizable human features. He thinks back to the time when he thought that language was Albanian. Now he knows better.

"Dude, they're right outside the door," he tells Carlton.

"I know. What do they look like?"

"Come see for yourself."

Carlton looks through the peephole and cringes. "Jesus."

"What do we do?" Eric asks.

"We wait for them to pass, then run like hell downstairs to the pool. We can't have them see us seeing them. Fuck, this place is overrun with those freaks."

The voices fade, and Eric pokes his head outside. They're in the room next door, cleaning.

"All clear. Let's go. Hurry."

They bolt down the hallway and quickly turn the corner.

"Stairs?" Eric asks, and Carlton nods.

They open the door to the stairwell and hear the familiar voices, apparently practicing English.

"BEEEP BUP great wedding."

"HA flllarggg bloog collapsed lung."

Eric and Carlton turn to each other. "Elevator," they say, simultaneously.

While waiting for the elevator to arrive, they are both visibly nervous. Come on, come on! Eric thinks, as the elevator dings. Thankfully, it's empty. They get in and he presses L for lobby.

"Dude, what the fuck?" Eric says.

"I don't know. We just have to make it through this night."

"Yeah, and the next one. And the next one."

They step out of the elevator and walk down the hallway to the pool. Nick and Ray are already in their Sunday worst, jumping in and out of the water like a couple of naked ten-year-old boys.

"Jackknife!" Ray shouts, and jumps.

"Not with your naked balls!" Eric yells, but it's too late. Ray comes up for air, and has that look on his face like he just discovered for the first time what it was like to do a jackknife completely naked. Eric can't help but laugh. What an Idiot.

He takes off his robe and dives in. A proper way to get in when nude. "Come on in," he calls to Carlton.

"No swim suits," Nick says, when he notices the colorful trunks.

"Shh, leave him alone," Eric says, and thankfully, Nick leaves it at that.

Ray, however, doesn't.

"What are you, chicken? Chip chip cheep cheep cheep," he taunts. "Come on, take off your clothes, stud."

143

DAVE!

Eric glares at Ray. "Shh. Vagina."

"Hmm-hmm, what?" he giggles.

Dammit. "You're a vagina. Now, leave him alone."

"Marco!" Nick shouts.

"Polo!" Ray replies. Both of them have their eyes open, so Eric's not sure what it is they're actually doing. All he knows is they're being frigging loud.

"SHHH!" he says.

"Marco!" Nick shouts again.

"SHHHH!" Eric shushes with one extra "H".

"What?" Ray asks, rather loudly.

"Do you want to call attention to us?" Eric asks.

"What, why? Because we're naked. It's as God intended!" Ray yells.

"For fuck sake, keep it down," Carlton says.

Eric clarifies. "Don't you see what's going on here? The employees? The vending machines? All that weird shit?"

"Your point?" Ray asks.

"The people that work here are not people, dummy."

"What are you, some kind of racist or something?" Ray asks. "We're trying to end racism, in case you forgot. I figured you'd be a little more tolerant of other cultures. Take a picture, it'll last longer!" he shouts.

"What the hell are you… oh shit."

Eric looks toward the hotel and sees there are more than a few lights on in the rooms. They're being watched. The faces in the windows staring out at the pool, looking like the faces on the chambermaids. They remind him of the faces peering out of the windows in the train scene in The Wall. Doughy, expressionless. Normally, this would have gotten him thinking about Starlet

144

once again, but not this time. He needs to get out of here, fast. They're in danger.

He gets out of the pool and puts his robe back on. "I'm going back inside. You all should, too." He is followed very quickly by Carlton. They don't look back to see if Nick and Ray are coming, and they really don't care.

"We need to leave," he tells Carlton.

"I know. But not now. I think we'll be okay for the night. We can leave in the morning."

"We'll be okay? Are you fucking high? We need to leave!"

"Shhh. We'll just draw more attention to ourselves. Let's get some sleep and we'll go first thing tomorrow, after the continental breakfast."

"I'm not eating anything that comes out of that kitchen," Eric says.

"I'm sure the muffins will be fine. Or some fruit."

"Fat chance of me getting any sleep tonight."

"Yeah. Me either."

CHAPTER TWELVE

June 5, 2031

She awakens in the morning to a pile of discarded clothing and wine bottles. She doesn't remember much of the night before. She spent the night on the sofa/table under a very hot blanket. She sweating profusely. Bella lies on top of the blanket, Starlet's arm wrapped around her furry body. When the dog senses her movements, she cranes her neck around and licks her face. Over and over and over. She must have to go out. She checks under the blanket and notices her bra and panties are still on. She must have won last night's game. She normally sucks at poker, but apparently Sarah and Greggg are worse players than her. The sun has yet to make its full appearance, but it's light enough to take a walk with the dog without feeling like she's in too much danger. Still, she knows she has to be cautious. She grabs a flashlight, even though what light there is outside is probably brighter than that.

She gets her clothes off the floor and puts them on. Bella is watching, patiently waiting. She's fairly sure the dog won't run off, but she decides to use the leash anyway. She doesn't want her disturbing anyone else that camped there for the night.

Starlet opens the door to the outside world, and Bella immediately tugs at the leash and squats the second she hits the grass.

"Good girl. You gotta go poo-poo?"

She heads over toward the wall, to survey the damage they did yesterday. Not bad. They still have quite a way to go, but if more people show up with more tools, there's no reason they can't get the job done within a couple days. She pities the people who have to knock down the concrete parts of the wall. This was actually quite easy. As she's thinking of all this, Bella is taking quite the healthy dump. Probably not the best place to go. Someone is bound to step in it. But the dog doesn't know any better. Starlet has no poop bags or anything. She contemplates leaving it where it is, but Bella's the only dog here, and she doesn't want her to catch hell for pooping right where someone will most surely step in it. On the ground, a couple big maple leaves. Perfect for scooping. Up the poop goes into the leaves, and over the wall. Fuck them Canadians. They want to complain about what's being done for them, let them walk in shit.

Starlet and Bella continue walking along the wall, doing more surveying. It's going to turn out to be an amazing morning. The rain from last night still hangs in the air, and it's quite refreshing. The sun is finally starting to peek through the trees against the horizon, and the rays catch Starlet's beautiful face as she steps in dog shit.

"Fuck me up the ass," she mutters. She thinks about turning around and calling it a day. She wipes her shoe on the grass and figures if this is the worst thing that happens to her all day, she's doing pretty good. Continues walking. It's too nice out to turn back and sit in the motor home. They head further along the wall, the stink trailing behind them.

Before she realizes it, they are in the thick woods. The wall here is untouched. She now fully realizes just what a big job it's going to be to break down the entire wall, especially with areas like this, that aren't even cleared out. It gets darker and darker, and soon the sun is completely hidden by the thick tree cover. She turns on the flashlight. It's probably a dumb move to be this far from camp, especially from what Eric's text said, but she gauges the danger by looking at Bella, who appears to be happy just to be outside, walking around. If there were any danger, Bella would let her know. Yet she can't help but feel like she is being watched. Suddenly, something has turned very wrong. The dog may be unaware, but sometimes dogs can be dumb. There are sounds the woods are making. Footsteps that are not her own, or Bella's. She needs to turn around and get out of there. Now. Something grabs her ankle. She looks down. Only a branch with some leaves attached. The walk back is taking forever. They couldn't have possibly gone this far. Just when she contemplates running, the clearing appears.

She walks past the damaged parts of the wall and heads toward the motor home. She's about fifty yards away when the front door opens, and someone steps out. Stone. What was he doing in there? She wonders if Sarah and Greggg are making breakfast for everyone.

Stone approaches her. "Hey, gorgeous. Nice day, huh?"

"Wonderful. What's going on in there?" She points at the motor home.

"In there? Oh, nothing I wanted to see if they wanted breakfast, but they'"

Bella sniffs at Stone's leg, which appears to have blood or something on it. She lets out a loud, sharp bark and bites right into Stone's meaty calf. He seems to not notice.

"Bella!" She shouts.

"Oh, she's fine," Stone says. "You headed in? I wouldn't disturb them if I were you."

"I gotta let Bella in."

"Okay, but be very quiet. Let them sleep. GEEEEG."

"Okay, we will. Come on, Bella. Let go of Stone's leg now."

Reluctantly, she lets go, but continues to growl and strain at her leash. Starlet has to yank the leash, dragging her to the motor home. She opens the door, still dragging her, hauls her inside, and shuts it.

The curtain that demarcates the bedroom is hiding Greggg and Sarah's sleeping bodies from view. Bella dashes for it and leaps between the partition. She hears a lot of yipping and panting from Bella. What she doesn't hear is any shouts of "Bella, get off of me," or anything even close. Just the dog.

"Guys?" She says. "We're home."

She pulls back the curtain, dreading the worst. That's exactly what she got.

Bella is straddling Sarah's chest, licking her face, whining and panting. Her throat is slit from ear to ear, a glazed look in her eye. Greggg is much worse off. The entire side of his head is caved in like a Cinco de Mayo day llama piñata, blood oozing out of his right ear. Half a tongue hangs out of his mouth, the missing piece lay on the bed between Sarah and himself. They have obviously both ceased to live, and the saddest thing of all was the sound coming from poor Bella. She needs to get out of here. Quickly.

She turns to leave and in the window is the face of Stone. He's grinning, of course. He breaks the window with his fist, and tries crawling through the little two-foot opening. She wonders why he doesn't just come through the door; it's unlocked.

As if reading her mind, he heads for the door. She beats him to it, though, and locks it.

He rattles the door, Bella barking all the while.

Shit, think, Starlet.

She needs to get out of here. The only way out is through one of the doors in the cab.

As if hearing her mind, Stone heads toward the front of the vehicle. She gets there first, however, and hits the power lock, bolting both passenger and driver-side doors.

Now the only way truly out is to drive the sonofabitch. Starlet looks around for a set of keys. There doesn't seem to be any laying about. She looks in Sarah's purse. Nothing. Checking the pants on the floor and again finding nothing, it's time for plan B.

She goes into Greggg's toolbox and finds a flathead screwdriver and a hammer. Pounds the screwdriver into the ignition. Turns it. Doesn't start. Time for plan C.

She thinks she remembers how to hot wire a car, but it has been a long time. She remembers it being ridiculously easy. Hopefully, motor homes are just as easy. Most new vehicles made it impossible to hot wire, but this is an older model, so here's hoping. Stone stops rattling the passenger side door and looks on the ground, presumably trying to find another rock. Time is definitely short.

She pries the casing away from the steering column with the flathead, exposing the ignition cylinder. She needs a wire cutter. There's one of those in the toolbox as well.

Starlet goes back to the steering column and examines it. The power wires need to be twisted together. Are they the red ones? She hopes. Wires-cut. Check. Twist together. Check. The dashboard lights up. Good sign. Now all she has to do is cut the starter wires. One wire cut. Second wire cut. The passenger window shatters, startling her, and she grabs hold of the bare wires. The shock she gets is barely perceptible. Stone unlocks the door, climbs inside, and leans over toward her, rock back in hand. He swings at her head, and she moves at just the right time. It misses her, and falls out of Stone's hand. His hands grasp around Starlet's neck and squeeze. She feels the blood flow being blocked on its way to her brain. If this is how she's going to die, she's not going to be too happy about it. She claws at his hands, and manages to wrench one of them free. Stone fumbles and when his arm comes up, he stops. His expression freezes in a grimace. His teeth clench, and he starts to drool. Weird, alien sounds come from his throat. His eyes burst from their sockets and dangle by his chin. She opens the driver's side door and jumps out. She considers running, but turns back instead to watch. His hand has brushed against the starter wire, and it is frying the shit out of him. Finally, the sounds stop coming from his mouth. He appears to be dead.

Approaching the motor home she silently prays to whomever will listen that he is, in fact, no longer alive. She gets in the driver's side and touches Stone's body. It is still surging electricity through it, but barely. Why, then, is Stone's body reacting so badly to it? A typical car battery is twelve volts; she thinks she remembers that. It's probably no different for this vehicle. She looks at his face, and the skin is sloughing off, revealing another face underneath. His empty eye sockets reveal rows of tiny teeth. Stone is not Stone. This is the first glimpse she gets of an actual alien. The rumors aren't rumors. "They're among us," she mutters to herself. "Holy shit."

She gets out of the cab, around to the passenger side door, and drags his body out. It's surprisingly light. Like he's stuffed with straw or something. She decides to leave him there. Soon everyone will be up, and they'll discover the body and they'll think that she did it. She needs to get the hell out of there. She slams the passenger door and sees something fall from the visor. When she gets around to the driver's side, there are the keys, on the floor.

The fucking visor. Of course. Why didn't you check there first? This whole mess could have been avoided. She could have driven away, and Stone would still be alive. And if Stone were still alive, he would kill someone else. No, it's for the best this happened. But what if he's not the only one of them here? What if there are more infiltrators? What if, what if? You need to get the hell out of here.

She twists the wires in the steering column back together, and uses the key. It starts right up. Thank God.

What are you going to do about the other bodies? The ones in the back? She will have to dump them somewhere; not here. You know, if you'd told them about what Eric's text said, they may still be alive. Jesus, don't think like that. They would. They'd still be alive and you could have come up with a plan to get out of here. No, she doesn't think so. Without proof to the contrary, everyone here seemed to be on the level, and they would have stayed right where they were. Their cause was too great to just leave. You don't know that. Those two bodies in the bed back there? That's on you. No no no no no! SHUT UP!

Bella nudges her with her nose, stirring her from her internal dialog. Motor home in gear, she heads out of the camp. She doesn't know where she's going, as long as it's away from here.

CHAPTER THIRTEEN

It had been a long night of uneven sleep, but Eric and Carlton made it through. In order to do so, Eric had to trick his brain into thinking that everything was normal. Despite the odd languages running up and down the hall. Despite what looked like slimy tentacles slipping underneath their hotel room door. Despite the fact that someone brought room service when they never ordered any. It looked delicious, too. Two steaks cooked to perfection, baked potatoes with sour cream and bacon, and asparagus. Neither one of them touched any of it.

Feeling like he is going to regret this, he asks Carlton what Ray and Nick's room number was, and dials their extension.

"Yyyellow," Nick answers.

"Hey, man. Just wanted to make sure you guys made it through the night all right."

"Oh, ya. Other than the fact that we didn't get any sleep, we're fine."

"Did you happen to get any what looked like slimy tentacles slipped underneath your hotel room door?"

"Yeah."

"Scary, huh?"

"Scary? No, not really. I get weirder shit than that slipped under my door nightly."

Eric has no idea what this means, and asks: "Did you get room service you didn't order?"

"Yeah. Steaks and potatoes and some green things."

"Those were asparagus spears."

"Yeah, well I calls 'em green things. Neither one of us ate them. You see, there is a completely worthless gene that humans have that make them detect a strong odor in asparagus pee. Some people don't have that gene and are fine eating the stuff. Me, I can't stand it."

"WORTHLESS GENES!" Ray shouts in the background, for no apparent reason.

"Yeah, worthless genes," Nick agrees. "Fun fact: There is also a gene that makes people hate cilantro. Says it makes it taste soapy. Some people don't have that gene. Me, I'm indifferent about cilantro."

"I'm indifferent about it, too. Most are. So I take it you ate the steak and potatoes."

"Sure did."

"And no ill effects?"

"No. Why?"

"No reason. So why were you up all night?"

"Me and Ray were playing reverse strip poker."

"Reverse strip poker?"

"Yeah. We already had our clothes off from the skinny dip, so we decided that we would start out naked. You know, reverse."

"Did you take your bets out of the pot instead of putting them in?"

"No."

153

"Did the cards start out on the table and the dealer dealt them back in the deck?"

"No."

"Then it wasn't reverse strip poker."

"The reverse was the strip part. Loser had to put clothes back on. Otherwise I would have said strip reverse poker. Or strip reverse strip poker."

"REVERSE!" Ray shouts in the background. He must have taken his Adderall already.

He has a point.

"You have a point. All right, well, get showered and everything. Let's move out. We wanted to be out of here before sun up, and it's already too late for that."

Eric hangs up the phone, heads into the bathroom, and closes the door. He turns the shower on to super-hot. One thing he loves in the morning is a scalding-hot shower. One thing he never expects to get in hotel rooms is a scalding-hot shower. (Liability reasons, he's sure. Just like McDonald's has been sued so much for having hot coffee that they now serve all their beverages at the temperature of human saliva, so the tongue detects that there is a beverage in the mouth only by taste.) One thing he didn't expect this morning, however, was an ice-cold shower. The water makes his teeth chatter and his joints ache. His balls, which he rarely uses nowadays anyway, shrink up into his throat.

He's not sure what kind of magical powers cold water lacks that it can't lather soap, but it doesn't. He would have been better off with no shower at all today.

A knock at the door. "You almost done in there?" He had literally been in there four minutes. Three of which were spent pushing his balls back down to where the belonged. "I need to shower," Carlton says.

Eric opens the door. "I wouldn't recommend it. Fucking cold as shit."

"Oh, come on. Don't be such a puss. How cold could it possibly be?"

The door shuts, water turns on. "Schmeeeeyikes!" Three seconds later, water shuts off.

Door opens. Carlton spits out a couple ice cubes. "You weren't jivin'."

"Heh heh, you old buzzard. Meet you downstairs."

The breakfast buffet is incredible. The continental breakfast looks inedible. Eric figures, why not? The food must be edible or Nick and Ray would be suffering some ill effects. As if on cue, the two Idiots spot him and wave him over. He gives them a "one second" finger, and asks the host, "How much for the full breakfast shebang, Shithead?" he reads the tag on the host's uniform.

"It's Shih-teed," he pronounced. "Five dollars, sir."

"Five dollars? Can't beat that with a broom handle. Here you go," he hands Yernkle a tubby, and gets back a Gary and a Peter in return. (A "Peter" is a ten-dollar bill, with Peter Tork of the Monkees on the face. A Gary is a fiver, with some lucky contest winner named "Gary" on it.)

"Mmmmm, omelet bar," he says to no one in particular.

"Yes sir, what would you like?" the strangely deformed omelet cook asks.

"Jeez, um, let me think, um. Ham, sautéed onion, and fuckin' cheese! Oh, and some tomato," he adds as an afterthought.

"Coming right up," the pleasant, although very ugly, cook says. How many eggs?" He asks.

"Three."

The cook brings out three of the tiniest blue eggs Eric has ever seen.

"Um, oh, uh, what kind of eggs are these?"

"Robin, sir."

Robin? Ugh.

155

"Better make that ten," he says.

"Very good, sir."

"Um, just out of curiosity, where does the ham come from?"

"New Jersey," the cook says.

"Animal?"

"Pig, of course." He looks at Eric like he has lost his mind. What else could ham possibly come from?

Eric leaves the omelet guy to cook his eggs, and he hopes to God it is better than the eggs he had at the diner. He goes to the waffle iron and makes himself one. "Batter up," he says, and laughs at his pun. Nobody else will. He checks out the syrups. Apple, maple, oak, pine. He samples each one, and the pine syrup tastes predictably like gin. He decides on that one. By the time his waffle is nicely coated with a thick layer of pine pitch, his omelet is done.

"Thank you, my good man," he says to the ugly fellow, and reluctantly grabs a seat by Nick and Ray. Carlton soon appears with an orange.

"Well, would you look at Orange Boy," Nick teases. He, himself, has an apple. So there really is no call for that kind of language.

"At least I have a breakfast fruit," Carlton says, and Eric gives him a look like Don't encourage him.

"Apples are a perfectly good choice for breakfast."

"No. They're not."

"What is, then?"

"Bananas. Kiwi. Fuckin' oranges. Anything but apples, really."

"Well, I like apples."

"Well good for fuckin' you," Carlton says.

"Jesus, what's crawled up your snatch?" Ray asks.

"Easy." Eric nudges him.

"What's crawled up my snatch? What the fuck has called up my batch? Fuck you, motherfucker. That's what."

"Eek," Ray says.

"He gets all uppity when anyone mentions genitalia," Eric says. "Just let's get back to eating our oranges and stuff. Man, this robin's egg omelet looks tight. Jussalookadathammmm."

"Ham looks nice," Ray says.

CHAPTER FOURTEEN

Starlet's only driven the handful of miles back to her house when she realizes she has no business driving this monstrosity. Up till this point, the largest vehicle she has ever driven would have been her father's pickup truck, back in her teenage years. This is a different beast altogether. With additional mirrors attached to the side-view mirrors. She isn't sure what they're for. Perhaps it's so the mirrors had a better view of other mirrors. There isn't even a rear-view mirror in this one. Not that she has anything to look at back there, 'cept for a couple of dead friends. It handles surprisingly well for an old piece of shit. The only problem she has is trying to keep it between the lines. She's not sure how much space she's actually taking up, so she hugs, and sometimes crosses, the yellow lines. Better to do that than get stuck in a ditch somewhere.

Bella is currently lying on the couch, crying. Probably afraid to go back and look at the bodies. Her parents are no longer with us. They're somewhere else, if you believe in that sort of thing. Bella believes in that sort of thing, as do all dogs. It's what gives them their sense of peace.

First order of business: Find a place to dump the bodies. She wishes she could find a place to dump the entire motor home, but she currently needs a ride. She can worry about switching vehicles later.

Second order of business: She doesn't know. She really wants to go home to grab more of her things, but her friends at the wall, when they notice she's gone, may come looking for her. She can't chance it. Some of those friends may not be friends.

Third order of business: Really hard to say when she doesn't know what her second order of business is. Maybe there isn't a second order of business. This would make her third order of business her second, in actuality. And that may just blow her mind.

Fourth order of business: See Third order of business.

Fifth order of business: Drive till she finds some place with cell phone reception.

She's not sure where she can dump the bodies. Has to be some place that she can get to with this monstrosity. A dirt road would be the obvious choice if she had a smaller vehicle, since there are so many of them up here. But she doesn't think she could turn this beast around, and there's no way in hell she could back up out. No, her best bet now is to hit Route 162, toss the bodies in Long Lake, and keep driving till she hit Route One, where she can head south till she reaches some sort of civilization.

When she gets on the stretch of Main Street where she can finally pull over along the side of the road, she parks and puts her hazards on. Which takes her quite some time to find. It's not anywhere near the dashboard, as one would think. No, the triangular hazard button is located in the middle of the cook-top stove, right between the knobs for the right and left burners.

She figures she'll start with the heaviest body. She grabs Greggg's body by its shoulders, and his mashed up face, which is currently stuck to the bed sheet, relieves itself of some of its flesh. There was no mistaking him for an alien. It was pure human meat beneath the skin. His eye falls out of its socket, as Stone's did, and she thinks how amazing it is that eyes actually stay in their sockets most of the time, if they can pop out so easily. There are no rows of gnashing teeth behind the eye, just an empty socket. More flesh tears and sticks to the sheet, which also tears in places. It occurs to her that if the body and sheet want to stay together, it may be easier to just wrap him up completely and drag the sheet with the body in it. And it is. Much easier. Although Greggg is still slightly overweight, and she is completely winded by the time she gets his fat ass to the door.

159

DAVE!

"A little help, here," she asks Bella, who couldn't be less interested. She's lying on the couch, still, with the ghosts of her mum and dad right beside her, petting her and giggling while watching the whole event.

Thankful she parked close enough to the side of the road that she doesn't have to drag the body through across the pavement. Total grass; easy to slide. She rolls the sheeted body into the water, and it doesn't seem to want to go anywhere. "Be right back," she says, and gets Sarah's body as well. Although much easier to move, she's pretty winded from having to move Greggg.

"Now a little help?" she asks again, and Bella seems even less interested than she did the first time she was asked. Perhaps if she were a wolf, she would have more experience moving corpses around. However, wolves are very spiritual animals, and they would probably also be very content just being petted by Sarah and Greggg's ghosts.

She drags the body down to the water. A car full of people passes by, perplexed looks out the windows. She gives a smile and an overly-cheerful wave, as if to say, Hello! Beautiful day, isn't it? Nothing to see here. Just rolling a couple dead folks into the lake, is all.

She rolls Sarah's body into the lake. The two bodies go nowhere, just hugging the shoreline. Perhaps this wasn't the best idea. She thought they would just float away. Maybe she should take the time and build them a little raft, put their bodies on it, light it on fire, and send it out into the middle of the lake. A true Viking funeral. But there's no time. She needs to get out of there before any more traffic passes by.

She gets back in the motor home and Bella licks her hand. So does Greggg's ghost, but she can't feel it. Sarah notices and sighs. What can she do? You can't control a ghost.

"Ready to roll?" she asks Bella.

She gets in the driver's seat, turns the key, and guns it.

She heads due south on Route 1. It's not till she gets to Caribou that she's actually able to get a signal. She pulls over and makes a call. It goes directly to Eric's voicemail.

"Eric? It's Starlet. I hope you get this. I'm heading south. I'm not really sure where I'm going, but I know I need to get out of Northern Maine. I'm just about to head into Presque Isle. I should have a pretty good signal from here on out. I'll leave my phone on. Please call me when you get this. Bye."

Hopefully Eric would get the message. She decides to try her dad next. He picks up on the second ring.

Jake answers his phone.

"Starlet?"

"Daddy!" She sounds like she's getting all choked up.

"Hey, I can hear you."

"I'm in Caribou. Seems to be pretty good reception here. Listen, Daddy, things have gone south rather quickly here. So I'm...going south."

"What happened?"

"D-daddy," sniff, "it was h-h-horrible. W-w-we were at...wall...and...infiltrators...they infiltraded...th-there was a guy n-n-named St-stone and...alw-ways cah-called me gorgeous...and...S-sarah a-and Greggg w-with th-three g's and... h-he k-k-killed them and i...r-rolled th-them in...lake a-and pretty d-dog n-n-named Bella."

"Honey, your connection is shitty again."

"N-no Daddy i-it's me. I c-c-can's st-stop crying. I can't breathe."

"Okay, sweetie. Deep breaths. Calm down." He hears her taking those deep breaths.

"Where are you now? You say you're inside a caribou?"

161

Another deep breath. "No, Daddy. I'm in Caribou. It's a town. I'm pulled over in a parking area on Route 1."

"Good. Good. Now, what happened?"

She tells him everything, without all the sobbing nonsense.

"Holy shit," Jake says. "Listen, honey. This is what I want you to do. Keep driving south. Get off from Route One as soon as possible. Don't stay on 95 too long, either. You do not want to be anywhere near the border wall. My buddy Pherl and I are heading to D.C. I want you to meet us there."

"What's going on in D.C.?"

Jake explains the Invader plan to her.

"Daddy, I just buried two of my friends. Well, rolled them into the lake, really. Why would I want to go to D.C. and get mixed up in all this? It's not safe."

"It's not safe anywhere, sweetie. I need you here, with me. You'll be safest here. I'll protect you. Don't worry. Just please, do your dad a favor and come down, okay?"

"Yeah. Okay, I will."

"Call me when you get closer, all right?"

"Sure, Daddy."

"And, pumpkin? I love you so much."

"Love you too. Bye."

Just as she hangs up the phone, there's a knock on her passenger side door. A deputy from the Aroostook County Sheriff's Department is standing outside.

"How you doin' today, ma'am?"

"Been better, to tell you the truth," she answers.

"Little problem with the window, I see?"

"A little."

"Could I see your driver's license, registration, and proof of insurance, please?"

"Certainly."

She hopes like hell the necessary papers are in the glovebox. They are. She hands them over, along with her driver's license.

"I'll be right back," the deputy says.

Shit, shit, shit. Should she take off? There's no way she can outrun a cop in this thing. It seems like an eternity before he comes back. She sees him in the passenger door mirror, examining the steps that lead to the side door.

"Who's Dennis Richter?" he asks.

"Who?"

"Yeah. Who?"

Fuck. She gave him her old license. She held onto it for a laugh; a conversation piece.

"Sorry, officer. That's an old license. I had reassignment surgery and changed my name. Here's my new one."

"You know you're supposed to destroy copies of old licenses?" he asks her.

"No, I had no idea."

"Yeah. At the very least, you can't carry them around with you. Highly illegal."

"Highly?"

"Quite."

"Sorry. I'll make sure to destroy it as soon as I find a shredder."

DAVE!

"I see. A little trouble getting the motor home started this morning?" He gestures at the demolished steering column.

"Yeah. I forgot I had put my keys up in the visor, like a dummy, and had to hot wire it to get it going."

"I see. You wouldn't happen to know a Greggg Puchinsky, would you?"

"Greggg…hmm. No. Can't say that rings a bell. Why?"

"Seems this motor home is registered to him."

"Hmm, well, yeah. Now that you mention it, that name does ring a bell…Yeah, now I remember. He told me I could use his motor home. See, I'm heading south, and I wrecked my car, so he said I could use his."

"I see. Did you report the accident?"

"Accident? Oh, you mean my car. Well, I figured since no people or property were hurt, except for my car, that it was unnecessary."

"I see. You know, you're supposed to report accidents, regardless. Right?"

"No, I had no idea. Really."

"I see. Mind explaining the blood all over the steps, here?"

"Blood?"

"Yes, ma'am."

She gets up to go look.

"Stay seated, please, ma'am."

"Yes sir. Well, I'm not sure about any blood. I have a dog in here. Bella. She likes raw meat. It's probably meat juice."

"Meat juice?"

"Yeah, you know. The juice from meat."

"So, blood."

"Yeah."

164

"I see. Please, step out of the motor home, ma'am."

"Yes sir."

He speaks into his walkie talkie thingy on his shoulder. "10-4, Charlie, Applesauce. We have a possible 6-15 here."

Another car shows up. Another deputy.

"Ma'am, do you mind if I search the vehicle?"

"Mind? Well, yes I would mind, thank you."

"Ma'am, I'm sorry to say, but since this vehicle is clearly not yours, we have the right to search it."

"Don't you need to notify the owner?" she asks.

He looks over at the new deputy, who shrugs.

"No, ma'am. We don't."

"Well, then I guess it's okay."

He is in there for about two minutes, and comes back out.

"Ma'am, could you please explain the blood all over the bed."

"Blood?" she asks.

"I'm sorry. Ma'am could you please explain the meat juice all over the bed."

"Must be the dog again. Bad Bella." Bella is just sitting there with a dumbass doggie grin on her face.

"I see." He steps out of the motor home.

"Mind stepping over here?" the officer asks. She does.

"Ma'am, the reason I came over here was this: There was a report of a vehicle house matching this description parked alongside Long Lake in St. Agatha earlier today. Someone saw what appeared to be a woman matching your description roll two bodies into the lake. The bodies were identified as Greggg and Sarah Puchinsky."

"Really? Well, that's peculiar."

"I assume you're going to say you have no idea what I'm talking about."

"Probably."

"I see. Ma'am, I'm going to ask you to turn around, facing away from me." The officer takes a few steps back. "Now put your hands behind your head and interlace your fingers." She complies. "Now, walk slowly backward toward the sound of my voice. Good. Stop. Now I'm going to ask you to stand on just your right leg. Good. Now just your left one. Good. Now neither of them. Good. Now I need you to put your hands down on the ground without the rest of your body touching the ground. Just your hands and feet. Like you're doing a push-up. Good. Now take your right ankle and place it over your left one. Good. Now raise your left hand in the air and balance on just your left foot and your right hand. Good. Now lay fully down on the ground. Good. Now slowly pull down your pants."

"Wha?" Starlet asks.

"Pull down your fucking pants. Underwear too. Come on. Get goin'"

"I have to say, this is highly unorthodox," Starlet says, but complies anyway.

"Good. Now just lay still. My buddy Chuck here is gonna enter you. Come on, Chuck. Carve yourself out a slice."

She cringes. Her body is shaking. This was not the way she wanted to spend her day.

Chuck pulls down his pants.

"Yeah, Chuck loves the ladies; don'tcha, Chuckie boy? Me, I like cock, so what you got don't interest me in the least. Get on it, Chuckie. Come on, before someone drives by. We ain't got all goddamn..."

166

From seemingly out of nowhere, a black shape comes whipping by. It's Bella. She grabs hold of Chuck's dick with her teeth, and shakes it like a rope toy.

"For the love of Evender Holyfield, get this mutt off me!" He screams, more in anger than in pain. With one great jerk of her head, Officer Chuck's schlong comes right off. Bella runs off into the woods with it as though it were a wiener sausage she was going to bury. "Dammit!" he shouts.

"Bitch, you're gonna pay for that," the first officer says. He pulls her up off the road and pulls her pants up. The handcuffs go on. "You are under arrest for the suspected murders of Greggg and Sarah Puchinsky. You have the right to remain silent. Anything you say can and will be used against you in a court of law. You have the right to an attorney. If you cannot afford one, an attorney will be appointed for you free of charge. Do you have any questions?"

"Yeah. Why are there only two Miranda Rights? You'd think there'd be more of them."

"Too much to memorize, is what it really comes down to. Come on. Watch your head please."

CHAPTER FIFTEEN

"Where we off to now?" Eric asks, when he notices Carlton taking a detour from the main route.

"We have a Skype with Dave at noon."

"Ah, here I thought all along we were just flying by the seat of our pants, and you actually have an agenda."

"Well, sort of. I have a plan to speak to Dave at noon. I wouldn't really call that an agenda."

"You seem a little hostile still."

"Hostile? Fucking right I'm hostile."

"Well, don't take it out on me, dude."

"You're the one I'm hostile at!" Carlton screamed.

"Me? What did I do?"

"You told them."

"Told us what?" Nick says from the back seat.

"Okay, first, I didn't tell them anything. And second, nobody gives a shit. It's 2031, not 2016. Nobody cares anymore. Watch. Hey guys, Carlton has a vagina."

"You mean a lady's vagina?" Ray asks Idiotically.

"And?" Nick asks, more intelligently.

"See?" Eric says. "They don't care. Ray barely knows what we're even talking about. The only one all hung up on this issue is you. You need to get over yourself. There are much bigger issues we're facing right now than what you have down below."

Carlton is silent for a moment, then says, "Fuck you."

"Why? Because what you thought you had that made you special and different nobody cares about? Because you have to give up that notion of being the black sheep? Look at those two Idiots in the back seat. Just look at them."

He does. Nick is picking Ray's nose, saying, "Haha, you really can pick your friend's nose. Who knew?"

"Give up. Let go. You're special because you're a leader, Carlton. Not because you have ladyflaps. Nick, Ray, they look up to you."

Now Ray is picking Nick's nose, saying, "Ha! It works in reverse!"

"I look up to you. That is your strength. Your hangups about your anatomy, that's your weakness. Don't mistake one for the other. Be proud of who you are inside. Forget all the body shit."

"Here," Carlton says, and hands Eric the directions to the hideaway. "We can't use GPS for obvious reasons, so I had to print the directions. Make yourself useful and navigate." That's his way of avoiding the subject, but Eric can tell by the look he gets that Carlton knows there is truth to what he's saying.

This particular bunker is much nicer than the one Carlton originally took Eric to. It's not as huge, but the amenities are exquisite. Comfy furniture. Huge refrigerator and stove. Even a better bathroom.

"I bet the bathroom in this one doesn't have the ventilation our old one does," Carlton says, as if reading Eric's mind.

169

"Let's see what's in the fridge," Eric says. "Schaweet. A leftover Subway sandwich and beer! I'm eating the Subway sandwich. You want a beer, though?" He asks Carlton.

"Love one. But I'm driving. Last thing I need is to get pulled over with alcohol on my breath."

"Chicken?" Eric says.

"No. Just practical."

"No, I meant there's Chik-Fil-A in here. Want some?"

"Chik-Fil-A sucks."

"Why, because of their antiquated views on homosexuality?"

"No. Because of their food."

"THEN DO YOU WANT THE SUBWAY SANDWICH?" Eric yells for no reason.

"Do you know how old that is?"

"DO YOU???????"

"No. I just got here. Same as you. Smell it."

Eric smells it. "There's no smell."

"It's probably good, then."

"No, like, there's no smell at all. No meat smell. No vegetable smell. Even the pickles have no smell. That's way past stale."

"Yep. Throw it to the dogs. They'll eat anything."

He opens the hatch, and offers the sandwich to Nick and Ray, who are both throwing a Frisbee around. Which, of course, is invisible.

"Here's a sandwich for you to share, boys. What you doing? Throwing the ol' Frisbee?"

170

Nick shakes his head. "Nah, couldn't find one. We're throwing a coffee can lid instead." What. The fuck. Ever.

"Alrighty, going back down. You guys need anything else, find it yourselves."

"How they doin'?" Carlton asks.

"Not sure," Eric answers.

"Status quo, then."

"Yup."

"So, it's eleven o'clock. Anyone else…" he is interrupted by a knock on the bunker door. "Coming?"

"Not sure," Carlton answers.

"Knock knock," says a voice from above. As if the actual knocking wasn't enough.

"Hi everyone!" There are only Eric and Carlton down here. Using the word "everyone" in this case is a little much.

"Pherl!" Carlton says. It seems he knows this guy and it seems his name is Pherl.

"Carlton!" Pherl says back. "Carlton, I want you to meet my friend and fellow invader…"

"Mr. Richter," Eric says.

"You can call me Jake," Jake says. Then: "Wait, you know me?"

"Sure do," Eric says. "You probably don't remember me, though. It was a long time ago."

"Hawaii!" Jake says.

"Wow, good memory."

"How could I forget? Pherl, this boy here was my daughter Starlet's first true love. Perhaps her only true love."

"Nice to meet you, Eric." Pherl says.

"This is wild," Eric says. "Of all the lousy bunkers in all the lousy towns, how the hell did you end up here?"

"I don't know. Fate? If this were a book, nobody would believe it."

"For sure. Hey, Jake, wanna go get some air? Let these two do their thing? You don't need us for anything, do you guys?"

"No, not really," Carlton says. "Go. Catch up on old times." Carlton does the old thumb across the throat bit.

"Still with that?" Eric asks.

Carlton does the thumb the other way, as if saying, If I don't catch your artery on the first pass, I'll slice it the other way and maybe catch it on the second. And if not, then I don't know, maybe a third? Or maybe I'll leave you wondering, you little miscreant. He wonders why Carlton is still posturing. He has no doubt that Carlton could kill him, he just doesn't think he ever would kill him. And he finds it hard to believe that Carlton actually thinks he can be taken seriously.

Eric climbs up the ladder and opens the hatch. "Watch out!" he hears Ray shout. Eric ducks as an imaginary coffee can lid flies by his head. Or, at least he thinks it does.

"Let's get off the playing field before someone gets hurt." He leads Jake by the hand, which is probably unnecessary.

"So, Eric, what have you been up to?"

"Not much. Pool sharking, mostly."

"Oh, ah, I see. And you make a living at this?"

"Pretty decent, actually. I just earned a thousand dollars last week doing it."

"Really? People pay that much for you to release sharks into their swimming pools? Sounds lucrative. Must be pretty dangerous work, though."

"Actually, people pay me to get them out of their pools."

"Oh, well that makes more sense."

"Listen, I'd love to sit here and chit-chat the day away, but I need to know if you've heard from Starlet at all."

Jake sighs, and looks away.

"Uh-oh."

"No," Jake says. "She's fine. She was in danger but she got out. Seems there was an infiltrator at camp."

"I knew it."

"Yeah, a couple of her friends got axed, but she got away clean. In fact, she's heading down to D.C. as we speak. She's even got a little dog with her."

"Oh, thank the Lord."

"Yep. She said she'd contact me later on."

"Does Pherl know?"

"Does Pherl know what?"

"That you've been in contact with her."

"Yeah, why?"

"Carlton seems to have a big issue with it."

"What, with you talking to her? Why would he have an issue with that?"

"He doesn't want any of the Topplers to know about us."

"Oh, who cares? Starlet can keep a secret. You just need to be more convincing."

"Maybe. I've tried, believe me. Well, what are we waiting for? Let's not wait for her to call us. Let's call her. I've been wanting to but Carlton took my phone."

"Carlton sounds like a real asshole."

"He can be, but he is mostly a good guy. He's just looking out for the greater good. Now hurry up and call!"

The phone rings. The person who answers is not Starlet. The person who answers is a man.

"Speak," The man says.

"Who is this?" Jake asks.

"This is Deputy Charles Riddley of the Aroostook County Sheriff's Department. And who may you be?"

"Jake Richter."

"Jake Richter...Any relation to Starlet Richter?"

Jake's face pales. "She's my daughter. Where is she? Did something happen to her? What's wrong?"

"Ohhh, nothin'. Other than the fact that she killed two people and stole their motor home, is all."

"You can't steal from the dead!" he hears Starlet shout in the background.

"Shut up, slut! Also, her dog ran away with my penis."

"Give me that," someone says, and the line goes dead.

"Did you hear any of that?" Jake asks.

"Yeah. All of it. Killed two people?"

"She must have gotten caught driving their motor home. I can see how that can look incriminating."

"We gotta go get her," Eric says.

"How do you propose we do that? We have no way to get there."

"We find a way."

"Okay, let's assume we find a way to get all the way up to Northern Maine. Then what? Bust her out of jail?"

"We bail her out."

Jake shakes his head. "You have no clue how any of this works, do you? First, they have to set a bail hearing. Then we have to come up with the money for bail. That's assuming they allow this bail thing to happen. Which they probably won't. It's pointless. What we need to do is stay the course here. We're at least doing some good here."

"You're right. I hate to say it, but you're right. Don't know if my heart's going to be in this while I'm thinking about Starlet rotting away in jail."

"Listen, she's my little girl. She always will be. There's nobody more concerned about her than I am. But I think I was more worried knowing about the impostors at the wall. I'm more worried about us and our safety. I wanted her with me at first. I told her I would keep her safe, but I really didn't have a plan as to how. She would be in as much danger here as we are going to be. No, I think the safest thing she could do right now is stay exactly where she is."

Eric feels defeated.

"What's wrong?" Jake asks.

"I feel…I don't know."

"Defeated?"

"No, not really."

Eric feels angry.

"I feel…"

"Angry?"

DAVE!

"No. That's not it."

Eric feels upset.

"You feel upset."

"Yeah, I guess. But that's not it exactly. I guess I feel...I don't know..."

"Helpless," Jake says.

"Yes, that's it exactly."

Eric feels helpless.

"Don't. We're doing our part. Which is huge. We're going to change the world. I really think this is the best way to help Starlet. Stay the course, my lad. Stay the course."

CHAPTER SIXTEEN

Speak."

"Who is this?"

"This is Deputy Charles Riddley of the Aroostook County Sheriff's Department. And who may you be?"

"Jake Richter."

"Jake Richter…Any relation to Starlet Richter?"

"She's my daughter. Where is she? Did something happen to her? What's wrong?"

"Ohhh, nothin'. Other than the fact that she killed two people and stole their motor home, is all."

"You can't steal from the dead!" Starlet shouts from her cell.

"Shut up, slut! Also, her dog ran away with my penis."

Deputy Flarp, the arresting officer, gets up from his desk. "Give me that," he says, and grabs the phone from Deputy Riddley. He presses "END" and tosses the phone in his desk drawer.

"You assholes," Starlet says. "Where's my one phone call I'm entitled to?"

"That was it," Flarp says. "You should have asked to talk. Anyway, that was your dad. Chuck told him everything he needs to know."

"What, that a dog ran away with his penis, or that I killed two people? Yeah, he's really the king of information."

"Your dad knows where you are if he needs to come find you. That's all that matters. Although he'll do best to stay away if he knows what's good for him."

"I notice he didn't use the word alleged."

"What?"

"Alleged. I allegedly killed two people."

"Whatever," Chuck says.

"Tell me this, Chuck. You seemed not to feel a thing when Bella took your penis. Why is that? Hmm?"

"I think you know why, lady," he says.

"I think I do, too. But I want to hear you say it."

"We're different, Flarp and I. In fact, most of us in law enforcement are. There are more of us than you know. But you will. Yeah, I suspect you will, soon enough."

"More of you what? What are you?" Starlet asks, her lip quivering.

"We're not of your world. But soon this world will be ours, and you'll be the one saying you're not of our world. The penis wasn't real. None of what you see standing in front of you is real. And if you saw the truth behind these costumes, it would blow your fucking mind."

"Jesus Christ."

"Tell me about it," Chuck says.

"You were going to rape me, weren't you?"

"I was going to sure as hell try. Although, I don't think I would have been successful, seeing as I was never able to maintain an erection with that fake thing."

CHAPTER SEVENTEEN

June 6, 2031

The hatch opens, and Carlton and Pherl step out. A panicked look is on Carlton's face, and an expression that looks like an expression only someone named Pherl can give is on Pherl's face.

"Guys," Carlton says, "we need to move out. Now."

"What's going on?" Eric asks.

"Change of plans." Carlton calls over to Nick and Ray, who appear to be tossing around a boomerang-like object, albeit invisible. "Hey shitheads. Let's go!"

"What's going on?" Eric asks.

"Yeah, what's going on?" Jake echoes.

"Can someone tell us what's going on?" Eric asks.

"I will once you get in the Elephant." Carlton says.

"I'm not getting in the Elephant till you tell me what's going on."

"For the love of crap, will you just get in the Elephant?"

"Fine. But I'd like to state for the record that I don't know what's going on."

"Duly noted."

Once everyone is in the vehicle, Carlton speaks.

"Okay, listen up because I'm only going to say this once. Well, I may actually say it twice if some of you didn't hear me well the first time. I will not, however, say it a third time. Ever."

"Come again?" Nick asks.

"Ugh. This is the second time. And I can't say it a third."

"What was that?" Ray asks.

Eric admires their tenacity when it comes to shenanigans. However, it doesn't explain why they are barreling down the road at over a hundred miles an hour.

"Wow, slow down, Carlton. You want to get pulled over? What's the rush?" Eric asks.

"Plans have changed. The invasion has been moved up a day. We need to get to D.C. and to our weapons cache as soon as possible."

"Why? What's up?"

"Word got out. They know what we're up to."

"Shit."

"Yeah. Shit. This is going to make it ten times harder. Maybe even eleven. They're pulling troops from the border and back to D.C. As far as Dave knows, they still think the plan is for the invasion to happen on the eighth. That's why it's been changed to the seventh."

"Tomorrow?"

"Yeah. Since today's the sixth. We have a lot to do in very little time. We're going to have to drive straight through, no stops."

"Don't you think you should slow down?"

"I will once we get closer to D.C. We're not in much danger of getting pulled over anymore, way out here. Police are too busy busting into our homes to pull over traffic violators. I wouldn't be surprised in the least if we don't pass one single cop on the road."

"Busting into homes? What are they looking for?"

"Intel. Anything they can to piece our plan together. This is why we have to get the jump on them. We need to catch them off guard. All plans say the eighth."

"So we get there a day early. That may give us a little advantage, but they know about everything else. The Distractors. The plan to kill the president. Et-fucking-cetera."

"So has the overall plan changed?"

"Dave doesn't think that's a good idea. There's no time to come up with another plan. The only other option is to turn around and go home. But we've passed that point. If we all go home now, we're all in huge fucking trouble anyway, and will most likely never see daylight again. Best thing to do is keep going."

"Do they know where our secret stash of weapons is?"

"I don't know. They may know where others are located, but they don't know where ours are at."

"You just ended your sentence in a preposition. What did you have to go and do that for?"

"See, there you go again."

"?"

"Stop changing the subject every time you get nervous."

"Right now I could shout something about antelope, but that would be obvious."

"Point is, we keep going."

"I'm as nervous as a little girl learning to pour her senile mother a cup of tea."

"?"

"Well, what does she want? Earl Gray? Green? Sleepy Time? Is she going to change her mind once it's all steeped and ready?"

"Your analogies need some improvement."

"What about Nick and Ray?"

"Their everything needs some improvement."

"The whole Distracting thing, is that still a go?"

"Well, there really is no point now, except to keep them out of our way. But yes. I want to keep them far, far out of our way. Like, if I could let them out right here, I would. But I don't think they'd be able to navigate their way home."

"We're no good with directions!" Ray shouts excitedly.

"All right, well, cool. Now that word is getting out, can I get my phone back? I need to call Starlet."

Carlton hands the phone over. "Knock yourself out."

The phone rings a couple times, then goes into voicemail. He's forgotten already; the police have her phone. BOOP BOOP his phone says, and goes dead. He's used up his battery.

The rest of the trip is fairly uneventful. They should be discussing the grand plan; instead there is silence. A cool, dull silence that soon lulls Eric to sleep. When he wakes up night has fallen hard, like an alcoholic priest trying to catch the subway.

"Rise and shine, sleepynuts. We're here." Carlton gets out and makes a big production of stretching his limbs. He yawns.

"Where's here?"

"Annapolis. Stay here. I gotta go meet my guy."

183

DAVE!

They're in front of what would normally be a busy section, if it wasn't the middle of the night. Carlton walks up to a random dude that appears to be milling around, hands in his pockets, minding his own business. The dude would have been known as a "completely random dude" if he wasn't the only dude hanging out. This dude was actually a lone dude, not a random dude. To Eric, milling around with your hands in your pockets looks suspicious and far from nonchalant. But apparently he's the guy, since Carlton is talking to him. He leads him into a laundromat, and Carlton waves the other guys in. Actually, he waves Eric in. He tells the other two yahoos to stay in the Elephant.

"Get a few hours' sleep, Idiots!" he shouts.

"Eric, this is some random dude. Random dude, Eric Stickney."

"Tisdale," Eric corrects.

"Tisdale? Are you sure? I always thought it was Stickney."

"Pretty sure, yeah."

"Hmph."

The random dude opens the door on a seemingly random horizontal clothes drier with a handwritten OUT OF ORDER sign on it and crawls inside. He fiddles around for a second and slithers back out. Then he leaves. They never see him again. He will never get billing in the credits.

"Follow me," Carlton says to Eric and crawls inside the drier. They crawl through a tunnel for about fifty feet when Carlton stops.

"Wait here," he says, and drops down out of the tunnel.

Eric listens to Carlton fumble around in the dark as claustrophobia starts to set in. "Hurry up," he calls out.

"Aha!" A light shines out from the darkness. "Found it. Okay, come on. Careful of the edge."

Eric crawls to the edge of the tunnel and drops a few feet to the floor. "Ow."

"Did you say Careful of the edge? I thought you said Werewolf on the ledge."

They're in another command center. Fairly standard, but smaller than the others. Laptop, snack rations, same old crap. On the wall is a movie poster, showing a very tall skyscraper in some unknown city, a very depressed-looking lycanthrope seemingly about to jump to his gruesome death. At the bottom, the movie title: WEREWOLF ON THE LEDGE!

"I did," Carlton clarified.

"Ugh, that was a depressing movie. I don't think there'd be anything more depressing to be than a werewolf."

"How about an alien trying to take over a strange planet, whose about to get his ass kicked?"

"That would most certainly be a huge bummer. I'm still going with werewolf, though."

"Right." Carlton looks at his watch. "It's 11:30 now. Let's get some shuteye till six or so."

"Sounds good. I just want to send a quick text to Starlet."

Carlton rolls his eyes. "Suit yourself. Good night." He turns off the desk lamp.

"Night, dude."

Eric turns his phone on. The battery is dead. He'd forgotten to bring his charger, and his phone is such an ancient piece of shit that no one has a charger that fits. Awesome.

CHAPTER EIGHTEEN

Get up, wake up, rise and shine," Cartlton sings to Eric.

"Ugh, must you sing?" Eric asks. "What time is it?"

"It's 6 in the morning. We need to get a move on before the laundromat opens."

Eric laughs at the thought of the customers in the laundromat, sitting and reading a magazine, or casually folding their clothes, as two guys crawl out of a drier like Mario and Luigi crawling out of a pipe. He grabs an orange juice from the fridge and they head out.

"Go wake the two Idiots up, and have them drive the Elephant around to the back," Carlton says.

Nick and Ray are fast asleep, spooning in the spacious back of the vehicle. It's almost a shame to disturb their slumber. Almost.

"Wake up, Idiots!" he shouts.

"Say whaaa?" Nick mutters.

"Whazaaa?" Ray asks.

"Dude, I told you no spooning," Nick says.

"Sorry. I forgot where I was. Thought you were my mom."

"So gross," Eric says. "Listen, guys. Carlton needs you to move his vehicle around to the back of the building and wait for us." He tosses Ray the keys and goes back inside.

Carlton has another OUT OF ORDER drier opened up. He pulls a lever hidden inside, and the whole panel opens around it. A safe appears, seemingly out of nowhere, if nowhere was the back side of a clothes drier. He punches in this ridiculously long code. The safe door opens, and laying there glistening is this mind-numbing arsenal of weaponry.

Not being much of a weapons expert, Eric hasn't much of an idea what it is he is looking at as far as firearms. He's fairly certain that there are a couple AK's. He only knows what those are because he'd seen a few rap videos back in the 90's. There are thirteen guns in all. Or rifles; what's the difference? The only people who corrected you when you used one term over the other were rednecks who needed to feel like they had one bit of knowledge that you didn't. Along with the firearms, there are boxes upon boxes of ammo, tear gas, grenades, and holy shit, is that a rocket launcher? Carlton opens the back door of the laundromat and starts piling weapons in the back seat of the Elephant. Ray and Nick get out to help.

The electronic chime of the front door ding-dongs. Eric hears someone say, "Hey, do y'all do dry-cleaning?"

"Shit," Carlton whispers. "You didn't lock the front door behind you?"

"You didn't ask me to," Eric whispers back.

"Did I have to? Come on, man. Common sense."

Eric looks over at the dude standing in the doorway with nothing but some old t shirts. Clearly he was one who was accustomed to overpaying for laundry services.

"What do we do?" he whispers.

"Keep loading. I'll get rid of him," Carlton says. He puts a handgun in the back of his waistband.

"You're not going to use that, are you?" Eric asks.

DAVE!

"Only if I have to. Keep moving."

Eric takes one more trip to the car quietly, as he listens intently to the conversation that Carlton is having with the customer.

"Of course, sir. We do dry cleaning. No laundromat worth their weight doesn't. Although, might I say, those ratty t-shirts don't need it. You can put those in the normal wash."

"They're the best clothes I have," the man says.

"Sorry to hear that."

BANG!

"NO!" Eric screams, and races over to Carlton. The man is lying on the floor, half his face missing. The floor, walls, and Carlton are covered in blood, brain, and bone.

"What the fuck, Carlton!? I thought you said you were only going to use the gun if you had to."

"Yeah, well, I had to." He locks the front door. "See? Had you just done that, just turned this little latch here, this man would still be alive, perhaps trying to find another place to do his dry cleaning. This is on you."

"On me? Are you fucking crazy?"

Carlton grabs Eric by the throat. Stars twinkle in front of Eric's field of vision.

"Don't you ever call me crazy. You hear me? Never!"

Again with the choking? Eric squeaks.

"Oh. Sorry." Carlton lets go.

"Not sure why you had to kill him," Eric mumbles

"This again?" Carlton asks, shaking his head.

"What do you mean, this again? Why did you have to kill him?"

"He saw our arsenal. We can't take any chances now." Carlton spins Eric around so he's looking him dead in the eyes. "I suggest you forget about this." He grabs the last of the weapons and shoves them in the back of the Elephant. "Come on. We're wasting time."

CHAPTER NINETEEN

Night fell slowly at the county jail. What I mean to say is, it fell at the same rate it did every night, rather, it was Starlet's perception of the rate at which the night fell that was slow. Am I over-explaining? I think I'm over-explaining.

Starlet spends the majority of her evening wadding up little pieces of toilet paper and throwing them at Chuck's head as he sleeps. She wasn't sure if aliens slept, but apparently they sleep pretty soundly. He doesn't awaken once during the barrage. Maybe all creatures in the universe need sleep. It may make an interesting study, someday. But right now, she's trying to concentrate on something other than the sleep habits of aliens. Like how to get out of here.

Deputy Chuck has been sitting at the desk overlooking Starlet's cell, leafing through an old pornographic magazine. He looks at it like a child at an art museum; like he's intrigued, but he has no clue what any of it means. He's showing her different photos, asking about different ones.

"What is she doing to him?" he asks.

"That's called fellatio. Or a blow job."

"And this is good?"

"Yeah. It's good. Men seem to like it anyway. I never cared for it when I had a dick, but then again, I wasn't supposed to have a dick in the first place."

"Wow, the mouth is used for so many things. Eating, talking, breathing, and that. How efficient."

"I guess."

"What about these people? What are they doing?"

"That's just plain sex. I think she's supposed to be his stepmother or something. I don't usually pay attention to the back story."

"Humans have sex with their mothers?"

"They're not supposed to. This is all fake, anyway. These people are just models. They probably don't even know each other."

"Ah. And what are they doing here?"

"That's sex again. Her legs are over his shoulders. Wait a minute. You don't know what sex is, do you?"

"It's something humans do for procreation and pleasure."

"Yeah, but you don't know the mechanics of it at all? What were you going to do to me on the side of the road?"

"I don't know. Perhaps wiggle it from side to side and let you look at it as it wiggled from side to side."

In a way, she feels bad for him. He wasn't going to violate her after all. Poor bastard didn't know how even if he wanted to. But then she remembers that he wasn't exactly pleasant to her last night.

"All right," she says. "If you don't mind, I'm going back to my bunk to mind my own business."

"Suit yourself," Chuck says.

She sits on her bed for a few minutes and is startled by a scratching at the door. It opens, and deputy Flarp comes in, led by a very familiar dog.

"Got some company for you," Flarp says to Starlet.

"Bella!" she shouts, jumping from her bed.

DAVE!

Bella rushes to the cell and licks Starlet's face through the bars, coating it in stinky doggy slobber; her tail wagging a hundred miles a minute.

"Oh, I missed you so much," she says. "How did you find her?"

"She didn't run off too far. It was pretty easy, actually."

"Did you find my penis?" Chuck asks.

"I did not."

"Dammit."

"Thank you for bringing her back," Starlet says. "But why?"

"I kinda like her. We all have quite a soft spot for most of the creatures that live on this planet. Dogs are right up there at the top of the list. Far better than any humans."

"Amen to that," Starlet says. "What a good girl." She scratches Bella's neck.

"Yeah, well don't get too comfortable with her. She's my dog now." His look turns sly. "You won't need her where you're going anyway."

Way to cast a shadow over the moment, asshole, she thinks but doesn't say.

"And where would that be?" Why did I ask that question?

"Well, once you get convicted of the murders you committed, you can't stay here. I know you like it here a lot, and we enjoy having you. But I think you'll be more suited for prison. Maybe even Death Row! Wouldn't that be cool?"

"No."

"Ah, well, to each his own, I guess."

She hears the familiar tone of her phone ringing from the desk drawer.

"For the love of fuck," Flarp says. "What is that infernal ring tone?"

"'Roofie Party' by the Cosby Kids. Everyone knows that," Chuck says.

192

"Well, I don't know it, and it's horrible. Whatever happened to good music, like 'Old Father Hubbard' by Tom Screws?"

"Man, that song is old news," says Chuck.

Flarp retrieves the phone from the drawer. "Looks like it's your boyfriend again."

"Can you please answer it and let him know I'm okay?" Starlet asks.

"You're not exactly in the position to be asking any favors." Flarp opens the back of the phone and removes the battery. "There, now we will never again have to listen to that shitty…" His words stop, and his head hits the desk. The chair rolls out from under him and he collapses to the floor.

"Flarp?" Chuck calls, and rushes over to him. He smacks him repeatedly on the cheek. "Flarp, wake up!"

He glares at Starlet. "What did you do??"

"What did I do?" Starlet asks.

"Yeah! What did you do?" He picks up the phone. "Is this some sick murder weapon you fashioned to look like an ordinary phone?"

"Um, no. It's just a phone."

"Yeah? Really? Then what is this?" he asks, and picks the battery up off the floor. "ZEEEEP!" he yells, and drops like a cold sack of cucumbers.

What the hell? She asks herself, and then she remembers. The motor home. The ignition wires. Stone dropping like a cold sack of cucumbers. The battery. For the love of God, is that all it takes to kill these bastards? A little bit of electricity? Very briefly, she wonders why, with so much static electricity everywhere, that they don't just drop dead while randomly walking across a carpet? Static carries up to 25,000 volts, yet here they are, seemingly immune to it. Exposition: They wear rubber shoes.

Bella pads her little way over to the two bodies, whines, squats, and pees on Flarp.

DAVE!

"Good girl," Starlet says.

Okay. Now, to find her way out of here. The keys are right there, in the desk drawer. If her arm were only ten feet longer, she would be able to reach them. She'll have to use Bella as her gopher.

"Bella, get the keys."

She looks at Starlet and tilts her cute little head, but does nothing productive.

"Bella. Keys."

Head tilt.

"Bella? Keysies. Keys, Bella. Keees."

Aha! Bella thinks. She stands up on her hind legs and puts her head in the drawer.

"Good girl, Bella. Good girl."

Bella gallops over to Starlet's cell, and puts down her prize. Ta-da! She thinks.

Starlet looks down. A block of cheddar sits on the floor by her cell.

"I said his keys, not his cheese."

For a few minutes they play this game. Bella brings forth a can of peas, a jar of bees, a pair of skis, a fresh breeze, a trapeze, a wage freeze, everything but the keys.

"Did someone get you a rhyming dictionary for your birthday? Just bring the keys. Please!"

Bella finally realizes that this is not a game, and that the situation is a dire one. Probably. At last, she brings the keys.

"Thank you. Good girl."

She finds the right key and lets herself out of her cage.

On the floor, the bodies of both Flarp and Chuck seem to be breathing. She doesn't know if they are still alive or if this is just reflex action, but she suspects it's the former. She picks up her phone and the battery. There are a lot of numbers and letters stamped on the back of the battery, but there's only one she's interested in. So, 12 volts kills them, and 3.7 volts knocks them out. If she ever gets out of this mess alive, she's going to write a book. How to Kill an Alien. It will be a relatively short book, perhaps only a page. But that one page will be very helpful, and just might help save the planet. She looks at the battery again. 3.7V D.C.

D.C.! She doesn't remember batteries ever having D.C. printed on them. People should just know that batteries are direct current, and printing D.C. on them is superfluous. Hence, she takes this as a sign. She knows where she has to be. Eric and her father are both heading to Washington as she stands here thinking about batteries. She knows how to fight these bastards. She needs to tell them! She puts the battery back in the phone and tries turning it on. Nothing happens. The shock it gave the deputies must have killed the battery, somehow. Her luck fucking sucks.

She needs to get to the capitol, and fast. And theres only one way to do it without getting caught. She strips Chuck of his uniform, and dresses herself in it. Flarp's looks like it will fit better, but it is covered in dog piss. She takes the key to his cruiser out of his pocket, says, "Come on, Bella," gets herself in the car, the dog in the backseat, and guns it. She calculates quickly in her head. It's two in the afternoon. All goes well, she can probably be in D.C. by 2 A.M. Whether or not she can find Eric or her father is another question entirely.

CHAPTER TWENTY

They drive off the main road down some beautifully paved side road that somehow reminds Eric of the entrance to Disney World (which has been closed for quite some time now). He almost expects there to be a booth at the end directing people where to park. But there is just a wrought-iron gate with a keypad and a video surveillance camera.

Carlton gets out of the vehicle and rings the buzzer.

"Who is it?" a voice comes from the speaker.

"It's Carlton et al," Eric hears Carlton say through the open window of the Elephant.

"What's the password?" the voice calls.

"PASSWORD," Carlton says, which everyone knows is the dumbest password ever.

The gate opens, and Carlton gets back in the car.

"The password is seriously password?" Eric asks. "That's the dumbest password ever. Everyone knows that."

"Yes, but it's ALL CAPS," Carlton clarifies.

"Hahaha."

"There's a video camera right there. Dave can see it's me. He doesn't even need a password."

"Right. In the age where aliens are wearing human skin. There couldn't possibly be someone who looks like you pretending to be you."

"Who'd want to pretend to be me?" Carlton asks.

"Well, normally no one. But now? I don't know. Hmm. How about someone who wants to get in the gate?"

"Dave knows what he's doing."

"Yeah, let's hope so."

They drive for about a mile down the driveway until they come to a rather large parking lot. It's almost filled to capacity. Carlton parks the car, and they walk to the end of the lot.

"Where's Dave's house?" Eric asks.

"It's yonder. We need to take the tram."

"This is like Disney World," Eric says.

"Wha?"

"Nothing."

The tram shows up with a few passengers already on, and all four hop on board.

When they're comfortably seated, Eric asks, "Why are we going through all the trouble of going to Dave's house? Aren't we wasting time?"

"We need to go over the plan."

"What plan? Don't you already know the plan?"

"Heh. Hardly. I knew the plan to get us to this point. The rest needed to remain secret until now. This is it. This is the big meeting I've been talking about."

DAVE!

"You never talked about any big meeting."

"I didn't?"

"Nope."

"Huh."

"I thought we were just going to grab some guns and storm the White House."

"Really?" Carlton looks at Eric like he's an even bigger Idiot than the two in the seat behind them. "And you thought that was going to work? Storm the White House? Do you even think the president is in the White House right now, with the intel he has? He knows everything. That's why we have to meet Dave."

"Why are we bringing the Idiots?"

"Well, just like us, they too need to know their parts. Plus, I don't want anyone notifying the Humane Society that we've left a couple Idiots in a hot car. They may come and take them away."

The tram pulls up to the front of the house, which roughly resembles Snow White's castle. Something tells Eric that Dave's been to Disney World.

Nick, spotting a couple friends, sprints out of the tram. It's Mary and Drew. And it seems they've brought a live chicken. And they're watching it scuttle to and fro. To be fair, Eric doesn't know if they've actually brought the chicken, but he wouldn't put it past any friend of Nick's.

Carlton turns to Eric. "Good people," he says.

"But you can't stand them."

"Right."

A stranger appears at the top of the extravagant stairs that lead to the front door. "The time has come!" he dramatically announces. "The hour is upon us!"

"We got that from when you said the time has come," Eric whispers to Carlton, who nudges him with his elbow.

198

"Everyone inside; Dave awaits!" the stranger shouts.

The inside of the castle is even more magnificent than Eric imagined it would be. Magnificent marble floors, gigantic Greek columns leading up to lavishly lofty ceilings. Divine draperies festooned the place, giving it a festooned look. In the middle of the front room, as expected, was a grand staircase leading up to a landing, the view of which is obscured by a giant theater curtain.

Waiters are waltzing through the congregation, passing out trays of hors-d'oeuvres. Eric never had developed a taste for horse eggs, so he passes. He's too nervous to eat, anyway. The crowd is so much bigger than he expected. Everyone, Idiots and Invaders alike, mingling and chit-chatting away.

"Silence!" a voice comes from beyond the curtain, and the chatter ends abruptly. Something tells Eric that Dave is a big Wizard of Oz fan.

"Thank you all for coming tonight. As you all know by now, my name is Dave. You'll have to excuse the dramatic curtain. Before I come out to meet all of you, I need to tell you, if there is anyone here who wants out of the mission, now is the time to speak up. No need to be embarrassed. You will be gently escorted out to the gate by my rather large guards and given a complimentary bag of chocolate chip cookies."

Everyone laughed. They knew that by complimentary bag of chocolate chip cookies, he meant painful death. As expected, no one raises a hand.

"All righty then. Let's get started. Marv?"

The stranger that had appeared before now appears at the top of the stairs. Obviously Marv. He slowly, suspensefully draws the curtain aside. "Introducing   DAVE!" he shouts

The drawn-back curtain reveals not the gorgeous man that Eric remembers, but instead a small desk, on which sits a rather unimpressive laptop. Behind the desk is a large movie screen, hooked up to the computer so that everyone can see. A picture appears on the screen. It's the Dave that Eric remembers. So handsome.

DAVE!

Murmurs of Huh? and Wha? and I don't get it bubble up from the crowd.

"Hello everyone. I'm DAVE. Your friendly Digital Artificial Virtual Executive."

Ray turns to Carlton. "Don't the first few words mean pretty much the same thing? Sometimes they try too hard on making acronyms work."

"A fucking computer? Seriously?" Carlton says to Eric, ignoring Ray. "This is going to be a long day."

CHAPTER TWENTY-ONE

Starlet can't believe how fast these cop cars can go. She's not sure about the politics of it all, but it always seemed like the police force in the cities got the fanciest cars, while the ones in the little Podunk towns, and the sheriff's departments of the counties no one outside of their own state has heard of, were always more than a few years behind in the modernity of their vehicles. This car is no exception; however, even being light years behind a police car in, say, New York, it's still far beyond anything she'd ever ridden in, let alone driven. Since the ability to afford a nice car is a rarity these days, most car manufacturers don't sink much money into civilian vehicles. A lot of them still look slick, such as your Ford Libidos and your Honda Elephants and your Hyundai Sinatras, but once their warranties run out thirty days later, they tend to start disintegrating. To keep them affordable, they needed to be produced with the cheapest materials possible. The cheapest materials, however, were used to assemble the wall, so cars were always made with whatever was cheaper than that.

Cop cars are paid for with government money, so they tend to be pretty fucking fancy. At this moment, Starlet is approaching 418 kilometers per hour. That's 260 miles to you and me. She has never seen the turnpike so barren. Lately people have way more important things to do than travel, such as killing, or avoiding being killed. Every once in a while, when the turnpike approaches the ocean, she catches a glimpse of people at the wall. In some places there are nothing but corpses left for the seagulls. In other places, people are still hacking away at the barrier, oblivious to what's to come. In a way, she envies them. Not really, actually. I'm not sure why I said that. I think I just thought it sounded poetic. Her father told her to avoid I-95, but he probably didn't predict that she'd be driving a police vehicle. She feels fairly safe in her cruiser and her uniform; no one's going to bother her today.

"Let's see what this motherfucker's got for some tunes!" She shouts to no one, cursing gratuitously. She turns on the radio, and "Lying Bitch Babykiller" by Anthony Casey is playing. Fuck yeah. She turns it up. Way up. She sings along with the track.

"Lying bitch lying bitch

Don't kill my baby

Kill my baby tonight.

Lying bitch lying bitch

Don't kill my baby

Kill my baby toniiiiiiight!"

Fuck yeah. Abruptly, she is interrupted by a grumbling noise coming from somewhere inside the vehicle. She turns the radio off and notices it's her own stomach reminding her she hasn't eaten in quite some time, and she should probably pull off the pike and get something quick to eat.

She turns off onto the Exit Q ramp in Lowell, Massachusetts, and drives a few miles in a direction that takes her nowhere. Figuring nowhere generally leads to somewhere, she keeps going. The road goes through a fairly affluent (or affluent once upon a time) neighborhood, mostly abandoned, but still quite nice. Gradually, the houses become more and more run-down, until there is nothing but rubble and old lumber littering what once was probably lawns. Thunder clouds quickly roll in, and the world gets very very dark. Soon she can see nothing but the inside of the cruiser. This is most definitely the wrong way, she thinks, and hangs a quick U turn to head in the opposite direction. It seems, however, that the opposite direction is not leading her back to the sunlight. She turns on her headlights. At least, she thinks they're on. Light is only visible when there's something to shine on. The only thing saving her is the fact that she remembers the road being very straight. As long as she keeps the wheel straight, she should, theoretically, stay on it.

Just as she starts having flashbacks of driving off the road and hitting the rock with her very own vehicle on the way to the wall, a very well-lit 7-11 appears like an oasis. Bella and her tummy both remind her that 7-11's have food. She pulls into the parking lot and up to the pumps. She puts her credit card in and fills the tank, knowing damn well that they can trace it if they need to. Whoever they are.

She goes inside the store, and heads right to the hot dog turny-thing. She chooses the least-wrinkled looking sausage, cradles it gently in a steamed bun, puts a great glob of mustard on it, and takes a bite. Nutritionally, it's garbage, and taste-wise it's even worse. So delightful, though, for her empty stomach. It's probably no more than twelve hours old, so what damage could it possibly do to her? She'll probably find out in an hour or so.

A finger taps her on the shoulder from behind. She turns around to find a police officer standing there. "Starlet Richter?" he asks.

"Yes?" she says, without thinking of the consequences of that one word, as a very hefty flashlight clubs her over the head and sends her sprawling unconscious to the floor.

Lights out.

PART III:

ENDGAME

CHAPTER ONE

A fucking computer? Seriously?" Eric says to Carlton. "This is going to be a long day."

"I literally just said that," Carlton says back.

"I KNOW WHAT YOU'RE THINKING," Booms D.A.V.E., whose voice is now booming apparently. "A FUCKING COMPUTER."

Nods of agreement all around. A murmur from the crowd: "Oh well I always thought…Nothing could have prepared me for…Well I suppose I better be…Computers nowadays…I'm not really all that…Got any more of them stuffed mushrooms?"

"YES. I AM A COMPUTER. BUT DON'T LET THAT DISSUADE YOU. DON'T THINK FOR ONE SECOND THE MISSION HAS CHANGED. I AM A COMPUTER PROGRAM DESIGNED BY A COMMITTEE OF COMPUTER GEEKS AND FUTURE POLITICIANS FORMED WITH THE INTENT OF STARTING A NEW WORLD ORDER…"

"Why did you deceive us?" came a voice from the crowd.

Two of the guards raced to where the voice was coming from, and escorted the man out. "Let's go get some cookies," one of the guards says to him. He will probably never be seen again.

DAVE!

"PLEASE DON'T INTERRUPT. THERE WILL BE TIME FOR QUESTIONS ONCE I AM DONE SPEAKING. BUT TO ANSWER THAT GENTLEMAN'S QUESTION, THE DECEPTION, AS HE SO RUDELY CALLED IT, WAS NECESSARY TO BRING YOU ALL HERE. WOULD YOU WILLINGLY HAVE FOLLOWED A COMPUTER PROGRAM ALL THE WAY HERE?"

Murmurs from the crowd: "Well no, I don't think that…I probably would have…It was probably integral to…Yo, stuffed mushrooms over here!"

"AND LIKEWISE, WOULD YOU HAVE COME ALL THIS WAY FOR SOME COMMITTEE? NO, YOU WOULD NOT HAVE. FOR GOOD OR BAD, PEOPLE HAVE EVOLVED TO FOLLOW ONE LEADER. THIS IS WHY GREEK MYTHOLOGY FAILED AND CHRISTIANITY GAINED POPULARITY. THIS IS WHY WE NEED A PRESIDENT, EVEN THOUGH WE KNOW FOR A FACT THAT HE IS THE LEAST POWERFUL PERSON IN GOVERNMENT. WELL, UP TILL THIS POINT ANYWAY. YOU NEEDED A LEADER. NOT MANY VOICES, BUT ONE VOICE. ONE WITH SO MUCH CHARISMA YOU COULDN'T HELP BUT FOLLOW. SO WE INVENTED ONE. AND HERE I AM."

Finally, it dawns on Carlton exactly how Dave was able to Skype with everyone at the same time, yet make each person feel like he was talking to them one on one. A human couldn't do that; a computer program, on the other hand…

"SO, NOW THAT YOU KNOW WHO I AM, TELL ME A LITTLE BIT ABOUT YOURSELVES. HAHAHA. JUST KIDDING. WE ALREADY KNOW EVERYTHING WE NEED TO KNOW ABOUT ALL OF YOU, AND DON'T CARE TO KNOW ANY MORE. ARE THERE ANY QUESTIONS BEFORE I CONTINUE?"

"NO ONE? COME ON, I PROMISE I WON'T BITE."

Nobody spoke up, for fear of being invited out by the guards for cookies.

"ALL RIGHT THEN. LET ME TELL YOU WHAT WE KNOW SO FAR. IN CASE YOU DIDN'T GET THE MEMO, WE HAVE BEEN INVADED BY AN ALIEN RACE. WE BELIEVE IT HAPPENED

SOMETIME IN 2016, JUST ABOUT THE TIME DONALD TRUMP WAS WINNING THE ELECTION. THEY DID IT WITH NO POMP AND CIRCUMSTANCE. THEY DID IT VERY QUIETLY. SO QUIETLY, IN FACT, THAT WE STILL DON'T KNOW HOW MANY OF THEM THERE ARE. WE KNOW THAT THEIR REACH IS FAR OUT OF D.C. THEY HAVE TAKEN OVER AN UNKNOWN PERCENTAGE OF THE HUMAN POPULATION. THEY INVADE THEIR HOSTS LIKE A PARASITE. WE'RE NOT SURE HOW THEY PICK WHO THEY PICK TO TAKE OVER, OR EVEN HOW THEY ENTER THE HUMAN HOST. WE DON'T KNOW THEIR MOTIVES OR METHODOLOGIES. WE DON'T KNOW WHAT THEY WANT FROM US."

"What do you know?" a voice from the crowd speaks out of turn.

"GUARDS?" Dave calls, but he doesn't really need to. They already have the situation taken care of.

"AGAIN, PLEASE DO NOT INTERRUPT. SAVE YOUR QUESTIONS FOR WHEN I ASK FOR THEM. AND I WAS GETTING TO THAT. WHAT WE DO KNOW IS THAT THEY ARE VERY DANGEROUS. WE KNOW THAT ONCE THEY INVADE A HOST, THE CONNECTIVE TISSUE WEAKENS AND THEY HAVE ISSUES KEEPING THEIR SKIN ON. ALTHOUGH, THAT FACT IS PROBABLY JUST ACADEMIC. WE CAN SPECULATE THAT THEY CHOSE THIS PLANET, AND MORE SPECIFICALLY THIS COUNTRY, BECAUSE THEY THOUGHT WE WOULD BE EASY PREY. WE ARE PROBABLY ONE OF THE DUMBEST RACES IN THE GALAXY, AND PERHAPS THE ENTIRE UNIVERSE. WE THINK IT WAS THE ELECTION OF DONALD TRUMP THAT TURNED THAT ASSUMPTION INTO PROOF. WE HAD BECOME A JOKE. PERHAPS THE BIGGEST JOKE IN EXISTENCE.

"AS FOR THE PLAN. OUR SOLE MISSION IS TO FIND AND KILL MEL GIBSON. OR RATHER, THE ALIEN PARASITE THAT HAS TAKEN OVER MEL GIBSON. THE REAL MEL GIBSON IS MOST LIKELY LONG GONE. WE ARE FAIRLY SURE THIS ALIEN IS THE ACTUAL LEADER AND NOT JUST A FIGUREHEAD. OUR HOPE IS

THAT IF WE KILL THE HEAD, THE REST OF THEIR UNWELCOME POPULATION WILL DIE. OR AT LEAST HAVE NO PURPOSE, AND THEREFORE BE INEFFECTIVE. OF COURSE, THIS IS JUST A GUESS, AND WE HAVE NO REAL EVIDENCE TO GO ON. WE HAVE COME TO THIS CONCLUSION BY COMPARING THEM TO BEES, OR ANTS. WE'RE NOT EXACTLY SURE WHETHER THIS IS A FAIR COMPARISON OR NOT, BUT THERE YOU HAVE IT.

"NOW, SOME OF YOU MAY HAVE NOTICED THAT I SAID FIND MEL GIBSON. WE KNOW FOR A FACT THAT HE HAS BEEN MOVED FROM THE WHITE HOUSE, AS THEY HAVE GOTTEN WIND OF OUR LITTLE OPERATION. HOWEVER, WE'RE NOT SURE WHERE HE IS, EXACTLY. WE HAVE QUITE A CREW HERE, AND WE'RE FAIRLY CONFIDENT THAT WITH A LITTLE STRATEGY AND INTEL, AND A WHOLE LOT OF LUCK, WE WILL FIND HIM. AFTER THAT, IT'S JUST A MATTER OF KILLING HIM, WHICH WILL PROBABLY BE EASY ONCE WE FIND HIM. IF WE FIND HIM. NOW, ARE THERE ANY QUESTIONS?"

Just then, Starlet's father Jake pipes up. "So, we followed you all the way here. You said come, and here we are. We assumed that you knew exactly what you were doing. Yet you really don't know much, do you?"

"AH, SO YOU WERE ASSUMING? AND NOW YOU CRITICIZE US FOR ASSUMING. DO YOU SEE THE IRONY?"

Jake isn't sure if he sees the irony. In fact, ever since Alanis Morissette was criticized for her song back in 1995, he always second-guessed himself every time he wanted to use that word.

"SO THE MISSION ISN'T AS EASY AS WE WERE MAKING IT OUT TO BE. WE THOUGHT IT WOULD BE EASIER THAN THIS. WE DIDN'T THINK THE GOVERNMENT WOULD GET WIND OF WHAT WE WERE DOING. DESPITE ALL PRECAUTIONS, HOWEVER, THEY DID. WE DIDN'T THINK WE'D HAVE TO HUNT DOWN THE PRESIDENT. YET, HERE WE ARE. WE WILL SUCCEED. WE WILL COMPLETE OUR OPERATIVE...PROBABLY...MAYBE...WE THINK SO."

There are a few more questions, most of which have no concrete answers, the rest of which were about the hors d'oeuvres. Nothing really helpful.

"NOW, BEFORE WE BEGIN GETTING DOWN TO THE NITTY GRITTY, ARE THERE ANY OF YOU WHO WISH TO LEAVE? WE PROMISE WE WON'T KILL YOU."

There are a few dumb shits who raise their hands up.

Dumb, dumb shits.

CHAPTER TWO

Starlet is deep in a dream. It's a beautiful dream. The wall is gone, and people are free to roam wherever they want to. She and Eric are married and are sitting on a beach in Barbados. The sky is the deepest shade of blue, matching the hue of the ocean perfectly. A gentle, refreshing breeze blows past her, keeping her from overheating. She's reading a new Stephen King book. He came out of retirement to write one more Dark Tower book, and it is a masterpiece. A bird swooped down to catch a fish. Waiters come by to bring her an endless supply of hot milk. It is a lovely place, and reminds her of her trips to Hawaii. The gentle breeze grows stronger. On the horizon, dark clouds come rushing in.

"Looks like we gotta pack it in," she says to Eric. She gets no response.

"Let's go get something to eat," she says to Eric. Still no response.

"Eric?" she asks.

Eric turns to her with a wide grin. The flesh on his face starts to ripple and fold. It falls into his lap.

"Eric? What's happening?"

His grin widens even more. He has that look like he knows something she doesn't. "A storm's a-brewin'" he says. His mouth opens and another mouth with jagged teeth juts from the opening. She gets up to run but is stuck in her chair. Everyone on the beach is morphing into something horrible. They are all closing in on her. The sky turns completely black.

She wakes up from her dream

"Did you hear me, bitch? A storm's a-brewin'"

A fist flies into her face, and knocks her head to the side.

The light is dim here. Where is she? Where are her arms? Holy shit, did someone take her arms?

A figure stands in front of her, presumably the one that punched her. This figure is not human at all, nor is it even pretending to be. The light is dim in this room, being only lit by a few torches on the wall, so she can't make out every feature on the face. She's glad that's the case, because what she can see is disturbing. The face is elongated, which is about the only thing that looks like the textbook gray man most people associate with aliens. It has no nose to speak of, and it looks like it has no teeth inside its beaklike mouth. The only teeth she sees are the ones jutting out of its eye sockets. The skin it's covered in, which is quite possibly not skin at all, is shiny in the flickering light, almost gooey.

"Where are my arms?" she asks, panicked.

"Right there on the ends of your shoulders, like always." The figure says.

She sits chained to a concrete wall, shackles around her wrists. Her arms look fake, as she has no feeling left in them. She must have been chained here for quite some time. It's hard to tell in the dim light thrown off by the torches, but she thinks the shackles are leather. If she could feel her wrists, she could probably tell what they're made out of.

"Whew. I thought you took them," she says.

"What would I want with your arms?"

"I don't know. What would you want with me?"

"You've been a bad girl, dear Starlet. You should have just stayed put in Aroostook County. But you had to escape, didn't you? You had to run away."

211

"Of course I had to run away. Isn't that what people do in jail, if given the opportunity?"

"You harmed two officers. Myself and deputy Flarp."

"Chuck?" she asks.

The creature nods.

"I didn't do anything to you. You're the one that grabbed the phone battery. So did he. How is old Flarp, anyway?"

The alien looks despondent, if that were at all possible. "He didn't make it."

"Oh. Sorry to hear that. I know he meant a lot to you."

"Flarp? He was an asshole. I couldn't fucking stand him. I'll never know why they paired me with him in the first place. Oh yeah, he thought he was Mister Big Shot, all high and mighty, then my wife up and leaves me for him, and he has the nerve to act like a father to my kids? That fucking pile of...Well, anyway. Now you have assaulting an officer of the law added to your list of charges, as well as one more murder. Oh, and let's not forget, theft of a police vehicle. You just don't know when to quit, do you?"

She looks around the room. The torches, the concrete wall, the shackles, the dirt floor, all remind her of those comic strips where a scraggly starving prisoner is hanging there, perhaps with a couple skeletons on either side, and there is a funny caption underneath. If only this were a comic strip. A frozen moment in time where she could say something funny, and then someone could turn the page and see a Wal-Mart BOGO ad or something. She tries to think of something funny to say.

"Did I ever tell you about the one..." she starts, but can't come up with any more words.

"Bahahahaha!" the alien laughs. "That's a good one." Is she really that funny, or do aliens not understand how jokes are supposed to work? She's not sure. She's a horrible mixture of lightheaded, tired, achy, hungry, and thirsty, and she's not sure if she could rank any of these feelings by urgency.

"You don't look so well. You hungry or something?" the Alien Who Once Was Chuck asks. He retrieves an object from a table in the corner of the room.

"Yeah, I could use a bite of…WHAT'S THAT???"

In his hand is a dried-up, shriveled tubular object. It emits a weak, squeaky cough from one of its ends.

"Oh my God, did you find your penis? That…is…fucking…gross; no offense. No thanks. Not that hungry."

"No, you silly twat. I didn't find my penis. This is the hot dog you were about to eat from the 7-11 when I clobbered you on the head. I saved it for you."

"Oh." For a second, she debates whether or not eating the hot dog was such a good idea. But only for a second. She is soooo hungry,

The Alien Who Once Was Chuck puts the frank up to her mouth. She takes a bite. It is much, much worse than she thought it would be. Her teeth pierce the skin and the meat crunches in her mouth like dried twigs, breaks apart on her molars as flakes, and disintegrates as a fine powder. It tastes vaguely of meat from another century. The mustard on it has dried, and does nothing to add to the taste, but does everything to add to the flakiness. She finishes it nonetheless.

"Thirsty?" he asks.

"Yeah. What you got for me? A cup of piss?"

The Alien Who Once Was Chuck looks guilty, if that's at all possible. "Thought about it; I did. But no, I got you a Slurpee."

A Slurpee? She tries her best to hide her enthusiasm. "What kind?" she asks.

"Watermelon. Hope that's okay."

Watermelon? Her favorite.

"It'll do. I would love a sip."

DAVE!

The Alien Who Once Was Chuck holds the cup to her lips. All the icy goodness has melted, and it's piss warm. She spits it out. There is nothing worse than a melted Slurpee. Nothing.

Unfortunately, the watermelon spit lands on the Alien Who Once Was Chuck.

"You're gonna regret that," he says.

"I already do."

The Alien Who Once Was Chuck crouches down, raising a hand to her face. The nails grow long and clawlike and he rakes one slowly down her face, cutting deep. It possibly hurts pretty bad, but Starlet is really too exhausted to tell just how badly it should hurt. I know one thing, she thinks as she feels a warm river dripping off her chin and soaking into the dirt floor, if I make it out of here alive, that's gonna leave a pretty nasty scar.

"You've seen what's behind my face. Now let's see what's behind yours." The alien grabs the flap of skin dangling from her cheek and pulls sideways. The skin tears easily off her face, with a little help from the alien's razor-sharp claw digging underneath with all the skill of a butcher. The squelching sound it makes as it comes off the flesh makes her vomit, which gets caught in her dangling lip. The bloody mix of vomit and saliva falls to the floor, and The Alien Who Once Was Chuck steps out of the way to avoid it.

"That was a close one," he says. "You're really lucky, bitch."

She's not sure how lucky she is, with her face hanging half off, but whatever.

"Now I see what's beneath. You stupid whore." Enough with the name calling, really.

"Why don't you look and see for yourself?" The Alien Who Once Was Chuck says, as if answering some question she didn't ask. He holds a mirror up to her face. She tries shutting her eyes, but only one of them will shut. The lids of the other one came off with the skin on her face. She can't help but look. Before her is a sight more grotesque than any horror movie. From

214

forehead to chin, half of the skin on her face has been peeled back, revealing a layer of tissue and cartilage.

Well, this day is really starting to suck, Starlet thinks.

CHAPTER THREE

The plan seems simple enough. Form a tight perimeter around Washington, moving in smaller and smaller circles, until they find Uncle Mel.

"How do we know he's still in Washington?" someone asks.

"WELL, TO USE THE BEE ANALOGY AGAIN, SINCE WE THINK MEL IS THE QUEEN BEE, WASHINGTON IS THE HIVE. AND DOES A QUEEN BEE EVER LEAVE HER HIVE?"

Looks of confusion all around.

"YEAH, WE DON'T REALLY KNOW EITHER. I GUESS WE SHOULD HAVE STUDIED UP MORE ON BEES.

"WE HAVE ASSIGNED EACH GROUP A ROUTE TO TAKE, AS WELL AS EACH LOCATION WE WOULD LIKE YOU TO SEARCH. WE WILL HAND THESE OUT BEFORE YOU LEAVE."

"There are a lot of buildings in D.C.," a brave woman in the crowd says, and everyone cringes, waiting for the guards to take her away. But instead, the voice is answered.

"YES, THERE ARE A LOT OF BUILDINGS, BUT YOU'RE NOT GOING TO BE CHECKING ALL OF THEM. WE HAVE PUT A LOT OF THOUGHT INTO WHERE THE LEAD ALIEN COULD BE HIDING, AND NARROWED IT DOWN CONSIDERABLY. NOW, MARV IS GOING TO PASS OUT SOME EQUIPMENT THAT SHOULD

HELP YOU IN YOUR SEARCH. YOU WILL BE USING THESE TO COMMUNICATE."

At first glance, these little pieces of equipment look an awful lot like cell phones. At second glance, these are, in fact, cell phones.

"WHAT YOU HOLD IN YOUR HANDS ARE SPECIALLY CREATED ECD'S, OR ELECTRONIC COMMUNICATIONS DEVICES."

"You mean cell phones?" a voice from the crowd chirps, then vanishes.

"THESE ARE NOT 'CELL PHONES', AS YOU CALL THEM. THESE ARE ECD'S, AND THEY HAVE TAKEN YEARS FOR OUR TEAM TO PERFECT. THESE AREN'T MEANT FOR CALLING OR TEXTING, AS CELL PHONES ARE. THE SOLE PURPOSE OF THESE ECD'S IS FOR SKYPING WITH ME AND WITH EACH OTHER. ALTHOUGH, THEY CAN ALSO BE USED TO CALL OR TEXT PEOPLE, OR TO LOOK UP RECIPES ONLINE."

"So they're cell phones," another voice said. Eric has a feeling these folks who speak out of turn are Distractors. At the very least, they are all Idiots. He looks to Ray and Nick, and puts a finger over his lips. Even though he can't stand them sometimes, it would be a shame to see them executed.

As though reading his mind, Ray thrusts his hand up in the air, no doubt to ask a stupid question.

"Put your hand down, dummy," Eric whispers.

"But it's important," Ray whispers back.

"YES," Dave says, "THE IDIOT WITH HIS HAND UP. YOU HAVE A QUESTION?"

"Yeah, well, um… I was wondering… I mean we were wondering, um…"

"SPEAK!" Dave commands.

"What about the Distractors? What's our role in all of this?"

DAVE!

A very intelligent question, Eric thinks.

"WELL, SINCE WE NO LONGER NEED DISTRACTIONS, YOU'LL BE JOINING IN WITH THE INVADERS' SEARCH PARTY. LORD KNOWS WE NEED AS MANY EYES AS WE CAN GET."

"But that's dangerous!" someone shouts.

"Yeah, we didn't sign up for this!"

"Phooey!"

"PHOOEY? REALLY? DO YOU THINK I SIGNED UP TO BE A COMPUTER? NO, I DID NOT. YET HERE I AM. I FEEL LIKE MAX HEADROOM, FOR GODSAKE."

No one in the room got the analogy, as most of them weren't born prior to 2000.

"YOUR OTHER OPTION IS TO LEAVE. AND IF I WERE YOU, I WOULDN'T PICK THAT OPTION. IT'S NOT A VERY GOOD ONE. YOUR COUNTRY NEEDS YOU. YOU SIGNED UP FOR THIS BECAUSE YOU WANTED TO HELP, AND TO MAKE THIS WORLD A BETTER PLACE, AM I WRONG IN SAYING THAT?"

Silence.

"WELL???"

Silence.

"I'M GOING TO GO AHEAD AND TAKE THAT AS A MAYBE. NOW IF YOU'LL JUST DO WHAT'S ASKED OF YOU, YOU'LL GO DOWN IN HISTORY BOOKS AS BEING AS BRAVE AS THE REST OF THE INVADERS. NO ONE WILL EVER KNOW THAT THERE WAS A PLAN TO KEEP YOU IDIOTS IN THE DARK. YOU'LL BE WRITTEN UP AS HEROES."

"Really?" No less than a dozen of them asked.

"I THINK SO. I DON'T KNOW. WHO WRITES THOSE THINGS, ANYWAY? I'LL TRY AND PUT IN A GOOD WORD. NOW LET'S GET CRACKING."

CHAPTER FOUR

Starlet hears whining coming from down the hall. Bella! How could she have forgotten about her? Suddenly remembering that her face is hanging half off, she decides to cut herself a little slack about not remembering the dog.

"You brought her?" she asks Chuck.

He opens a door out of her range of sight and Bella comes rushing in. When she catches sight of Starlet, she pauses, unsure whether or not she should approach. "I couldn't very well leave her where you left her. Do you know you abandoned her in one of the most dangerous parts of the great state of Massachusetts?"

"Abandoned? I was blindsided!"

"I was trying to save you from eating that old hot dog."

"The one you just fed to me?"

"That's the one. Do you know the cashier said it had been on the rack since he started working there in 2016? You just ate history!"

"Couldn't you have picked me up a can of Spaghettio's or something?"

"Actually I did, but the dog was hungry, so she ate it."

"Spaghettio's? She's going to have diarrhea."

"So? All of your Earth foods give me diarrhea. What is it with that stuff?"

"You, being from another planet and all, are not used to the chemical compositions of most of our foods. Your body was not made to digest what we have to offer, so it can't properly break it down like a human body can."

"Do you think I'm stupid? Do you, bitch?"

Suddenly something dawns on her. She has a plan, which may or may not work. Most likely it won't, but it's a plan. And as they say, a plan is a plan. Do they say that?

"Stupid? Well, yeah. Kinda, yeah."

The Alien Who Once Was Chuck jabs his claw into her gut. Not deep enough to do any real damage, but deep enough to draw yet more blood.

"I'll have you know, you dumb bitch, that we've been watching your planet now for several of your Earth centuries. We have watched stupidity blossom and grow with time. We are not the stupids, little girl. It is you. You who are the stupids."

"Oh yeah, then why didn't you frisk me before you brought me in here? Laziness? Or maybe it's because you're stupid?"

"Why should I have to frisk you? You're tied up. That was a stupid thought."

"You're stupid," Starlet responds.

"You're stupid," The alien retorts.

A silence passes, both contemplating the stupidity of the conversation.

"Well?" she asks.

"Well what?"

"Aren't you going to frisk me, stupid?"

"Is this a way to get me to have sex with you? Because frankly, I'm turned off at this point."

She sighs. "Never mind."

"All right, all right," the alien says. He pats down the front of her and feels the lump in her pocket.

"What do we have here?" he asks, and reaches in to grab the object that's in her front pocket. And collapses to the floor. Score one more for the ol' cell phone battery. It was a long shot, and she could have sworn there was no more juice left in it, but she was wrong. It must have been the phone itself that wasn't working.

Bella still hides in the corner, whimpering.

"Bella," Starlet tries to call to her, but her skinless lips that have crusted over stick together, so not only does it cause a gush of blood to spew forth from her mouth and a horrid pain, it also makes the dog's name sound more like Mella. It's fine, though. Bella seems to understand her anyway.

She walks over slowly to Starlet, still a little cautious.

"It's okay, sweetie. Here, girl. I need your help."

She pads her way over to the body of the alien, squats, and pisses. Her favorite trick, apparently.

"That's great, honey. But I need you over here. Come on, girl."

She goes over to Starlet and jumps on her. "Woah, girl. Be careful!"

Her tongue bobbling out of her slobbery mouth, she proceeds to lick Starlet's skinless face. Whether it's out of love for her or love for fresh meat, she's not sure. It feels somewhat soothing to her, and Bella seems to really be enjoying it. Even though she knows Bella is polluting her face with dog ass germs, she doesn't have the heart to tell her to stop. She gets a little too close to the dangling face flap that's hanging off the side of her head, and sinks her teeth into it a little, like nibbling on a corncob. It tickles a bit.

"Okay, Bella. That's not a toy. That's enough. Hoo-hoo-hee-hee. Stop it!"

"Bella? Bella. Listen to me, okay. You gotta help. Look up."

It dawns on her that dogs aren't so smart with the whole Hey, look up there thing. She tries a different approach.

222

"Bella, look what I got. Look what Starlet's got." She holds her hand like she has something in it. This works pretty well, but Bella is more interested in what she doesn't have in her hand than on chewing through the leather strap. She wiggles her arm a bit to cause some commotion, and finally Bella decides she finds the strap interesting after all, and starts chewing on it.

"Good girl. That's a good pup."

After about ten minutes of this bullshit, she finally chews her way through the strap. Once one arm is clear, she unclasps the other strap. She's free.

She takes a minute to look at her surroundings. An honest-to-God dungeon. She didn't think these existed outside of ancient Rome or modern day Middle East. Yet here's one right in the United States. Possibly Massachusetts. It seems pretty old, but is it? Or was this specifically built for occasions like this one? Are there more of these? It does seem pretty cool, though, with the torches on the walls and the whole bit. There's even an iron gate at the front.

Her flesh is starting to dry out and feel uncomfortable. The dog saliva probably didn't help things any.

It's time to stop being selfish, Starlet, she thinks to herself. Let's go save the world.

CHAPTER FIVE

So," Carlton says, "looks like we get to start out at an Irish pub. Lucky for us. I love Irish pubs. Hmm. Imeacht Gan Teacht Ort. What a pleasant-sounding name. I drank one time at a nice pub in Boston called Róisín Dubh. It means The Black Rose. I wonder if this is just has just as nice a meaning."

The cracked windows at the front of the pub are held together by sun-dried and flaking masking tape. The wind blowing down the street causes the glass pieces to rub against each other, making a horrible skreek like an ice pick on a chalkboard. Adding to this annoying noise was the squeaking sound of the old wooden sign hanging above the door, held on by just one eyelet in the corner, and swaying back and forth. The patrons are being thrown out at regular intervals by the bouncer, landing on various parts of their bodies and breaking some important bones in the process.

"I wouldn't call this nice or pleasant," Eric says.

"True, but it does seem authentic. Let's go see what all the fuss is about."

Eric doesn't remember hearing any fuss over this bar, but whatever; it's on their itinerary. He finds it hard to believe that this is one of Mel's hangouts.

"Let's keep the drinking to a minimum, please," Eric cautions Carlton.

"Don't think I know my limits, do you?"

"I don't think your limits know you," Eric answers.

They walk into the pub, the jukebox blaring loudly the new hit from the Pentagons called "That Plane Could Not Have Possibly Fit in that Hole, Dummies." At least, Eric thinks that's the title. Some Pogues or old Dropkick Murphys would fit better, but then again, he thought his shoes would have fit better by now, and look where that got him.

Just look!

All eyes turn toward the dummies as they enter.

"HEY!" Nick shouts. Oh, God. "Any of you unpolished turds know where I can find Mel Gibson?"

As Nick sits out on the street, his face abraded from the abrupt meeting it had with the sidewalk, he thinks perhaps he should have phrased his question a little better. Idiot. Maybe a softer approach is in order? He walks back into the bar, this time making a wide berth around the very large bouncer.

"Say there!" Nick starts.

"Shhh," Carlton warns. "No one here made you the spokesperson. Just chill."

He approaches the bar. The bartender has one eye on him and one on the shotgun he keeps behind the bar. The gun is way down at the other end of the bar, so for most folks it wouldn't be an easy task to watch both. However, the bartender has Marty Feldman eyes, which makes it impossible not to look in both directions at once.

Carlton has no idea about the shotgun behind the bar, so don't mention it to him.

The bartender taps on the bar with a shillelagh. "Arrggh, what can I fix ye?"

Apparently he doesn't know the difference between an Irish accent and a pirate's accent.

"Four pints of Guinness, my good man." He looks over at his compadres. "And whatever these Idiots want."

They place their orders, and the bartender retrieves four cans of Guinness. Cans? What kind of an Irish pub is this?

"I'll take drafts, please," Cartlton specifies.

"Aye, we only have 'em in cans."

"What's on tap?" he asks.

"We only have two. For domestic, we have Millerrrrr. And for imports we have Budweiserrrr, that fine Gerrrman beerr." "r."

"Right. Well, whatever. Cans will have to do."

"Aye, and I'll tell ye one thing. Don't act up here or we'll t'row ye out, and I'll never tell ye where to find ye olde Mel Gibson."

"Oh, and where is that?" he asks.

"He's over there," Eric says, and points to a dark corner at a man looking an awful lot like Mel Gibson, Ray seated next to him, jabbering away.

"Oh, shit," Carlton races over, pausing just long enough to get a grip on his four beers.

"…oh and I really like Tina Turner you should get her to do the music for the next movie is she dead? I think she may be dead (pant, pant, pant). Sorry for your loss." Friggin' Adderall.

"Ray, take a breath," Carlton says, as he puts his four beers down on an adjacent table. "I'm sure Uncle Mel has better things to do than listen to you talk about soundtracks. Hi," he says, and holds out his hand for Mel to shake. "I'm Carlton. You've already met Ray. Don't mind him. He's just a little high-strung, is all."

Mel stares at the outstretched hand like it is a three-week old baked potato that someone has left in the fridge by mistake. If only they remembered it was there, they could have had a delicious starch to go along with their baked seagull.

"They don't understand handshakes," Eric whispers to Carlton.

"??" Carlton looks at Eric.

"Don't ask about their alternative. It ain't pretty."

A look of impatience and perhaps a little incontinence crosses Mel's face.

Carlton puts his hand down. "This here is Eric, and this douchebag that almost got us thrown out is Nick. If Ray annoyed you, I would really not recommend chatting with Nick."

Nick puts his hand out for Mel to shake. We all know he's slow-witted, but this is really getting out of control.

"Mind if we sit with you?" Carlton asks. Mel just looks down at his whiskey sour and takes a sip. Carlton takes that as a yes, and sits down, his hand feeling in the back of his waistband for the Ruger he has stashed there. It had been there for so long, his back had gone numb to the sensation, but it's still there.

The rest of the crew take seats at the table as well. Carlton's really not sure what to do next; there was no plan, really. Maybe they should have thought it out a little better, but they were never sure where or when they would find Mel. This had been too easy. He could just shoot him right now; nothing's stopping him. But something tells him that he needs to be a little more slick. He's going to have to wing it.

He opens his mouth to speak, but he's out of words. "Help me out here," he whispers to Eric.

"Pleasure to meet you, Mr. Gibson. So yeah, Mad Max, right?"

The president cocks his head, like a dog who hears the word walk or cookie.

"MacQs?" he says, like he has no idea what the fuck.

"Yeah, you know, Mad Max? Thunderdome, motherfucker? Hell yeah."

Mel's head cocks the other way.

"I know, some say that Braveheart was your defining moment, but there's something about Mad Max that just gets me every time I watch it." He's lying. He likes Braveheart so much better.

"MadfuckingMAXXXX!" Ray screams, and starts running around the bar like a buffoon, taking little bitty sips out of everyone's drinks.

"Ray! Chill the fuck out!" Carlton shouts. "What the fuck are you doing?"

"Sampling!" Ray answers.

"Why don't you ask the bartender if you can sample, instead of polluting everyone else's drinks with your nasty-ass saliva?"

"Hey barkeep can I…"

"Arrrgh, no samplin' fer ye."

"See dude? Can't sample."

Ray stands up on the bar, and yells at the crowd. "I NEED SAMPLES!!!" He runs from one end of the bar to the other, yelling and screaming about Grey Goose and Old Crow, Hendricks and Absolut SKWID.

The bartender, severely agitated, rushes to the end of the bar and puts his hand on his shotgun, still keeping it hidden from view.

"Ray, sit down!" Carlton yells, but Ray pays no attention.

"IT'S A VERITABLE SMORGASBORD!" He yells excitedly. "Where do I begin?" He jumps behind the bar and starts opening bottles, taking swigs from each one in line.

"Ray, calm the fuck down!" Carlton shouts. But Ray is too far gone.

"Argggh get away from me bar or ye'll regret it," the bartender says.

"Excuse me for a second," Carton says to Mel. He races toward the bar and hops over it in one leap. He wraps his arms around Ray in a bear hug, and says in a calm voice, "There there, little guy. It's all right. Daddy loves you. You just took too much Adderall, that's all."

Ray begins to flail wildly. "Let go of me!" he shouts, and elbows Carlton in the lip.

"Okay, that's it, goddammit," Carlton says, pulling the handgun out from behind his back and pushing it against Ray's temple. "Chill the fuck out!"

The bartender takes his shotgun out from behind the bar. "Aye, there'll be no firrrrearrrms in herrre."

"But you have one," Nick shouts over from Mel's table.

Uncle Mel gets up from his chair, grabs his whiskey sour, and sneaks toward the door.

"He's getting away!" Eric shouts.

Carlton spins and aims the gun at the president. "Not so fast, Uncle Mel." He fires a shot, which hits Mel in his whiskey glass. Uncle Mel's eyes go wide, and he continues to sneak toward the door, as though nobody is noticing him.

"Not so slow, Uncle Mel," Carlton says, and fires off another shot, this time hitting him in the back of the head. A spray of goop, which is most likely blood, hits the door, but Mel seems unfazed. The little bit of flesh that flew off his skull quickly grows back, and he continues sneaking.

"Aye, that'll be enough" the bartender says, and aims his shotgun at Carlton's head.

Carlton rushes the bartender, taking a huge chance, and the shotgun goes off, grazing his shoulder.

"Ow," he says, which is quite an underreaction, if I do say so myself.

Forgetting he still has a gun in his hand, and he could have just shot the bartender instead of tackling him, he fires off a shot right into the face of the makeshift pirate, who promptly stops breathing.

"Darn," Carlton says, when it dawns on him that this is the first person he's ever killed. He sure is the king of the understatements today.

He grabs the shotgun from the bartender, which is thankfully a double barrel, aims it at Mel, and pulls the trigger, which blows half of his head clean off. Whatever patrons are left at this point bolt out the front door. Even the bouncer, that chickenshit. However, Uncle Mel continues to sneak his way toward it.

DAVE!

"The fuck?" Carlton says. He grabs more ammo from the Ziploc baggie that was stashed behind the bar and reloads. He fires again, the other half of Mel's head flying off, yet following a different trajectory than the first half did. Carlton takes a brief moment to wonder why it flew in that particular direction, then he realizes he got a C in Physics as well as Anatomy and Physiology, so he probably can't answer that question. He did really well in English Lit, however.

Mel's headless body continues to slowly sneak toward the door, only this time he is feeling around with his hands. He bumps into the front wall, missing the doorway by a country inch.

Eric gets up (finally! Jesus.) and picks up the handgun that Carlton has abandoned. He opens fire on what's left of Uncle Mel as Carlton plugs another round of buckshot into his body and reloads.

Round after round of bullets and buckshot riddle Mel's body, until soon there is nothing left but some slithering pieces that try sneaking their way outside. Persistent little fuckers.

"Okay, um, guys, I'm not really sure what happened, but can I come out now?" Nick asks from underneath the table.

"No," Eric answers. He's pretty sure it's safe for Nick to come out, but he doesn't really want him to.

"Is he dead?" Ray's words seep out from behind the bar.

"Umm, I…ohhh….ummm…" Carlton says

"We're not really sure," Eric answers.

"What do you mean you're not sure?" Nick asks.

"Well, little pieces of him are oozing down the sidewalk as we speak. Come on; let's go watch!" Carlton says to the gang.

Eric peeks his head outside, making sure there are no aliens or police around.

"Is the coast clear?" Nick asks.

"I don't know, have you seen the beach lately, motherfucker?" Carlton shouts

"Sorry, Carlton," Nick says. "Soon the wall will come down, and we'll have our coast back, and you can go hang out with your jellyfish friends."

"I miss them."

"I know you do."

"What the fuck?" Eric says, as he steps out of the doorway and into the street.

"What is it?" Carlton asks.

"I don't know."

"Look at the pieces!!" Ray shouts. "They're growing!"

They are, too. The little unrecognizable pieces of Uncle Mel are getting bigger the further they crawl down the street. Making a sluurrrp sound as they go. Soon they begin to orient themselves vertically. Soon after that they start sprouting limbs. They're forming people. Each one becomes identical to the next, and within a minute, there are twenty or so fully-formed naked Uncle Mel's. They being charging toward the gang.

"Holy sheepshit," Eric says. "Let's get the hell out of here!"

They book it around the corner to their waiting Elephant. They all pile in, Nick getting in the front seat and slamming the door. Eric reopens Nick's door. "Out," he says.

"Dude," Nick says.

"Out. I'm shotgun. I called it times infinity. You can't be in this seat."

The Mels round the corner. They get closer. Thirty feet. Twenty five.

"Just get in the fucking car!" Carlton shouts.

Eric sighs, gets in the back seat, and shuts the door just as his leg is grabbed by a Mel.

DAVE!

Carlton floors it, and Eric opens the window to toss the newly-severed arm out before it can sprout another president.

"What. The. Fuck. Was. That?" Eric asks.

"I don't know," Carlton answers, "but I think our problems just got exponentially bigger."

"Ya think?" Ray asks, and gets a stern look from Carlton.

"Come on," Carlton says. "Let's head back to headquarters. It's time to regroup."

CHAPTER SIX

She rattles the big iron gate. Locked. Of course it is; why wouldn't it be? There has to be a set of keys, but where? She looks over to the horrible, urine-soaked alien's body. Most likely, the keys are in his pocket, but does she want to go over there? She doesn't really want to touch him. And it's not because he's covered in urine. We've all been covered in pee from time to time, Starlet included, so that doesn't really bother her. What bothers her is the fact that she doesn't know if the alien is dead or just out cold. What if he comes to while she's searching him? She'll be dead, for sure. Well, no time like the present; the longer she waits, the greater the odds of him waking up.

She crouches next to his body. He doesn't seem to be breathing, so that's a good thing. But then again, maybe that doesn't mean jack shit. She checks the left pocket of his pants, and begins pulling out objects. Antifreeze, cottage cheese, Socrates, Crohn's Disease, Alicia Keys. Close, but no. Right pocket: A copy of Degrees of Separation, a dalmatian, a space station, a Croatian. No fucking keys. She pats him down from his disgusting head to his gnarly toes (gag). No lock-opening devices, but she does find a gun in a holster on his hip. She snags that; it may come in handy at some point.

"Okay, Bella, let's go exploring."

The dog follows her down the corridor. It's fairly well-lit with torches the entire way. She wonders if Chuck actually took the time to light all of these. Why bother lighting the entire cave? Seems like a waste if they were only going to stay in the front room. And if Chuck didn't light these torches, who did? Are there others in here with her? She shudders at the thought, and realizes it's pretty stupid to keep going any farther in. She doesn't see any alternative, however.

There are rooms lining each side of the corridor. These are shrouded in utter darkness, and they give her the creeps as her mind starts to churn over what could be lurking in them. That thought no sooner enters her mind, when she hears something shuffling in one of the rooms off to her left. Maybe a squirrel or something. Bella hears it too, and darts into the room after it.

"Bella, no!" she yells.

She hears the dog barking angrily.

"Bella, get back here! Bella! Come!"

She hears the scampering of the dog's paws as she chases whatever it is in the room. And judging by the loud thumping it makes, it ain't no fuckin' squirrel.

"Greeee!" a voice shouts from inside the room, and Bella barks again in reply.

Oh shit. It's not a something. It's a someone. Another alien! Fuck!

"Bella, goddammit, get out here!" she screams.

"A creeeed e croood!" the voice shouts. More barking.

Well, she can't just stand here calling for Bella to come back out. She needs to go in there and save her. Bella's saved her hide many times; it's time to repay the favor.

"I'm coming, girl!" She crosses the threshold just as Bella and the intruder come bolting out, chasing each other. The stranger has a funny pointed red hat and a big blue coat held shut by a belt with a rather large buckle. He has big black boots and a long beard that reaches down to his midsection. Also, he stands about three feet tall. A fucking gnome? You gotta be kidding me, she thinks. She puts her hand on the butt of her new gun, getting ready to do whatever is necessary.

"Heh heh. A greeep a grope a groot!" he shouts as he chases the dog down the corridor. He stops abruptly, and runs back toward Starlet, letting Bella chase him. They stop in front of Starlet, and he bows gracefully. Bella copies him and puts her head low to the ground; her own way of bowing. Starlet takes her hand off the gun.

"Well, hey there little fella," she says. "Where did you come from?"

"Little fella, you say? Why I oughtta bust ye open with me boot. I come from me mum, I wager."

He turns and faces away, looking over his shoulder at Starlet. "Ye'll never catch me!" he yells, and runs away. And he's right. She won't catch him. I mean, she would if she could, but she's not really in the mood. She's surprised Bella isn't chasing him, but maybe she's fed up with his shenanigans as well.

"Wait!" she calls. "How do I get out of here?"

The gnome doesn't answer; he just giggles and keeps on scampering. Oh well.

"Freak," she says. "Come on, Bella. Let's keep exploring. There has to be a way out."

They come to a fork in the corridor. "You take the left, I'll take the right," she tells Bella. "If you see any keys, or any way out, report back to me immediately. The dog salutes her and pads her way down to the left.

Starlet continues down toward the right. No exit yet, but she does stumble across a bathroom. Whoever built this room actually did a pretty good job. There's a shower, a soaking tub, and a sink. The only thing it's missing is a toilet. Just a hole dug in the ground to poop in. She turns the sink tap on, and water comes out. Unbelievable. Although she's thirsty, she decides to not drink it, just in case. To come all this way in her journey just to die of e. coli or something, well, that would be ironic. Maybe. She's not sure what ironic means. She knows "The Gift of the Magi" by O. Henry was ironic, but apart from that, she's not sure what fits the definition. She remembers the day that she found out that "sarcasm" was not the same as "irony". Sarcasm, she found out, has nothing to do with saying the opposite of what you mean. That's irony.

Sarcasm just means to make a negative comment. She's confused, but her face is hanging off right now, and she doesn't have the time or patience for semantics.

One thing this bathroom does have that every bathroom needs, is a medicine cabinet. But this medicine cabinet lacks the one thing every medicine cabinet needs: Medicine. It does, however, have eight pairs of toenail clippers. Makes sense, if this is where the aliens hide out. Their toenails are nasty and thick. Makes her shudder just thinking about those nasty, horribly disfigured toes. Blech.

Also in the medicine cabinet, thankfully, is a pint of rubbing alcohol. She knows what she has to do if she wants to fight infection, but it's going to suck. It's going to suck so bad. She thinks of drinking some just to take the edge off, but her brain shuts that thought down quickly. There's no way in hell she can drink this shit. However, her hands don't fully realize what her brain is saying, and before she knows it, she has a mouthful. Her mouth gets what her brain is saying, when the taste hits her palate. Fuck! Also, her skinless lips shoot an intense pain directly to that brain of hers, as if to say You were right, dude. Holy shit, the agony! Whatever, though. She takes a couple more swallows and prepares herself for more of the same sensation, only all over her goddamned face. Well, here goes nothing, she thinks, and dumps the bottle on herself. The last thing she feels before she passes out is the torturous pain of a thousand suns simultaneously shooting off solar flares and chicken bone shards directly into her brain stem.

Starlet awakens to a screaming headache. Both the front her of her head, as well as the back, from banging it on the sink during the fall, most likely. She gets up, which makes her head pound more. She briefly thinks of killing herself with a pair of the toenail clippers, but they're so friggin' dirty, she decides it's a bad idea. She may as well try to fix her face instead.

She looks in the cabinet underneath the sink, on the hunt for medicine. Nothing there except a couple rolls of toilet paper and a toolbox. Inside the toolbox, she finds a hammer. Perhaps she can bash herself over the head with it and end her misery. Why is she having these suicidal thoughts? Is it the pain? Or is it out of frustration? As brutal as the pain is, she decides that it is in fact frustration that's causing her to be so down. She can't let that bit of irritation decide her fate for her; she's come way too far to give up. She puts the hammer down. Digging farther in, a stapler appears. Not a desk stapler, but an open-ended industrial one used for securing cables to walls as well as various other home improvement projects. This would be the perfect thing to secure her face back to her head. Well, not the perfect thing, but under the circumstances, she doesn't have a choice. They use staples in surgery all the time, and these look fairly similar. She needs to put her face back before her flesh decides it's time to scab over, and there's no hope left in the tissue reattaching itself.

She pulls her face back over her skull, the feel of it like papery mannequin skin. Perhaps it's already too late to reattach. The blood on the backside of it has become flaky. But there's nothing to lose at this point. Either it takes or it doesn't.

She shoots one into her head. Pow. At least it doesn't hurt as bad as she was thinking it would; nothing can hurt a badly as the alcohol did. She plugs another and another; twenty in all. Checking in the mirror, she still looks like a total freak show, not even a shadow of her former beautiful self.

The staples are holding well, but she needs something to cover the seam with so her face doesn't get inadvertently ripped away. Duct tape! The fix-all. She tears off a decent strip and carefully adheres it over the divide. There. That takes care of that issue.

No sooner does she finish when she hears a yelp coming from far off, followed by whimpering. Bella.

"I'm coming, girl!" she shouts, and it feels good to be able to worry about others and finally forget about herself for a change.

She follows the sound of Bella's voice, which leads her back in the direction from which she came, and down the other side where the dog headed. She doesn't have to go too far when she sees Bella lying in the hallway, a sad expression on her face.

"What's the matter, girl? Come on, let's go. Let's continue exploring this way for a while." When Bella doesn't move, she says, "Well? Come on sweetie, let's get out of here."

DAVE!

She still doesn't move. Starlet reaches down to pet her, and she sees what's wrong. Someone carelessly left a bear trap out here, and her tail is caught.

"Oh, no. Oh, you poor thing." She grabs the trap with both hands, and with all the strength she has left, opens it. Straining to do so causes her head to pound even more. A wave of dizziness hits her, and she's forced to sit down.

Bella gets up and licks her face. "Thank you, girl. Ugh. Let Starlet see your tail."

She turns the dog around and looks at her tail. It has been cut in half; the bone completely severed and the end of it dangling off like the, misplaced comma in this sentence.

"Well, kid, looks like you and I are in rough shape. Thank God it was just your tail and not your cute little puppy face. Let's get you fixed up."

First thing Starlet needs to do is get rid of the dangly bit. She searches in the toolbox and finds a pair of pruning shears. She pats Bella gently on her head, and cuts through. Suprisingly, she gets no reaction from the dog. Okay, that was easy.

"Good dog. Now, I gotta warn you, this is gonna suck." She grabs the bottle of rubbing alcohol and pours it on her tail. The most awful noise she's ever heard in her whole life comes from Bella's mouth, as she runs away. She gets up and chases her down the hallway. "Bella, wait!"

Bella doesn't stop, but she slows down enough for Starlet to catch up to her. "Come on back, sweetie. The bad part's over. Let's cover this up before you get it dirty.

They go back into the bathroom and she bandages her up, getting surprisingly little resistance, and even a kiss from Bella at the end of it all.

"There. All better. Ah, look at us. The amputee and and faceless wonder. Let's find a way out of here."

Slowly they make their way down the hall till she finds a door on the left with a sign tacked on that says CONFERENCE ROOM. Conference room? In a cave?

The door is unlocked, and she steps inside. Thankfully, there is a light switch on the other side of the door. She turns it on, and the room lights up. Electricity? Down here? What the hell's with all the torches, then? Ambiance, she guesses.

The room is rather empty, save for a table smack dab in the middle of the room with six highly polished wooden chairs around it. The remains of someone's creamy coffee is in front of one of the seats. Someone has been here recently. Although the coffee mug is cold to the touch, coffee with cream molds within a few days. This is slightly congealed, but far from moldy. Off to the side, on one of the walls, is a poster with a smiling handsome fellow on it. Underneath the face is the word DAVE! Around his head is a bullseye, and although there are no holes in the poster itself, there are darts jammed in the wall all around it. Whoever was throwing darts at Dave sure had bad aim.

She is jarred from this by the sound of approaching footsteps. "Well, well, well, what have we here? Dear Starlet. And her little dog, too." Bella growls at the voice.

She turns. "Oh, come on. Not you again."

"Hahaha! You're scared, aren't you?"

"Mmm, no. More annoyed than anything, really."

"You're shaking in your boots!"

"Yyyyyeah, no."

"You rue the day you ever met me!"

"Well, yeah, but not because I'm scared. I'm just tired of your bullshit. I was kind hoping you were dead back there."

"Yeah, well, hope again, stupid."

"You're the stupid."

"You're the stupids."

239

She puts her hand on the gun on her hip, prepared to shoot if need be. "You're gonna tell me how to get out of here, right, stupid?"

Chuck chuckles. "You didn't notice the big iron gate at the front? I guess you are stupid."

"It's locked."

"Oh."

"So...?"

"Oh. I suppose you're looking for the keys. They're hanging up on a hook right by the gate. All you had to do was look, stupid."

"Well you don't have to be so rude about it."

"The key to the cruiser is hanging up with it. Take the car. Take whatever you need. Just get the hell out of my life. I rue the day I ever met you."

"Aha! How the tables have turned," Starlet says, smugly.

"You're more trouble than you're worth. I was supposed to keep an eye on you. You were supposed to be this big threat. You're no threat; you can't even repair your own face without duct tape. You're just a flea in a small pond. Of fleas."

"Hey, I can be a threat if I wanna be," she says, offended.

"Just go."

And with that, Starlet and Bella leave the cave. The cruiser is parked right outside the gate, and she opens the door for Bella to hop in the back. She turns the key in the ignition and checks the time on the dash. 2 P.M. It'll still be somewhat early when she gets to D.C., provided there aren't any more of these hiccups.

CHAPTER SEVEN

The gang are on their way back to headquarters, Ray and Eric fighting over arm room, when a text comes through to their D.A.V.E.-issued phone.

Carlton takes the phone out of his pocket and is about to read it when Eric reaches over the seat and grabs it from him. "Gimme that. Keep your eyes on the road. You've had a couple beers and I'd rather not die in a fucking car crash."

He reads the text aloud.

ATTENTION: IT IS CONFIRMED. THE PRESIDENT HAS JUST BEEN SHOT AND KILLED ON 14TH AND COLUMBIA. PLS AWAIT INSTRUCTION.

"Woo-hoo!" Nick shouts, followed by an echoed, "Woo-hoo!" from Ray.

Judging by the look Carlton gives, those two are the only ones gullible enough to think it would be that easy. Right on cue, another text comes in, which Eric also reads aloud.

UPDATE: NEVER MIND.

"Fuck," Carlton mutters.

Another text comes in. Eric reads.

DAVE!

ATTENTION: IT IS CONFIRMED. THE PRESIDENT HAS JUST BEEN SHOT AND KILLED ON 17TH AND MASSACHUSETTS. PLS AWAIT INSTRUCTION.

"Wait for it…" Carlton says.

UPDATE: NEVER MIND

"I have a feeling…" Eric says, and is interrupted by yet another text, which he reads to the crew.

ATTENTION: SEVERAL MELS HAVE BEEN SPOTTED IN THE D.C. AREA. WE R NOT SURE HOW, IT SEEMS THAT THEY R MULTIPLYING. PLS AWAIT FURTHER INSTRUCTION.

"I need a drink," Carlton says.

"Me too," Eric agrees, then drops the phone on the floor, mouth dropping at the same time.

"STOP!" he screams at Carlton, who slams on the brakes, just in time to avoid a kid named Fritz Weber, who happens to be riding past on his hoverboard, doing a front-360-kickflip, paying absolutely no attention.

"Wowie! Thanks for that. That kid came out of nowhere."

"Kid?" Eric asks. "What kid?"

"The one you helped me avoid hitting when you yelled stop."

"Oh, him? That's not the reason I yelled stop. Look!" he says, and points to a bar across the street.

"Ráicleach?" I'm not going to another Irish pub. I'm done with those for a while, outside of Boston.

"No, not that one. The one next to it."

"Starlet Bar and Grille? That some queer joint? God I hope so. All right, let's go try it out."

"Dude. The name," Eric says.

"Yeah, what of it?"

242

"Starlet."

"So, what is the...ohhh, is that the name of your little transgirl? Aww, ain't that cute?"

"Man, what are the odds?"

"That your girl would be named after some Bar and Grille? Pretty good, I'd say. It's an odd name."

"Well, let's go, let's go. This is fate I tell you."

"Yeah, it's fate. I'm hungry and thirsty and we found a bar and grille. Let's go get a burger."

The place is pretty packed and, unlike the bar they just left, pretty clean.

"How many in your party?" the host asks.

"Four," Carlton says, then regards Nick and Ray. "Well, two and a half."

"Right this way."

When they're all seated, the host says, "Your server will be right with you."

"Thank you," Says Eric.

Of course, Carlton starts perusing the cocktail menu right away. "Wow. These all sound yummy. Thirty-eight styles of margaritas? Oh, man. Oh, look, they have scorpion bowls. Wanna share one?"

The guys all shake their heads. Scorpion bowls are not to be trusted in burger joints.

"Hmm, what should I get? I'm in the mood for something with coconut in it. Coconut and, ooh, pineapple. If only there were some drink that has both of those things in it, that would make me really happy."

Carlton's foofy drink fantasies are interrupted by a "Hello, gentlemen. Welcome to the Starlet Bar and Grille. My name is Mel and I'll be your server." He looks up at the waiter. You gotta be kidding me.

"Can I start you guys off with some drinks?"

DAVE!

Carlton looks the president in the eye. "A fuckin' bottle of whiskey."

CHAPTER EIGHT

Starlet drives south for two uneventful hours; so uneventful that her eyes are starting to get heavy. Although she'd like to get to the capitol as soon as possible, she needs to pull over and get some air. She stops in front of a park, plenty of room for letting Bella run around for a few minutes while she wakes up. Bella whines and wags her half-tail. She knows what's up.

"You must have to go to the bathroom, huh, little girl?"

Her tail continues to wag. Starlet opens the back door and Bella bolts to a clump of trees, looking to do her business. A sign by the clump of trees shows a cartoon of a dog with a perfect swirl of doo-doo underneath and flies swarming around it. PLEASE PICK UP AFTER YOUR DOGGIES, it says, with a roll of poop bags underneath it. She pulls a couple from the roll and watches as Bella crouches and lets forth a light brown puddle of gelatinous poop. Sweet, she thinks. She tries the best she can to pick it up with the bag, but mostly what she's doing is smearing it further into the grass, wafting forth a horrible stench which smells like a mixture of bad pasta, anal gland mucus and old Popsicles. She gags. Fucking SpaghettiOs. She puts the bag inside a second bag, ties it, and throws it in a nearby receptacle while the dog pees in another spot.

Starlet spots a little coffee and pastry shack by the main entrance. Mmm, coffee. That's exactly what she needs. Perhaps she can get Bella a little something to eat there. Something that isn't canned pasta wheels.

DAVE!

The barista gives Starlet a look like she has a loose face being held together by duct tape or something, then quickly falls into her boring barista routine. "Good afternoon and welcome to the Coffee Shack what can I get you?"

"I'll have the Cuban coffee and a blueberry scone."

The girl looked annoyed like she really didn't want to go through all the trouble of making a Cuban coffee for just one person. It is a complicated beverage, but why offer it if you don't want to make it?

"And do you have anything for dogs?" Starlet asks.

"We have a carrot-carob cruller that is nutritious and delicious for canines."

"Okay, one of those, please."

"Anything else?" the barista sighed.

"No, that'll be it."

"That'll be $38.02."

Starlet takes out her Discover card, which is the only thing she has on her after being kidnapped.

"We don't take Discover. Nobody takes Discover."

"Ummm, can I owe you?"

The barista looks super-annoyed. "Just take it," she says. "I'm super-annoyed."

"I can tell. Thank you."

"Whatever. Have a great day," says the barista, as she quietly slits her wrist with a bagel knife.

Starlet watches her bleed out and eventually drop. She turns to Bella, reaches down, and grabs a fallen tree branch. "Come on, girl. Wanna go chase a stick?" Bella's stump wags like crazy.

She throws the stick, and Bella sprints off. As she's waiting for the dog to return, she takes a sip of her coffee. ZING! Holy shit. She had forgotten just how potent Cuban coffee is. KA-POW!

On the forty-eighth throw, Bella has had enough. Starlet feels like she can throw the stick at least forty-eight more times, but with no one to fetch it, what's the point?

"You have a beautiful dog," a voice from behind her says. "What happened to her poor tail?"

"Oh, it got caught in a…" her words halt as she sees who is behind her- the President of the United States.

"A bear trap, you say? Well, that's just awful. Doesn't look like it fazed her one bit, though, does it?"

Her hand goes instinctively to the butt of her gun. Even though she knows it's not going to do her any good, she's willing to fill him full of lead if she has to.

He extends his hand in a fist-bump gesture. "Nice to meet you. Starlet, isn't it? My name's Gleeerg. I mean, Mel Gibson. Did I say Gleeerg? Who's Gleeerg? I'm not Gleeerg."

"I know who you are," she says, her hand still on the gun, leaving him hanging on the fist-bump front. "Pleasure to meet you, Mister President. How do you know who I am?"

"Oh, I know who you are." He smiles. "We all know who you are. You're famous." A hint of the gnashing teeth shows behind his cornea, appearing to be floating in the aqueous humor.

A figure approaches from across the field. Help is here. Maybe Mel will leave now. As the figure gets closer, she rubs her eyes, not believing what she's seeing. It's Mel. He extends his hand in a fist-bump gesture. "You have a beautiful dog. What happened to her poor tail? A bear trap, you say? Well, that's just awful."

"What the fuck?" she says out loud.

247

DAVE!

"Doesn't look like it fazed her one bit, though, does it?"

Soon several more figures race across the field toward her, all saying the same thing. "You have a beautiful dog. What happened to her poor tail?" They're not all saying it in unison, however, and the voices jumble and scramble and soon become one garble of speech, along with a low-volume high-pitched squealing that makes Bella bow to the ground and cover her ears.

"What the fuck?" she says again. She heads to the cruiser. "Bella, let's get the hell out of here."

She makes it to D.C. by nine o'clock. A boring trip; the only excitement watching Bella stick her little head out the window, letting the air currents flap her little doggy lips. The only company besides the dog is the voice in her head. And the more the coffee wakes her up, the more and faster the voice blathers on.

Why did Mel know who I am? Why did he say We all know who you are? I'm famous? Was he serious? What on Earth did I do to become famous? Am I being paranoid? Should I be paranoid? Why all the presidents, and where did they all come from? How many are there? Are they clones? Are they all just wearing the same disguise?

The further she drives on, the more random Mels she spots- riding bikes, crossing the street, in cars passing by or stopped next to her at a red light, playing hop scotch in the dark- until she gets to D.C. and sees them everywhere. Some appear to be brain-dead, shuffling to and fro like zombies.

"What the hell is going on, puppy?" she asks Bella, as though the dog has the answers.

Her stomach growls, reminding her she's had nothing but coffee in it for quite some time. "You hungry, girl?" she asks, and Bella whines excitedly. "Let's go see if we can find a burger or some wings around here." But where to go? There are so many choices. Who serves delicious burgers this late at night?

She pulls over to the curb in front of a group of presidents and rolls her window down. "Any of you Mels know where a lady can get some decent wings this time of night?"

They all point in different directions, and upon noticing their little faux pas, they consult with one another. Finally, one of them speaks up. "Who is asking?"

"Starlet," she says. I thought they all knew who I am. Word must not have gotten this far.

Suddenly, they all point straight ahead. "Two blocks," the supposed leader says.

"Thank you very much," says Starlet, and speeds off.

Two blocks later, she pulls up in front of the Starlet Bar and Grille.

"Well, that's just plain weird. Bella, you stay here and be a good girl. I'll be back very soon." She gives the dog a kiss on her head and exits the cruiser.

CHAPTER NINE

Night came without warning. Even though night happens every night, technically nobody warned them that night was coming. They decided to call it a night, which is usually what you call night, unless you call it "evening". They did not decide to call it an evening.

The crew is pretty much trashed. They had finished off the bottle of whiskey very quickly. Eric doesn't like whiskey. A small glass of single malt scotch is good, for a nightcap, but he was never one to slug down shot after shot of Jim Beam. The taste was something he hoped he'd get used to by the end of the bottle, but it just kept getting worse with each sip. Why did he drink that shit? Nick and Ray had stuck to beer and white wine, respectively. He should have done that. Maybe if he crams some food down on top of it he can stuff his rising gorge back in. "Lersten," he slurs. "We butter get some food in our bellies before we end up hanging over."

"Agreed," Carlton agrees. "How bout some wings?"

"Nonsense," Eric says. "How bout we get some wings?"

"Sounds dandy," Carlton says.

As if reading their minds, the Mel-waiter-thing comes over. "Can I get you guys something to absorb all that whiskey?" he asks.

"Wings!" Eric shouts excitedly.

"What kind of wings would you gentlemen like?"

"What kind you got?"

"We have Lemon Pepper, Parmesan Garlic, BBQ, Garlic BBQ,Chipotle BBQ,Desert Heat, Curry, General Tso's, Honey Mustard, PB&J, Salt and Vinegar Dry Rub, Teriyaki, Thai BBQ, Thai Chili, Albany Dark, Buffalo, Buffalo Bacon Nacho, Buffalo Garlic, Hot Buffalo, Honey Chipotle, Redneck, Thai Peanut, Valley Girl, Blackened Dry Rub, Jamaican Jerk Dry Rub, Diesel, Diesel BBQ, Deisel Garlic, Sour Diesel, Hot Mango, KGB, Spice Girl, Spicy Redneck, Chernobyl, Firehose, Fukushima, and Ghost Pepper Ass Fuck."

"What was the fifth one you said?" Eric asks, which gets a face-melting stare from Mel, which is probably hotter than any wing they offer.

"Wanna try the Ghost Pepper one? That sounds good," Carlton says.

"Sure, why not?"

Mel looks annoyed. He shouts to someone in the back, "Mike! We got any more forms?"

"I think so," Mike shouts back.

"I'll be right back," Mel says.

He comes back with a dusty box, which he blows off onto the table, and pulls out two pieces of paper from it. Handing one to Eric and one to Carlton, he says, "Sign, please."

"What's this?" Carlton asks.

"This is a waiver stating that you release the Starlet Bar and Grille from any and all liability, should you become disabled, damaged, or deceased from a wing."

"Seriously?" Eric asks.

"It's no joke. Every now and then, and it's only when someone is severely intoxicated, they order the Ghost Pepper Ass Fuck wings. These wings have killed thousands. Granted, a couple of those deaths were from the chicken not being cooked well enough, but the rest were from the sheer heat. Of course, this only occurs when someone tries to finish their portion. Most take one bite and we have to end up tossing them in the trash."

"So they either end up dead or hungry?" Carlton asks.

"That's right."

"Then why do you make them?"

"I've been working here for years. Still have no clue."

"Let's go with the Valley Girl," Eric says.

"Very well. And what would you like for dipping sauce?"

"What do you have?"

Mel sighs. "We have Blue Cheese, Ranch, Blanch, Spicy Beer Mustard, Garlic–Chive Greek Yogurt, Queso Fundido al Tequila, Strawberry Honey Mustard, Spinach Artichoke, Cheesy Horseradish, Vanilla Bean Ketchup, Lime Cilantro, Roasted Red Pepper Tartar Sauce, Chipotle-Citrus Mayonnaise, Espresso Barbecue Sauce, Gasoline, or any of the wing sauces I mentioned earlier. Also, you have just plain fucking Heinz kethcup right there on the table. Assholes."

"Ooh, let's get the Blanch, that sounds like fun," Eric says.

"Very good, sir," Mel says, and mutters as he walks away, "You have the menus right in front of you, fucking dirtbags."

"Oh, look," Eric says. "We have the menus right here."

"Hey!" Eric shouts to Nick and Ray. "You guys want some wings?"

"Sure!" Ray yells. "What kind do they have?"

"Waiter?" Eric shouts.

"Fuck off!" shouts Mel, throwing a menu at Ray.

A couple minutes later, Eric pipes up. "Should we have a meeting? We should probably make a plan."

"I think we should wait for instructions from headquarters," Carlton says.

"That's a plan, isn't it? We need to at least discuss what's going to happen. Let's get the two Idiots over here."

Carlton shakes his head.

"Why not?" Eric asks as Carlon points his thumb over at the bar.

Although there is no music playing, Nick and Ray are both standing on the bar, stark naked, showing what they got and gyrating and pulsating to the beat in their heads. There they are, the two dingalings, showing off their dingalings. One a show-er, the other a grower. Maybe. Who knows? Although Eric is quite drunk, there aren't whiskey goggles thick enough to make this interesting. The audience seems to like it, though.

"Anyway, what are your thoughts?" Eric asks.

"I think Ray is definitely a grower."

"Me too, but that's not what I mean. What are your thoughts on all these Mels? Do you think we can possibly put a stop to them? Do you think the human race is doomed?"

"Yes."

"Not the answer I wanted to hear," Eric says.

"I don't see how we can possibly stop all these Mels," Carlton says. "Especially since they can regenerate so easily. Dismembering is obviously out of the question. Maybe we can burn them. But all of them? Who knows how many of them there are? They seem to be everywhere."

"Maybe D.A.V.E. knows what to do."

"Yeah, I'm starting to lose faith in that, too. Oh, I wish someone had the answers."

The front door opens, and the streetlight glow frames a familiar face. Is Eric hallucinating? He hasn't had that much to drink. He rubs his eyes, which creates stars in his field if vision and makes the room swirl, but does nothing for his focus.

"Eric?" he hears from the direction of the new face.

"Starlet?"

He stands up and rushes to the door, catching his leg on a chair and toppling over, landing on his chest with an ooof. He gets back up, red-faced from the embarrassment exacerbated by the alcohol, and throws his arms around Starlet.

"Oh, Eric, I've missed you so," she says.

"I missed you too. Oh, I was so worried. I'm so glad you're okay." He kisses her face, his lips a little dry and pasty from being dehydrated by the whiskey, and thus sticking to her cheek and pulling on the skin a little.

"What on Earth happened to your face?" he asks.

She sighs. "It's a long story."

CHAPTER TEN

They're all gathered around the table, Nick and Ray included, enthralled by Starlet's story.

"...and so I told them I was Starlet, and then they pointed here, thinking I was talking about this place haha. It's all a bit ironic. Don't ya think?"

"I'm not really sure," Eric says. "But I'm sure glad to have you back. Let's get married!"

"Woah woah, slow down. Wait, was that a proposal, or Tourette's?"

"Um, a proposal?"

"Okay, well sure, but we need to solve this whole alien invasion problem first."

"She said yes!" Ray gets up and runs back and forth, shouting the phrase over and over.

"What's his deal?" Starlet asks Eric.

"Mostly? He's an Idiot," he says, "with a touch of Adderall intolerance."

"I hate to break up all this narrative filler," Carlton says, "but are you saying that all we have to do is shock the president with a car battery?"

"Well, yeah. I think. I mean, it's worked before. But of course, now it has become exponentially more complicated."

"You're telling me," says Carlton. "I mean, do we have to kill all these Mels, or just the original? Or are they all originals? And if there's only one original, how do we find him?"

"Right, that's why I said it's become exponentially more complicated."

Mel the waiter approaches with a heaping plate of Valley Girl wings and a teensy little dipping cup of Blanch. "Here you go, fellas. Enjoy."

"Um, hold on a sec," Eric says. "We may need more wings now."

"Sorry, guys. Deep fryer is off for the night."

"Can we at least get some more Blanch?" Eric asks.

"No. We're only allowed to give out one tablespoon per every pound of wings. However, you're more than welcome to use as much of the table ketchup as you like."

"Stingy pricks," Carlton mutters.

"Hey," Starlet says to the waiter, "Anyone ever tell you you look like someone?"

"Hmhm, no I'm not Travis. Why does everyone ask me that?" He walks away.

"So I say let's go see if the hotel next door has a vacancy, get some rest, and we'll wait to hear back from headquarters," Carlton says.

"Agreed," says Starlet. I could sure use some rest."

It was decided that no matter what the cost at this short notice, they would get three separate rooms. One for the Idiots, one for Carlton, and one for the love birds, as they had a lot of making up for lost time to do.

A sign on the front desk says NO DOGS.

"Dammit," Starlet says.

"What's the matter?" Eric asks.

"No dogs."

"Oh, that's right. You have a dog. Where is she? I love doggies."

They walk out to the cruiser together. Bella is lying in the back seat, her head on her front paws, eyes looking up with a sad expression.

"Oh, Bella. Mama's sorry for leaving you in the car. You must have to go pee."

"Hi, Bella," Eric says, but is completely ignored, as Bella races to find a spot of grass to pee on. Once relieved, she rushes back, gives Starlet a kiss on her hand, and then Eric.

"Oh, thank you. What a pretty dog you are," Eric says.

"Oh, thank you," Bella says. Just kidding. There are no talking dogs in this story, but she does wag her stump.

"Poor girl," Eric says. "That must hurt like a sonfofabitch."

"Yeah. She's a trooper," Starlet says.

Eric looks at Starlet. "Trooper? My God, you're almost missing a face. You're both troopers in my book."

"Thanks."

"DOG?" comes Nick's voice, racing around the corner. "I LOVE DOG!"

Bella sees Nick, bowls him over, pins him, and kisses him all over.

"Aww, that's so nice. Look, Nick, somebody finally likes you."

"Haha," he says, as he gets up. "What a sweet puppy. Come on, Bella. Let's go inside."

"Can't," Starlet says.

"Why not?"

"Sign in there says no dogs. I'll sleep in the cruiser tonight with her."

257

"No," Eric says. "We'll both sleep in the cruiser with her. I don't mind sleeping in the car."

"No dogs? Why, that's discrimination in the highest degree. But hold on, I think I have a plan."

"Oh, no," Eric says.

"What?"

"Your plans suck, as a rule."

"When have I ever made one?"

"True."

"But this one's good. Bella's black and white, right?"

"Yeah, so?"

"What other animal is black and white?"

"Zebra," Eric says.

"Not gonna work. That's stripes. Plus, she's not big enough. What other animal is black and white?"

"Pandas," Starlet says.

"Hmm, cuddly, but again, too big. I'll give you a hint. They live in the North Pole."

"Polar bears?" Starlet asks. "But they're all white."

"Think smaller," Nick says.

"Elves?" says Eric.

"Nope. Think more bird-like."

"Hmm, I give up," says Eric.

"Penguins, you dope!"

"Penguins live in Antarctica, you dope," Eric says.

"That's what I said; the North Pole."

"Nick…oh, never mind. What's your idea?"

"We say she's a penguin. The sign says nothing about penguins. Think about it."

Eric did. It made his brain hurt.

"Look at her tail. Don't you see? It's fate. It's a blessing it got chopped. Otherwise she would look nothing like a penguin."

"Yes, you're right," Eric says. "That long tail would have been the only thing keeping her from looking like a penguin."

At this point, Eric has no better ideas. He would sleep in the cruiser with Starlet and the dog if he had to, but it sure would be sweet to be in a nice, warm bed. They all need rest.

"All right; let's try it. We have nothing to lose."

They stroll back into the hotel. The front desk clerk looks suspiciously at the quartet coming in. "Penguin," Nick mouths, and points to Bella. The clerk nods his head in recognition, and gives him a thumbs-up.

Eric would have been content with just a night of making out with Starlet. After explaining to his drunk ass the inherent dangers of pulling her face off with his sticky lips, he decides that there are other places to kiss. Places more…exotic. It has been a while since he's been around a vagina, Carlton's notwithstanding, and it has been never since he's been around Starlet's vagina, so he's not quite sure what to make of it, or how to operate it. He kisses her neck, which thankfully is still attached, and makes his way down to her breasts. She moans with delight. He has always loved her tits; she had the greatest set. Even still, after all these years, they were very supple and fun to play with. He spends quite some time with the nipples, and Starlet's moans fade after about twenty minutes.

"You know, you can move down, if you want to. It's ok."

DAVE!

He looks to Bella for reassurance, but thankfully, she is passed out in the corner.

"Umm, all right. I guess."

"You don't have to."

"No, no, future wife. I want to. It's just, well…"

"What?"

"Ah, forget it."

"No. What is it?"

"I don't really know how to."

Starlet looks confused. "What do you mean? I thought you had a girlfriend before. One with a ladysnatch."

"I did. We just never did…that."

"Never?"

"Never."

"No blowjobs?"

"Oh, no, I got plenty of those."

"No offense, Eric. But I would have slapped you silly. No wonder she left your ass to join a cult. I bet it's a cult just full of cunnilingus. A cunnilingus cult."

Eric shudders.

"What?"

"Could you please not use that word?"

"What, cunnilingus?"

He gags a little.

"Okay, fine. But why?"

"It reminds me of going to a Jewish delicatessen and ordering a tongue sandwich, for some reason. Just the sound of that word."

"Well, you won't be disappointed when you get down there, then."

He gags.

"It's okay. Come on back up."

"Really?"

"Yeah. We have our whole lives together. You don't have to do that tonight."

"I love you, Starlet."

"I love you too. I'm so glad we found each other through all this."

"Me too."

"Hold on," she says, and reaches in her purse. She comes out with a pencil. "Now, put this pencil in my backside and ram me in the front with your huge cock."

His eyes widen. He's so excited he drools a bit. "Ohmygod, I can't believe it!"

"I know!" she says. "Sounds like fun, right?"

"You better believe it! A pencil? God, I haven't seen one of those in twenty years or so. Whatever happened to those?"

"Umm, I'm not really sure. They kind of fell out of fashion."

"Why would they even invent such a thing? I mean, pens were invented first, right?"

"Yeah."

"And the pen has always been a far superior product. Why would they even bother with this? You have to sharpen it constantly. Pens never need to be sharpened. When they run out of ink, you just toss them out. Pencils are kind of stupid. Jeez, I wonder how much this is worth?"

261

DAVE!

"Not much, yet. Someday, maybe."

"My God, a pencil. Wow."

They spend the rest of the evening talking about pens and pencils, and never really get down to business. That's okay, Starlet thinks. We have the rest of our lives. I'm getting married!

CHAPTER ELEVEN

They sit there at poolside. It had taken a lot of convincing Nick and Ray to leave their clothes on; they seem to disrobe at every possible opportunity. Even at those opportunities that aren't really opportunities.

"But why, Carlton? Why can't we skinny dip?"

"Um, because it's a crowded hotel, and it's the middle of the day, and can't you guys just be normal for once? Just relax, go for a dip. Let's take some much needed downtime while we wait to hear back from D.A.V.E." He goes up to the pool bar and orders a round of Bloody Marys for everyone.

He comes back with the tray. "Ugh, I don't think I can drink another drop of alcohol. Plus, Bloody Marys are disgusting," Eric says.

"Have you ever had a Bloody Mary?" Carlton asks.

"No."

"Then how do you know you don't like them?"

"Because I can't stand any of the ingredients in them. Except for vodka, of course. I hate tomato juice, or V8, or any of that other crap. Reminds me of cold, tasteless marinara sauce. I'm more of a mimosa man."

"Mimosas? Grow up. And anyway, these aren't made with tomato juice or V8."

DAVE!

"What are they made with, then?"

"Clamato."

Eric heaves a chunk of something from his stomach into his mouth, contemplates it for a second, chews it, and swallows.

"Well, these can't be any worse than whatever it is you were just chewing on. Come on, try it. It's got plenty of Tabasco."

"Oh, I like Tabasco."

"Perfect."

"I'll take yours if you're not gonna drink it," Starlet says to Eric.

"No, no. I'll drink it. Hopefully the Tabasco will... What the fuck is this? Celery?"

"What does it look like?" Carlton asks.

"It looks like celery," Eric says.

"Then I would say it's celery. It sure as hell ain't rhubarb."

"I can't drink it. Celery is the worst. I can't stand the smell of it. Even after you wash your hands, the smell stains, like onions stain. No way, no how, nope."

Carlton takes the celery stalk out of the glass and wings it into the pool.

"Celery dive!" Ray shouts, and goes diving for the celery, never once realizing that celery floats, and it's bobbing on the surface the whole time.

"I love celery dives!" Nick shouts, and goes underwater as well.

I hope they never come up for air, Eric thinks, but he realizes it's the hangover talking.

"All right, gimme the drink."

At first, it's as horrible as he thought it would be, but once he's halfway through, it's starting to not taste too bad. Bonus is, it's alleviating his hangover a bit.

"Could you get me another one, with a little more Tabasco?" he asks Carlton.

"No. One's enough."

"One's enough? When has one ever been enough?"

"We're never sure when we'll be needed. We have to maintain our wits. If your hangover starts coming back, you can have another. Meanwhile, want to go play some volleyball?" Carlton gestures to the sand pit by the pool with the volleyball net.

"Yeah, that would be fun. Come on, let's…"

Carlton's special-issue phone rings. "It's D.A.V.E. calling."

"Hello?" Carlton answers. "Yep. Hmm. Okay. Bye."

"So?" Eric asks.

"That was D.A.V.E."

"No shit," Eric says.

"The real president has been spotted on the set of his new movie: The Cheeseburger Monologues."

"Wow!" Eric says. "How do they know it's him?"

"Deductive reasoning," Carlton says.

"Deductive reasoning?" Eric asks.

"Deductive, inductive, conductive reasoning, I don't know. The point is, they found him there on set, directing. We're the first to know, which makes me feel pretty goddamned special. They're filming not too far from here.

"This ought to be interesting," Starlet says to Eric.

"Ugh, to say the least," Eric says. "So, uh, we'll follow you guys, hey?"

Carlton gives Eric a look. He mouths silently: If you think you're gonna stick me with these two assholes while you have your little rendez-vous in the police cruiser with your long-lost girlfriend and her dog, you got another thing coming. Then again, you have been a good companion to me throughout this adventure, and you deserve happiness. I only hope I find the kind of love you two have some day, if we make it out of this alive.

Eric mouths back: You will, buddy. Just keep your chin up and your vagina fresh, and some day you, too, can have what I have. You have been a great friend, and an excellent partner-in-crime, and I think of you as a brother.

Carlton mouths: Me too. Actually, I don't have any family of my own. I never knew my mom and dad. I grew up in a stranger's attic and wasn't released until I turned sixteen, when I could get a work permit and start washing windows on skyscrapers. I quit that job when my partner Bob Chiselstein fell thirty stories to his untimely death. Those lifts are no joke; you should be really careful on those things.

Eric mouths: Sorry to hear about your friend.

Carlton mouths: Don't worry about it. He wasn't a friend, anyway. He was actually kind of a douchebag.

Starlet mouths: If you boys are quite done air-kissing each other with words, let's go. I want to get this over with. Plus, I want to see what this new movie is all about.

CHAPTER TWELVE

David Hasselhoff is lying shirtless on the floor, drunkenly manhandling his cheeseburger. His daughter says from somewhere off-camera: "Dad, you need to promise me you're not gonna get alcohol tonight, okay?"

"Whuut?" Hasselhoff rudely asks his daughter to clarify, although her message was pretty clear the first time.

"Promise me you're not gonna get alcohol tonight," she repeats.

"Okay?" she asks, as he drunkenly takes a bite of his floor burger. "'Cause if you get alcohol tonight, you're gonna get fired from your show tomorrow."

He gazes at her, still not comprehending the words she is speaking.

"And the doctor's coming over here in the morning to check your alcohol level. And if there's any alcohol in your system, you're gonna be fired from the show."

His gaze becomes even more glassy, if that's even possible, as he takes a bite of an errant lettuce leaf or something.

"Tomorrow," she says. "You hear me? No alcohol."

"Shed," he mumbles, as a chewed piece of burger falls on his lap.

DAVE!

He's seventy-nine years old. Eric thinks how although it's quite unfortunate that Germans still enjoy Hasselhoff's music to this day, it's even more unfortunate that this is what Americans remember him for.

"Cut and print," Mel shouts. "That was wonderful, David. Great job."

"Did I do a good job?" Hasselhoff asks, not because he's drunk (he'd given that up years ago), but because he's quite hard of hearing.

"YOU DID A GREAT JOB!" Mel shouts, and gives him a thumbs up and a smile.

"Thanks, Pamela," he says, and wanders off, taking a bite of his burger. (I should probably also mention that he's senile as an old bat in a basement.)

"Don't eat that, David," Mel calls out after him. "That's just a prop. That's Play-Doh."

"Thanks for the snack," David calls over his shoulder.

Mel turns around, surprised to find an audience of five humans and one dog standing behind him. "Help you folks?" he asks.

"Oh," Carlton says. "We're your biggest fans. We heard about the new project and are just thrilled!"

"You are?"

"Oh yes."

Mel shakes his head. "I don't get it. Biggest piece of shit I'll ever make. And that's including The Beaver. I wanted to make another Mad Max, but the producers said, 'You can make anything you want, after you make this movie.' Garbage."

"What's the plot?" Starlet asks.

Mel laughs. "Plot? Plot? There is none. Nobody cares about plot anymore. Have you seen a movie lately? Have you read some of the books out there? All authors care about is emotion. Making you laugh. Making you cry. I don't see how they do it with dumb story lines, or worse, no story lines. Plot is secondary, sometimes even nonexistent. No character development. Just scene after scene of weird shit happening."

"Yeah," Starlet agrees. "Some books are pretty stupid. I'm reading a new series by Richard Marx, remember him? I think it's called STEVE! Or something. Funny as hell, but the plot is dumb."

"But you're still reading it, right?" Mel says.

"Yeah."

"See? I don't get it. So yeah, there is no plot here. Just a bunch of celebrities reenacting their worst moments. I don't see what the fascination is with watching celebrities crumble. We're human too."

"Maybe that's why people like it so much," Starlet says. "It shows you're all just people, same as them. They can relate to you a little better, and that makes them feel a little better about themselves."

"I just think people like to take pleasure in the misery of others."

"Or that," she says.

"We're wrapping up for the day. Want to see what I have so far?"

"Hell yeah," Nick says. Mel gives him a look like he's some kind of Idiot.

"How do you find the time to do this, being president and all?" Eric asks, as Mel is setting up his holographic projector.

"Presidents gotta have their hobbies. Some play golf. Some have affairs. I make movies. Okay here it is."

The opening title sequence begins, Alec Baldwin's voice playing over the credits.

"Hey, I wanna tell you something, okay? And I wanna leave a message for you right now. It's 10:30 here in New York on a Wednesday, and once again I've made an ass of myself trying to get to a phone to call you at a specific time…"

LEEPIN LIZZERDS PRODUCTIONS PRESENTS

DAVE!

"When the time comes for me to make this phone call, I stop whatever I'm doing, and I go and I make that phone call, at 11:00 in the morning in New York, and if you don't pick up the phone, at 10:00 at night. And you don't even have the goddamned phone turned on…"

AN UNCLE MEL FILM

"I want you to know something, okay? I-I-I'm tired of playing this game with you…"

ALEC BALDWIN

"I'm leaving this message with you to tell you, you have insulted me for the last time. You have insulted me. You don't have the brains or the decency as a human being. I don't give a damn that you're twelve years old, or eleven years old, or that you're a child, or that your mother is a thoughtless pain in the ass…"

DAVID HASSELHOFF

"…who doesn't care about you as far as I'm concerned. You have insulted me for the last time. You have humiliated me for the last time with this phone. And when I come out there next week, I'm gonna fly out there for the day just to straighten you out on this issue."

LINDSAY LOHAN

"I'm gonna let you know just how disappointed in you I am, and how angry I am with you, that you've done this to me again. You've made me feel like shit, and you've made me feel like a fool over and over and over again."

CHARLIE SHEEN

"And this crap you pull on me with this goddamned phone situation, that you would never dream of doing to your mother. And you do it to me constantly, and over and over again. I'm gonna get on a plane, and I'm gonna come out there for the day, and I'm gonna straighten your ass out when I see you"

MICHAEL RICHARDS

"Do you understand me? I'm gonna really make sure you get it. Then I'm gonna get on a plane, and I'm gonna turn around and I'm gonna come home. So you better be ready Friday, the Twentieth, to meet with me. I'm gonna let you know just how I feel about what a rude little pig you really are. You are a rude, thoughtless little pig."

AND MEL GIBSON

THE CHEESEBURGER MONOLOGUES

Starlet sheds a tear. She feels bad for Alec Baldwin's daughter. She also feels bad for Alec. All these celebrities, all well past their prime, and all we remember them for is the bullshit. It's not right. Then again, it sounds like a fun movie.

Opening scene: a cop car, flashing the ol' red and blues. A familiar face steps out of the vehicle. One all too familiar nowadays. Uncle Mel. He obviously has a great makeup team, as he's looking thirty years younger. Starlet's pretty sure she knows what's going to happen. She vaguely remembers this scene going down years ago.

Gibson drunkenly stumbles out onto the road.

He turns to the group watching. "I was so wasted back then. I have since given up drinking, much like my friend Mr. Hasselhoff."

The officer puts him through the usual field sobriety exercises, and makes his determination.

"Mr. Gibson, you are under arrest for driving under the influence."

"No, I don't!" Gibson shouts nonsensically. "Everything's fucked. My life is fucked!"

"Mr. Gibson, sir, it's just a DUI. Your life is fine."

"My life was fine. I should have just shut my mouth at this point," he says.

"Come on, I won't even handcuff ya if you just get in the back seat here."

Gibson turns and runs back to his own car. "You'll never catch me! I'm the gingerbread man!"

"Mr. Gibson, you are not the Gingerbread Man, sir."

"Then I am the gingerbread man's son!" he shout/sings, as he races toward his car. The cop catches up to him and slaps the handcuffs on.

Next scene: They're in the car, headed toward the precinct.

"You motherfucker!" Gibson shouts. "You cow-catcher. Don't you know I eat people like you for breakfast? You probably eat cheeseburgers off the floor! I'm going to fuck you in your asshole!"

Mel turns around again. "I wouldn't do that, just to clarify. That's bravado speaking."

"You piece of salami. You trash-heap pig. I own Malibu!"

"I don't really own Malibu. Back then, I had a pretty nice house there on a couple acres. But I never owned the whole city."

"I'm going to get even with you! You stupid Jew!"

"His name was Liebonipowitzsteinberg. I mean, was I wrong in assuming he was Jewish?"

"You look like a pig in heat, and if you get raped by a pack of niggers, it will be your fault!"

"I never said this to the cop. Here's the point where I repeat everything offensive I've ever said."

"I will burn your fucking house down, after you blow me. Do you take it up the ass, homo? Butts are for shitting, not for sticking dinkies in, dummy. I want to kill you. I want your intestines on a stick. I want to kill your fucking dog!"

"I rambled incoherently a lot back then," he said, and stopped the movie.

"Well, you get the gist of it, I suppose. Nothing but garbage. This is worse than watching a turd circle the bowl. I'm sorry you have to witness this. The worst part is, this movie will make billions. I just wanna make a Mad Max!"

Starlet feels sorry for him. He seems so nice. Are they sure he's really the president? It doesn't make sense. The president's an asshole. If this is the real deal, could it be they've had him wrong all along?

"Something tells me there's still Jews in Hollywood. I can't wait till we find those few strays and toss them over the border with the rest of them."

Okay, maybe not.

"Listen, kids. I gotta wrap this up and get going. Presidenting to do. Nice meeting you all. Have a great day, and remember, never let go of your dreams. Even if they're screaming for mercy."

"Nice meeting you, Mr. President," Carlton says.

"What are we gonna do now?" Starlet asks Carlton.

"I don't know. Somehow we need to find a way to shock him."

"How?" Eric asks. "Do we jut run up to him and ambush him with a car battery and a pair of jumper cables?"

"No. No, we can't do that. That would be too easy," Carlton says.

"Or too difficult," Starlet says.

"Or that," Carlton says. "We need something with just the right amount of difficulty. Something middle-of-the-road. Something that will continue this story for just the right amount of pages... uh, time. Just the right amount of time."

"Did I hear someone mention jumper cables?" an actor says through a mouthful of cheeseburger. He looks familiar, but Starlet can't quite place him.

"Oh, hi, Scott Bakula. No, nobody here said jumper cables. Or car battery, for that matter."

"Scott Bakula, what are you doing here?" Eric says. "You are one of the most respected men in Hollywood."

Bakula looks far away with a faraway look. "This is true. I am quite respected, and very respectable."

"I didn't think anyone was respectable in Hollywood anymore," Starlet says.

"Scott Bakula is," Eric says. "Do you know his Star Trek: Enterprise contract stated that they had to wrap up filming at 6 P.M. every Wednesday so that he could be home in time to have dinner with his family?"

"No!" Starlet says.

"It's true," Eric says. "Why, Scott Bakula is an absolute anomaly. You'll never see him eating a cheeseburger off the floor. You'll never hear any recordings of him cussing his twelve-or- eleven-year-old daughter out. You'll never see him with cocaine and tiger's blood pumping through his veins. Why, Scott Bakula is about the only man I know with no skeletons in his closet. Am I right, Scott Bakula?"

"Well, one time I…"

"Terrific," Eric says. "So that begs the question: Why are you here?"

"Got myself hired as a Key Grip."

"What's a Key Grip?" Nick asks.

"Nobody knows for sure," Scott Bakula says. "He pretty much just sits around, telling the Best Boy what to do."

"So you're not even in the movie?" Eric asks.

"No. I wasn't brought on as an actor. This movie is about a bunch of old guys who made fools of themselves in their prime. I have never made a fool of myself."

"Nonsense!" Nick says. "I watched Quantum Leap."

Eric grabs Nick by the arm, hard enough that his fingers touch each other through the bone. "Quantum Leap was a fucking masterpiece! Watch your mouth!"

"Now, now," Scott Bakula says. "Everyone has the right to their opinions. That's what makes this country so great. Or, what made this country so great, once upon a time."

"Well, I'm sorry, but he's wrong. I mean, week after week, the same premise, but a different story line. The writing was genius. And Dean Stockwell? My God."

"I always thought of him as the poor man's Ray Wise," Ray says, which makes Eric's grip tighten even harder on Nick's arm.

"Hey, come on. I didn't say that," Nick says.

"Sorry," Eric says, and lets his arm go.

"Hey, how is old Stockwell, anyway?" Eric asks.

"Dead," Scott Bakula says.

"Sorry to hear that. Please, continue."

" I'll never be one of the guys. I'm too respectable to hang out in their social circles. These guys don't even know who I am. Which makes infiltration that much easier."

"Infiltration?" Carlton's eyes light up.

Scott Bakula clicks his tongue, winks, and gives the finger-gun.

"I knew it!" Eric shouts. "All my life I have always felt a certain kinship with Scott Bakula. This seals the deal!"

"Sure does," Scott Bakula says.

"Wow, so you're an Invader, like us," Eric says.

"Yeah. Been here keeping an eye on old Uncle Mel the whole time. You folks, on the other hand, aren't infiltrating as well as you thought."

"What do you mean?" Carlton asks.

"He knows what you're up to."

"Really?" Carlton asks. "Doesn't seem that way. He was very cordial; showing us the movie and everything."

275

"Jeezum Crow," Scott Bakula says. "He's an actor. And, may I say, one of the finest actors of my time. Lethal Weapon? Come on, now."

"But it's not really even Mel Gibson," Carlton says.

"Oh yeah, I forgot. But these aliens are damn fine actors, too. Anyway, I've got a surefire plan, guaranteed to work."

"And how do we know we can trust you?" Nick says.

"How do you know you can trust me?" he asks. He smiles and a sparkle flashes in his eye. "I'm Scott Bakula."

"He's got a point," Carlton says.

"So anyway," Scott Bakula says, "We can't be sneaky about this. The president has eyes everywhere. If we try and sneak up on him with a pair of jumper cables, we won't get within ten feet of him. No, we have to do this fairly, and honestly. We have to appeal to his ego."

Charlie Sheen comes up from out of nowhere. "Did I hear someone mention ego?" He gives Starlet a warm embrace.

"Ick, get off of me, Charlie Sheen!" The words squirt out of Starlet's mouth like toothpaste out of a tube that got left on the bathroom floor and stepped on by a heavyset person with a pair of old shoes.

"Starlet! It's me. Your pap pap." Sheen's face lifts up and Starlet catches a glimpse of her daddy.

CHAPTER THIRTEEN

Daddy!" she exclaims and wraps her arms around him again, even though his Charlie Sheen mask is a huge turnoff.

"Shhh," he says. "These guys think I'm really Charlie Sheen. Act like you know him."

"Charlie!" she shouts. "How's…" she stops in her tracks. She suddenly realizes she doesn't know much about Charlie Sheen. "Uh, come on. Let's go grab a sandwich from the line."

She chooses egg salad, which is an odd shade of gray. Either they overcooked the eggs, or these aren't from a chicken. It tastes pretty good, though. Her father Jake chooses to make himself a sandwich out of the cold cuts they have, and slaps some mysterious blue meat between a couple slices of marble rye. She gives him a look.

"Relax," he says. "I'm not gonna eat it. I'm just trying to look casual."

"What are you doing here?" she asks.

"Well, when word got out of the filming of this movie, they asked for a couple of volunteers to act as spies on the set. Pherl and I offered our services."

"Oh, Daddy, um, Charlie," she corrected, making sure to say the name loudly "it's so good to see you. I missed you so much."

277

"I missed you too, pumpkin. Now, what are you doing here? I see you found Eric."

"Yes. And we're engaged!"

"Congratulations, honey. That's just wonderful."

"Thank you. I really love him."

"Me too. Now, what are you doing here?"

"Daddy. Charlie. I know how to end this whole mess once and for all."

"I'm listening."

"What would you say if I told you we could end the whole alien invasion overthrow the U.S. government with a simple car battery?"

"I'd say you're full of malarkey. But go on."

She recounts her entire story, most of which he's heard already, and as his mind starts to walk off he starts wondering just what in the hell that blue meat is. He is certainly quite hungry. Perhaps he should just take some chips from the bowl, but he's always had a hard time eating food that others have had their grubby mitts all over. He actually doesn't like buffets for that exact reason. There's no telling who sneezed on the food, or who decided to not wash their hands after their trip to the bathroom and then handling every plate of carrot cake there before deciding on the perfect slice. Someone's hands have probably been wiped all over the blue meat. Even if it is edible, he doesn't want to risk catching any germs. He decides that it's too risky, and puts the sandwich down.

"So what do you think?" she asks.

"I think it's a great idea. But listen, honey, I don't want you in any sort of danger. You just let me and Pherl take care of it and stand out of the way, okay?"

"Stand out of the way? What are you..."

"Just watch, and learn."

"Guys, you remember Pherl," Jake says. "Uh, I mean Lindsay Lohan."

"Sure," Carlton says. "Nice to see you again, Lindsay."

"Now," Jake whispers. "Who's got jumper cables?"

"Not us," Carlton says. "I took them out of the Elephant's trunk to make room for all of our completely useless weapons. What are you planning on?"

"We're gonna shock the president."

"Yeah," Carlton says. "We got that covered already."

"Then what's your plan?"

"Well, we were just in the middle of discussing it with Scott Bakula, till you showed up," says Carlton. "What's your plan, Scotty?"

"All right, now I've heard that Ol' Uncle Mel loves to gamble. He'll never turn down a bet. So what we need to do is come up with something we can bet him on. We win, we get to kill him."

"And if he wins?" Jake asks.

"The um, the stakes have to be even."

"So he gets to kill us?"

"Maybe he'll settle for just one of us," Carlton says.

"Maybe," Scott Bakula says. "But more likely he's going to want to kill all of us."

"Why all of us?" Carlton asks.

"Because if we kill him," Scott says, "his whole race dies out."

"This is ridiculous," Jake says. "I'm going to end this once and for all. Linsday, find me some jumper cables."

Pherl holds up a pair. "Way ahead of you, hoss."

"Let's go catch up with Mel before we lose him," Jake says.

DAVE!

"Daddy, no," Starlet pleads.

"It's okay, sweetheart. Nothing bad is going to happen."

"Well, I beg to differ," she says.

Scott Bakula pipes up. "I have to say, I totally advise against this. I think we should wait and do this a different way."

Jake turns to Scott. "No offense, okay, but you're Scott Bakula. I never did care for you."

"Do what you want," Eric says, "but don't you dare say anything bad about Scott Bakula. He's the Greatest American Hero, for gosh sake."

"Yeah, I wasn't in that," Scott says.

"I know that," Eric says. "I mean you are literally the Greatest American Hero. You should be on Rushmore instead of Roosevelt."

"That's a little much," Scott says. "But thanks."

The Scott Bakula ego stroke fest is brought to a halt when Carlton says: "What the fuck are they doing?"

Jake, a.k.a. Charlie Sheen, and Pherl, a.k.a. Linsday Lohan are standing in front of a car with the hood propped open.

"Hey Mister President, you wanna see if you can give us a hand?" Jake asks. "The damn thing won't start. We need a boost."

"Oh, no thank you, kids. I don't play around with electricity. Best to just get yourself another vehicle and forget about that one."

"But sir," Pherl says, "it's not a big deal. Look."

He grabs the jumper cables, attaches them to the car battery, and grabs a clamp in each hand. "Zooiiinnk!" he shouts, but other than that, nothing really happens.

Mel's look of suspicion turns to one of anger. If Pherl were one of them, he would have dropped dead. "Infiltrator!" he screams. His head cracks open like an eggshell, and a creature emerges from inside. Somehow, the monster is larger than the body it just came out of. No masks and makeup here; this time it's wearing an entire human exoskeleton.

"Kill him!" the alien yells, and the rest of the cast and crew of The Cheeseburger Monologues toss off their masks, bust out of their shells, and begin their attack. All except for Hasselhoff; he's the real deal.

They all swarm, hundreds of them, onto Jake and Pherl. It doesn't take but a few seconds before their screams are silenced and they're completely ripped to shreds.

"Daddy, no!" Starlet shouts, but at this point she's shouting to a discarded meat pile.

"Oh God," she speaks to the heavens. "What was the point of bringing him back if you were just going to kill him off like that?"

"Seize them!" Mel yells to the rest of the aliens.

They approach the group, all sharp claws and teeth.

"Don't hurt them," Mel instructs. "I want them alive. They need to answer some questions."

CHAPTER FOURTEEN

Starlet. Eric. Carlton. Nick. Ray. Scott Bakula. All tied to director's chairs, in an open field adjacent to the movie set. The president makes his appearance, once more in full Uncle Mel garb.

"I would like to offer my congratulations. You have all successfully been the biggest pains in my ass since I took office. What. The fuck. Are you doing?"

"We're the Invaders!" Nick shouts proudly.

"No shit," Mel says. "I know all about you damn fools. Why are you doing this to me?"

"We're tired of the way you're running the government," Carlton says. "We want out planet back."

Mel laughs till tears roll down his eyes. "Oh, ho, ho, ho. That's rich. You want your planet back. And how do you propose you're going to do that?"

"We're going to kill you," Starlet says, still sobbing from thinking about her daddy being a pile of meat.

"Yeah, well, obviously." Mel laughs again. "Not working out so well, is it?"

"Not up to this point, no," Carlton says.

"You guys don't have much in the brains department, do you?"

"Actually, we're all very smart, and very capable," Carlton says. "Well, except for Nick and Ray. That's why we were trusted to head up this mission."

"Wow, if you're the best the human race has to offer, then you have my condolences." Mel says. "Why are you trying so hard to destroy us? Your kind is doomed. We're the only hope you have of surviving. We're trying to save you."

"Save us?" Carlton asks. "By taking our freedoms away? By turning this country into a Nazi regime?"

"Believe me, we didn't want it this way. But your race is soft. You have all turned into a bunch of pussies. We need your planet. And we need to build the world our way. Whether or not you choose to live in it, that's up to you."

"Well, we don't," Starlet says.

"Well, then I can kill you all right now. Easy enough."

"Or we can kill you," Starlet says.

Mel laughs again. "Oh ho ho, you sure got balls, I gotta give you that. What's your deal, anyway? A bunch of vigilantes? You can't possibly be working alone."

"Dave sent us," Eric says.

"Dave? Dave? You have to be shitting me. Well, that explains it, I guess. Makes total sense."

"What does?" Carlton asks.

Mel shakes his head. "You fools think you're getting out of a pile of shit by killing me? By siding with Dave, you've just stepped into a bigger, stinkier, pile of shit. Do you know they want to integrate the races? Make everyone the same?"

"So?" Eric says. "Nothing wrong with that."

"There will be when your union is no longer legal because you're both white."

DAVE!

"Bullshit," Starlet says.

"They're planning on putting laws in place banning offensive speech," Mel says.

"Good," Carlton says. "There's been too much of that lately. I, for one, can get behind a country that tries to be sensitive to people's needs. There's no need to offend people."

"But everyone is offended by something. Don't you see? Your freedom of speech will be stripped away."

"Oh, you're being dramatic," Carlton says. "Freedom of speech doesn't mean the freedom to act like an asshole."

"Actually, yes it does," Mel says. "You think your freedoms are impinged upon now, just wait and see. Better yet, don't. I'm going to put an end to this once and for all. Guards!"

The aliens come out from behind a clump of trees, poised for slaughter, when Scott Bakula cries out, "Stop!"

The guards all stop in their tracks.

"How did you do that?" Mel asks.

"I'm Scott Bakula," Scott Bakula says.

"Yeah, I still don't know what that means," Mel says.

"Time to appeal to his ego," Scott says to Eric.

"Uncle Mel, I hear you're a bettin' man."

"That's true. Never turned down a bet I thought I could win, and never lost a bet I never turned down."

Scott thinks about this for a second, but it confuses him.

"I also hear you like to play billiards," Scott says.

"That's true. Never played a game of billiards I couldn't win."

He thought about this, too. He thinks it makes sense grammatically, but he's not sure.

"Well, our friend Eric, here, is a pretty good pool player himself."

Great, Eric thinks. Scott Bakula obviously doesn't know the first thing about hustling, which is to pretend like you're terrible, or at the very least, be modest about how great you are.

"Oh really?" Mel asks.

"Yep," Scott says. "I'll tell you what. Let's make a wager. We win, we get to kill you."

"Sounds good so far," Mel says. "And what if I win?"

"You get to kill whoever you want to."

"But I can already do that."

"Yeah, but do you know where Dave is?"

"I assure you, I always..." Mel obviously thinks, Why lie at this point? "No. I have no idea."

"Then we will lead you right to him. You can do with him what you will."

Mel Gibson unties Scott Bakula, pulls his pants down, and inserts his finger into Scott's anal cavity. "My friend," he says, "you have a deal."

CHAPTER FIFTEEN

Well, some men go to war, and fight for what's ours

Others are content to drink pints in bars

Some watch the Olympics for patriotism

While others give hummers and spit out the jism

Some men bust down walls, and some stand and fight

And some carry signs as they yell about rights

Some men lead the country and act like a fool

And some are content playing pool."

Marcia puts down her guitar, smiling; proud as a hummingbird on a honeysuckle bush.

"That was a little song I wrote a few minutes ago, as we were preparing for this broadcast. You can download the full version by following the address below." A URL appears on the screen. "Please, take a moment and click on the link. I'll wait."

"Uh, Marcia, don't you think it's time we get to the real news?" her co-host, Dirk Ripley, says.

"This is real news, Dirk. Why, if I sell enough copies of this song, I can quit this stupid, dead-end job, reporting the same thing day in and day out, six days a week, for very little pay, and follow my passion."

"With that song?" he asks.

"I'll have you know, that song, as you call it, is very personal to me. I wrote it a few years ago when I was going through a very tough time. I was going through a painful divorce and my ex-husband was suing me for custody of our 23-year-old twins, Ricky and Lucy. I couldn't take the pain any longer so I overdosed on paint thinner and woke up in a hospital bed with this song in my head."

"I thought you said you just wrote it a few minutes ago," says Dirk.

"Don't judge me. Haven't you ever wanted to chase a dream?"

"Well, yes, as a matter of fact. I always wanted to be a stunt car driver."

"Then do it. Do it, Dirk. You drive your stunt cars and I'll sing my song and we can get the hell out of this shit hole studio."

Dirk laughs. "You know I can't do that, Marcia, as I'm just a head in a jar."

That's not some weird sort of figure-of-speech. Dirk is, in fact, just a head in a jar.

"Well, that's fine for you," Marcia says. "I'm still cursed with arms and legs and a torso and a neck and a golden voice. And this amazing song. This billiards game that's taking place tonight will change everything. And this will be the theme song. This will be the go-to song every time they rerun the footage of this evening. I'm gonna be bloody rich! Haha! Suck it, Dirk!"

"Ahem." Dirk would have cleared his throat, were he to have one. Instead, he just has to settle for saying 'Ahem' to get Marcia back on track.

DAVE!

"Sorry, folks. Well I, for one, never thought this day would come in my lifetime. Yet here we are. Some are calling it a turning point in history. Some are calling it just a pool game. As most of you know, just last week, what was gearing up to become a war of the worlds came to a screeching halt when a simple bet was made. One man versus one president in a friendly game of pool. The stakes? Death for an entire race of people. I guess we'll see if both parties live up to their end of the bargain or not as to whether it was just a pool game. We take you once again to Mister Danger himself, Chaz Mufflebeard, who is live on the scene in Baltimore at the soon-to-be-famous Joe's Pool Hall, where the game is almost underway. Chaz?"

The camera cuts to Chaz, who is sitting on top of a pool table.

"Thanks, Marcia. Yes, once again, it's your fearless reporter Chaz here, to bring live to you the biggest sporting event of the century. No, the biggest sporting event in Earth's history. It's Eric Tisdale versus Uncle Mel Gibson, folks. The end of civilization and the beginning of a new one all comes down to this moment."

"Hey Chaz, get off the felt!" a voice calls from out of view. Chaz scoots down off the table as a beer bottle goes whizzing past his head and smashes on the dartboard on the far wall.

"Bullseye!" Chaz shouts. "Another close call. It doesn't get any more dangerous than this. Thank you, young man. You saved my life."

"Fuck off, Chaz!" the voice yells.

"Yes sir, you can sure smell the excitement," Chaz says.

"Sorry, that was me," the bartender says, and gives an I'm sorry look with a cute little shrug.

He holds a microphone up to a face in the crowd. "Tell me, sir, what are your predictions on the outcome of this match?"

"F-f-fuck off, Ch-ch-Chaz," the man says. This man, whose name is James, had been traumatized as a child when his parents were murdered in cold blood by a burglar while he sat there watching. The burglar tipped his hat and was on his way, getting all caught up in the moment and forgetting to actually steal anything. It wasn't the trauma that caused his stutter; rather, it was his mother's blood, which contained an unidentified pathogen and landed on the popcorn he was eating. The bloody popcorn, once digested, sent the pathogen to his brain, re-wiring his frontal lobe and affecting his ability to produce speech effectively. After years of both mental therapy as well as speech therapy, he was able to talk again, but could never seem to shake the stutter. It was especially pronounced in times of excitement such as this one. He isn't one to speak much in front of strangers, but of course, he can't resist the urge to tell Chaz to fuck off.

"Very well, then," Chaz says cordially, and turns his attention and his mic to Starlet. "And what about you, Miss? Are you just thrilled to be a part of this?"

Starlet breaks down in tears. "F-f-fuck off, Ch-ch-Chaz," she sobs.

"I'm sorry," Carlton apologizes for her. "She lost her father last week and is still very upset."

"No worries," Chaz says. "I'm sure he'll turn up. Okay, the players are all prepped, and chalk is… ACHOO… flying. Hey, gimme some of that."

Chaz takes a fingernail full of the fallen dust and sniffs it up his left nostril. "Woo-hoo! Oh yeah, that's the good stuff. I haven't snorted chalk dust since middle school, when our teacher Mr. McKenna used to eat it. What am I saying? I'm sorry Mr. McKenna."

"Get off the felt, Chaz," Eric says as he chalks up his cue.

"Very well. Let the game begin."

They flip for break. Mel wins the toss.

"No cheating," Eric tells Mel. "I've played pool with your kind before and I can tell a cheat when I see one."

"I never cheat on a bet," Mel says. "I always win my bets fair and square. Now, if you'll excuse me, I have some ass kicking to do."

He puts the cue ball directly in the center, and studies the future trajectory for about five minutes.

"My God, just break," Eric says.

"Shhhh.," says Mel, standing erect. "I'll call a foul if you break my concentration again. Now, where was I? Oh yeah." He lines up the stick and pulls it back and forth in his lead hand sixty-eight times. One last pull, and he fires. The cue ball hits the 1 ball dead center, and sends the balls scattering, sinking the 2 and 3 balls in the process.

"Shit," Eric says under his breath.

Mel turns and winks at him. "Looks like your luck has run out, Bubble Boy."

Eric shakes his head. What luck? So far, his luck has been pretty horrendous.

The Prez aims for the 4 ball, and sinks it in a side pocket.

"Ooh," Chaz whispers. "This is it, folks. If you're watching at home, and I'm sure you are, say goodbye to your loved ones. Uncle Mel only has to sink five more balls, and our time on Earth is done. This is the end of the human race."

Eric glares at Chaz, even though he could be right. This could very well be the end. He starts to sweat; he hasn't even gotten a chance to play yet.

Mel lines up to sink the 8 ball.

"Woah, hold on a minute. Looks like the President is trying to sink the 8 ball. This could lose him the game and save humanity forever," Chaz says, a little too loudly.

"Shhh," Eric says.

Mel looks at Chaz. "What do you mean?"

"You can't sink the 8 ball till you have the 1 through 7 all in. You'll lose."

"I thought I was solids?" Mel asks.

"You are, but the 8 ball doesn't count. You don't know the rules?"

"Not really."

"Well, that's one of 'em."

"Don't you have something better to do?" Eric asks Chaz.

"Like what? Go and download Marcia's new song? Haha. Come on. Woo, this chalk dust is getting all up in me tits!"

Mel aims for the 6 ball instead, and misses.

"All right," Eric says to the crowd. "Read 'em and weep," which is probably more appropriate for poker, but whatever.

The 15 ball is nestled right in the corner. It takes no lining up to sink this in. Next is the 12. It's all the way on the other side of the table resting on the rail, but Eric is great at long shots. He sinks it very easily. It's going to be tricky to sink unlucky 13, since it's hiding behind one of Mel's balls, but if he banks it just right, he thinks he can get it in the side pocket. He hits the cue ball and it ricochets off the rail, hitting the 13 ball in the totally wrong direction, shooting it into the 8 ball, which spins madly toward the corner pocket. What a horrible shot. Time slows. Eric can hear the tick of the clock as the 8 ball creeps slowly closer and closer to the pocket. Sweat is pours off his head and splashes onto the felt.

The 8 ball is quite old. 26 years old, as a matter of fact. He has taken part in several thousand games of pool, and has been knocked around so much that he can barely form a coherent sentence. "Myyeahhhh," is about the best that he can muster, and that's only on his birthday. All the other balls make fun of him because of the color of his shell. He has given up telling them that they're all white underneath; they never listen to him. He had been a major disappointment to his family all while growing up. His grandfather would go on and on about being knocked in the pocket by Minnesota Fats, winning him some championship. He never cared much for piano players, or player pianos, so he never really listened to what anyone had to say. But at this point, it's all too much. Perhaps they're right. Perhaps he is a failure. Maybe he should have finished his time at the college his parents tried to push him into. He could have become a doctor or a lawyer, even in this racist society. Alas, during his first year of college, he got caught up too much in the party scene. Everybody wanted to bring an 8 ball to their parties. Soon, he was a wreck. Despondent, he dropped out, ended up at the first bar he saw, and rented space on a shitty table. The felt was torn, the pockets were coming undone, and he ended up crashing on the floor most nights. Eventually he worked his way up in life to this dive, Joe's Pool Hall. If this was as good as life was going to get, he's had it. And now, here he is, edging closer to the pocket, ready to jump. Should he? Shouldn't he? Will it make any difference? Will anyone miss him when he's gone?

The spectators all stand around, staring at the ball, mouths agape. Is it going to stop in time? Does it have too much velocity? Are they all going to die now?

Fuck it, the 8 ball thinks. I'll give life another chance. But goddammit, if one more thing goes wrong, I'm calling it quits, I swear to God.

"Close call," Mel says. "Now, here's where I end it." Across the table, the 1 ball is pretty much lined up for an easy shot. But Mel doesn't take the easy shot. "Trickery!" he shouts, and shoots the cue ball in the opposite direction, hoping to hit three banks before knocking the 1 ball in. However, not even an accomplished professional would do something this asinine, when the shot is lined up so perfectly. Up till this point, Eric had been under the impression that all aliens have an Einsteinesque understanding of trigonometry. This is not the case, however, as the cue ball goes in a completely wacky direction, and touches the 8 ball ever-so-slightly, but just enough to knock it in.

So much for that second chance, the 8 ball thinks.

"Woo-hoo! I won I won!" Eric shouts like a seven-year-old boy.

Uncle Mel hangs his head in shame. Game over.

CHAPTER SIXTEEN

The broadcast flips back to Marcia. "Well, that certainly was an exciting game, wasn't it, Dirk?"

"To tell you the truth, Marcia, I was expecting just a few more nail-biting, edge-of-your-seat moments. If this is the end, it's kind of anticlimactic."

"Oh, you talking heads are all the same. Nothing's ever enough for you. Let's go back to Joe's Pool Hall where Chaz Mufflebeard is probably in the way and pissing someone off. Chaz?"

"Thanks again, Marcia. Yes, it's time for the bet to be settled, and for Uncle Mel to pay up. They have him tied to a chair, and Scott Bakula is spitting on him. This is completely out of character for the actor."

"All right, Uncle Mel. Time to pay the piper," says Eric.

"Yes yes, you won. Just get this over with."

"Bartender?" Eric asks. "Get me an ice pick. We're gonna de-mask Uncle Mel. People need to see who we're really killing."

The bartender tosses the ice pick like a javelin, and it lands in Chaz's left eye.

"Oh for the love of!" he shouts, and drops.

Eric pulls the pick out of the corpse's body with a squelch, and buries is deep in Uncle Mel's head. Once more, it cracks like an egg, and the alien head appears, all jaws and fangs and scaly plates. "EEEEAAAAAAAHHHH!" It screams, trying to terrify the humans for the last time.

But wait. That's not a scream of terror. That's a scream of pain. The ice pick is still in its head. The skull is cracking,

"There's something underneath," Carlton says excitedly.

"All right, alien. Time to see who's behind this once and for all." Eric jiggles the pick back and forth until the fissure widens and two halves of the skull fall away, revealing a human face.

No way. Uh-uh. It can't be. He'd recognize this face anywhere. The fat, doughy eyes, the horrible haircut.

"Donald Trump?" Eric says.

"That's right," Donald says. "And I would have gotten away with it too, if it wasn't for you pesky Invaders."

"Cables!" Eric yells to Carlton, who hands him the jumper cables attached to the car battery.

"Please don't," Donald says.

"Fuck off, Donald. We've had enough of you."

"A couple more years?" he pleads.

"You've had your turn. Goodbye."

He fastens the jumper cables to Donald's nipples, and soon he is dead. Within minutes, his body begins to melt and then evaporate. Soon, random people, who obviously aren't people, start melting and evaporating as well. Within a couple hours, every impostor all across the country, every alien being, is completely gone. The world is saved.

Kick ass.

EPILOGUE

THREE MONTHS LATER...

"Dearly beloved, we are rather here today to calibrate the love between Elvis Tidswell and Scarlet Johnson, to be forever unionized in a state of holy macaroni. If anyone objectifies this unionization, please speak now or forever hold it."

"Woof!" says Bella, and everyone laughs.

"I now pronounce you man for life you may kiss the bribe."

Starlet and Eric share the best kiss of their lives. This is a very special day. Not only is it the day of their marriage, but they are going to witness the wall coming down.

To thank them for saving the human race, Dave had given them three million, with which they bought a gorgeous house in Frenchville, and still had 2,999,000 dollars left. Carlton moved in to their spare bedroom, and Nick and Ray moved into the in-law apartment above the garage.

Although Starlet's face had become quite infected, it had healed nicely, thanks to a two-week stay in the hospital and lots of antibiotics and super glue.

Quite a large crowd has turned out for their wedding at the wall, both to witness the wall coming down and the marriage of two of the heroes who saved the world. They are quite famous. After their vows are said, they grab some sledge hammers and pound at the remaining boards. They're down to the last layer of planks, and the crowd shouts.

"10, 9, 8, 7, 6, 5, 4, 3, 2, 1."

On one, they all pound together and one of the planks comes loose. The crowd cheers. They can see Canada, for the first time in a long time. Some for the first time in their lives. Starlet's first order of business: Take a dip in the St. John River in her wedding dress. Quickly they rip the remaining boards down. The cheering slowly becomes murmurs and whispers when they get a good look at what's beyond.

Something isn't right. Starlet expected there to be people on the other side to greet them. This has made worldwide news, she thought. But there is nobody. Not only is the land devoid of people, the whole landscape is gone. No trees, no grass, no St. John River. A stiff wind blows a miniature sand storm across a vast, arid desert. She steps across the threshold to the other side. The sun seems abnormally close, and it's hot as blue blazes. She's joined by Eric.

"What the hell?" he asks.

"Where are we?" Nick chimes in.

Starlet shakes her head. She can't believe her eyes. "Something tells me we're not in Canada anymore."

Want to read more? Don't stop here, the action is just beginning. Go to www.marcrichardauthor.com and sign up to the mailing list to get lots of cool stuff not available elsewhere.

Please don't forget to post reviews on Amazon. They mean everything to a starving artist. Thank you!

MARC'S OTHER BOOKS

DEGREES OF SEPARATION

It's a tale of idiots. It's a tale of life. A dumb cast of characters you have to see to believe. See how the actions of one can affect the lives of many in these Degrees of Separation. Meet a pyromaniac stripper and a faithless priest. Marvel at the woman having intercourse with lasagna. Sit back as you're taken on a downward spiral through hell. Through beauty and nightmares, through comedy and tragedy. Where is this all headed? Is this The End? Strap in and enjoy the ride.

HARM'S WAY

The junkie. The goth girl. The redneck. The nerd. The gangsta. The gay kid. The jock. The twins who can't even tell themselves apart. A loveable cast of walking clichés, out for a week in a cabin in the middle of nowhere. What could possibly happen? Murder, that's what! Who left that dead girl skewered on the porch, anyway? All are suspect, as the slayings become more and more ridiculous. Hell of a way to spend a vacation. Will they find out who the killer is in time to stop this madness, or will this mean the end for all?

THOSE EYES

Archangels in the sky have one job: Making sure our souls get to new bodies. But sometimes they screw up. Ronnie Jones is an ambitious teenage boy about to ask his Helen to marry him, till an accident cuts his life short. Like that annoying joker someone forgot to take out of that deck of cards before shuffling, his soul ends up where it doesn't belong; miles away. When he reawakens as Freddy, his spirit is on a mission. He must find the girl that has his heart. The good news: He finds her again! The bad news: It's thirty years later, and she's a baby. Seriously. He can't catch a break.

IT'LL END IN TEARS

Doc is a psychologist struggling with mental illness. After eight years, his wife Elisa has finally reached her breaking point and they separate. Bryan is Doc's new client. He comes into the office with a crippling caffeine addiction and a severe case of schizophrenia. Or maybe he's just a weirdo. Doc really likes Bryan at first. Till he suspects Elisa may be sleeping with him. In the office, he tries to help him. Outside the office, however, is a whole other story. Revenge is on Doc's mind. It starts off harmless at first, with childish pranks. Soon these high jinks turn into something more sinister. Will Doc and Elisa reconcile? Will Bryan survive? Will he at least switch to decaf?

SORRY!

The perfect bathroom reader. Includes dumb ramblings and poetry that will probably make you feel better about yourself. Witness an ice skater being eaten by sharks! Unwrap odd Christmas gifts! Find out who the familiar stranger is living next door! All this and more!!!

OR GET THEM ALL IN THE ULTRA-LOW-PRICED

SIX OUT OF FIVE: THE MARC RICHARD BOX SET

45842504R00167